AN EXCERPT FROM
TORMENT ME (ROUGH LOVE PART ONE)

"Since this is an introductory session, we should talk for a minute before we go any further," I said in a firm voice.

"Oh, I think I'm going to run this rodeo, especially considering what I'm paying to have this 'introductory session' with you."

Don't freak out. Don't freak out. Just because his voice was deep and harsh, just because he felt big and muscular, just because I couldn't see a thing, just because my hands were zip-tied behind my back...it didn't mean I was turning my last trick.

"Don't struggle, or those ties will hurt your wrists," he said. He picked me up and deposited me in a chair, one of those slick, padded, modern chairs they had at all the W hotels. I usually liked being manhandled, but I didn't like it as much when I couldn't see or move my arms. The room was silent. He was still. I didn't know if he was close to me or far away.

"Will you take off the blindfold?" I begged in my sweetest voice.

"No." Not his sweetest voice. More like his deep, rough, mocking voice.

"Pretty please? I'm dying to see what you look like."

"I'll describe myself, then. I have black hair, piercing blue eyes, a chiseled jaw, and an 8-pack. Or maybe I have white-blond hair, high cheekbones, bronze skin, and a smattering of freckles."

The latter part was describing me. He was lying, which clients always did, but I felt too powerless to be okay with it. I thought about ending the date. Henry would be angry, but panic was crowding in on my dark world. I took a shuddery breath. My heart was beating too fast, and my brain was thinking too fast.

I felt his palm against my cheek, cool but warm. Static. Non-violent. "Calm, Chere. Be calm. I'm not a bad guy. I just like to be in control. Breathe in. Breathe out."

"Okay," I whispered...

"A Chorus Girl" by E.E. Cummings was originally published in *Eight Harvard
Poets*, New York, Laurence J. Gomme, 1917. It and the following poems are used
in this work by rights of public domain:
"Mystery" by D.H. Lawrence was originally published in *Amores: Poems*, New
York, B.W. Huebsch, 1916.
"Choice" by Angela Morgan was originally published in *The Second Book of Modern
Verse*, Boston, Jessie B. Rittenhouse, 1920.
"She Walks in Beauty" by George Gordon, Lord Byron was originally published
in *Hebrew Melodies*, London, 1815.
"Sonnet 147" by William Shakespeare was originally published in London,
England, 1609.
"Longing" by Matthew Arnold was originally published in *Empedocles on Etna, and
Other Poems*, London, B. Fellowes, 1852.

TORMENT
ME

ROUGH LOVE PART ONE

ANNABEL JOSEPH

OTHER BOOKS BY ANNABEL JOSEPH

Mercy
Cait and the Devil
Firebird
Owning Wednesday
Lily Mine
Disciplining the Duchess

FORTUNE SERIES:
Deep in the Woods
Fortune

COMFORT SERIES:
Comfort Object
Caressa's Knees
Odalisque
Command Performance

CIRQUE MASTERS SERIES:
Cirque de Minuit
Bound in Blue
Master's Flame

MEPHISTO SERIES:
Club Mephisto
Molly's Lips: Club Mephisto Retold
Burn For You

BDSM BALLET SERIES:
Waking Kiss
Fever Dream

PROPERLY SPANKED SERIES:
Training Lady Townsend
To Tame A Countess
My Naughty Minette
Under A Duke's Hand

1.

THE INTRODUCTORY SESSION

There are a lot of fucking weirdos in the world. I know because some of them are my clients. Something about money and privilege turns men into perverts, and you don't want to expose the wife to those unseemly urges. Not when you can hire a high-class call girl and meet her in an upscale hotel.

It was the W Hotel today, near Union Square. I crossed to the elevators and checked Henry's email again. *New client, two hours. Super asshole about privacy. Put on the blindfold before you knock on the door.*

I slid a hand into my designer bag, past condoms and sex toys, to locate the black eye mask the client had provided. It couldn't be a pink, fuzzy, soft blindfold, or one of those cucumber-scented spa things. No, it was heavy black leather with a buckle in the back. Like I said, fucking weirdos. Here's some news for the privacy assholes of the world: We escorts are as concerned about our privacy as you are. The escort-client relationship is a covenant. You don't out me, I don't out you. Let's keep things pleasant and professional. I know how much you're paying. To the best of my ability, I'll treat you well.

I stopped outside a corner room on the eighth floor and double-checked the number. My stomach jumped a little. You never knew what you were going to get with new clients. Henry checked them out pretty thoroughly, but still, you never knew. Money and respectability didn't mean you weren't going to death-choke a whore on the eighth floor of the W Hotel.

I'd had pretty good luck the last ten years, so it wasn't that hard to pull out the blindfold—okay, let's be honest, leather fetish mask—and strap the thing onto my eyes. Maybe he was really *that* concerned about privacy. Maybe he had some kinky games in mind, which might be fun. Maybe he was butt ugly. There was no way for me to find out. I couldn't see a damn thing.

I knocked on the door and hoped he answered before someone came strolling down the hall. What would they think of me in my pale pink, skintight, high-class-whore business suit and stilettos, with the black blindfold strapped onto my head? They'd probably think, *pfft, New York*, and go about their business.

I heard the lock click and I felt very, very nervous, since I couldn't tell if or when the door opened, or who might be standing there to guide me inside. I jumped when the client took my arm.

"Miss Kitty, I presume?" His voice was deep and lacking inflection, or maybe I was just lacking the vision to see his expression.

"Meow," I said, flirting into the darkness. "That's me."

Miss Kitty. Sweet, petite, sensuously feline, but not in a pet-play kind of way. Unless the client was into it. I had long, white-blonde hair (fake, so fake) which I straightened to a bouncy shine twice a week. Unlike my hair, my size D boobs and curvy body were all natural. I was a friendly, pretty, brown-eyed, bleach-blonde kitty, ready to crawl into your lap and blow your mind.

The faceless stranger pulled me into the room and collected my wrists behind me in a rough, strong grip. "I'm not going to call you Miss Kitty. What's your real name?"

And my real name—Chere—came spitting out of my mouth. I can't say why, except that his forceful grip compelled me to reveal it.

"Chere?" he repeated, like a taunt. He was cinching my hands behind my back with, *oh my fucking God*, zip ties. I could hear the susurrating sound of the tiny tabs and feel the unforgiving plastic. Jesus. Zip ties. So murder-y.

"Since this is an introductory session, we should talk for a minute before we go any further," I said in a firm voice.

"Oh, I think I'm going to run this rodeo, especially considering what I'm paying to have this 'introductory session' with you."

Don't freak out. Don't freak out. Just because his voice was deep and harsh, just because he felt big and muscular, just because I couldn't see a thing, just because my hands were zip-tied behind my back...it didn't mean I was turning my last trick.

"Don't struggle, or those ties will hurt your wrists," he said. He picked me up and deposited me in a chair, one of those slick, padded, modern chairs they had at all the W hotels. I usually liked being manhandled, but I didn't like it as much when I couldn't see or move my arms. The room was silent. He was still. I didn't know if he was close to me or far away.

"Will you take off the blindfold?" I begged in my sweetest voice.

"No." Not his sweetest voice. More like his deep, rough, mocking voice.

"Pretty please? I'm dying to see what you look like."

"I'll describe myself, then. I have black hair, piercing blue eyes, a chiseled jaw, and an 8-pack. Or maybe I have white-blond hair, high cheekbones, bronze skin, and a smattering of freckles."

The latter part was describing me. He was lying, which clients always did, but I felt too powerless to be okay with it. I thought about ending the date. Henry would be angry, but panic was crowding in on my dark world. I took a shuddery breath. My heart was beating too fast, and my brain was thinking too fast.

I felt his palm against my cheek, cool but warm. Static. Non-violent. "Calm, Chere. Be calm. I'm not a bad guy. I just like to be in control. Breathe in. Breathe out."

"Okay," I whispered.

"You're not doing it. Breathe for me."

Sharp voice. Dominant, demanding voice. He was clearly a liar, and might machete me at any moment, so I sucked in a big breath and let it out nice and slow.

"Good girl," he said. "It's not like I'm going to hurt you. Or kill you. Your agent has all my information." He chuckled. "All my bank account numbers, anyway."

"I hate this," I blurted out. "I hate this date so far. I want to take off the mask."

"No, you'll leave the mask on, and I'll keep my identity secret. You'll sit there and let me do things to your body, and we'll keep it civilized. Okay?"

Civilized. More sarcasm.

"Are you still breathing?" he asked. "I paid for two hours, and I'm using two hours, whether you're passed out or not."

His jokes weren't funny. His voice was too intent and too scary to be funny. I could feel him close to me but I didn't know what he looked like. He ran a hand up my leg under my pencil skirt.

"Why are you wearing panties?" His voice was smooth now, like silk.

"It's a thong."

I gasped as he twisted it in his fingers and ripped it off. "Which is a form of panties. Don't talk back to me, Chere. I don't like it."

So that thong was history. Okay, I had a thousand of them. More pressing: this guy was terrifying me.

"I think we should talk about what you like, and what you want to do," I said, before my courage left completely.

"Talk is cheap. Basically I want to fuck you."

His fingers were inside me now, probing through slickness. Why was I wet when this guy was freaking scary? "Well, what kind of things do you like? I mean, what kind of fucking? What positions? Do you like toys?"

"I should have made you wear a gag in addition to the mask."

I wasn't making any headway at trying to get this guy in line. Henry was my agent (because high-class call girls did not have "pimps.") He was supposed to protect me from these kinds of situations.

I was just summoning the words to end the date when his thumb pressed my clit. Ah, God, he'd found my spot. My legs opened wider of their own accord. This was the part of the date where I was usually thinking what to do to get the client off most quickly. Right now, I wasn't thinking about anything except that he knew his way around a clit.

Then the fingers were gone and he was gone, moving around, doing something. Rummaging. He returned and knelt in front of me. He zip-tied one of my ankles to the chair before I knew his intent. I tried to save my only remaining free limb but he grabbed that ankle in his big, firm fingers and *zzzip*. Tied. Fuck.

I tried to stand up but he pushed me down again. "Don't move."

The stern voice. The control. I wanted to hate it, but I also wanted him to finger fuck my pussy until I came.

"What's your name?" I asked. "What do I call you?"

"Nothing. You don't get my name."

"But you know my name. My real name," I said in my cutesy Miss-Kitty whine.

"It's not my fault you told me your real name like a fucking idiot." He touched my chin, my hair. "If you want, you can call me W."

I knew from the way he said it that W had nothing at all to do with his real name, and everything to do with it being the name of the hotel. He moved away. More rummaging. This time when he came back, he put something thin and cold and metal against my thigh.

"What are you doing?" I asked in a panic.

He clapped a hand over my mouth. "Undressing you. Hush."

He let go of my mouth, and I heard the snip-snip of scissors through fabric. Your hearing really is heightened when your other senses are dulled, because I could hear every thread of my thousand-dollar designer skirt being cut in two.

"Stop," I yelled. "What the fuck are you doing?" This was one of my best, priciest outfits, a classic Lanvin number that fit me like a second skin. It was ruined now. "You're paying me for this suit, motherfucker. While you have the scissors, cut these zip ties and let me go. I'm leaving."

"You're not leaving yet."

"It's a *designer suit.*"

"I know. Shut the fuck up and sit still, or I'll graze you with the scissors."

His calm voice confounded me. He got through the skirt and started cutting away the blouse. He could have just unbuttoned it. He was doing this out of spite.

"This isn't sexy," I spat at him.

"Good."

"I would have taken my clothes off when I got here, if you'd only asked."

"I like cutting them off better. Now shut the fuck up."

One of my favorite lace bras was removed with a snip at the front. The cool air hit my breasts, tightened my nipples to rebellious peaks. I didn't want to be turned on. My pussy shouldn't have been clenching at the cool, selfish hauteur in his voice. He cut right up to my collar and then through it. I turned my head to the side because I didn't want to get stabbed in the neck.

"You're a fucking asshole," I said.

"That doesn't sound very classy. I thought you catered to a finer clientele."

"I do, usually. I cater to clients who'd never destroy a Lanvin suit."

His hand replaced the cold metal of the scissors against my neck. He squeezed a little. I could feel his body against the front of me, clothed, not naked. He smelled rich, like power and money. I felt his lips against my ear.

"The only thing you like more than this designer top, Chere, is the feeling of me cutting it off when you can't do anything about it."

"That's not true. And you can't *do* this. You can't bind me with zip ties and use scissors on me, and make me wear this black leather mask."

"I think I can."

"You're not supposed to."

"Your pimp didn't say anything about limits. He said I could do whatever I wanted for two hours. Oral. Anal. Fingerfucking. Pussy fucking. Mindfucking. Clothes cutting." His hand left my neck but he was still close. I reeled from his heat, his presence. "Don't be scared," he said. "You're going to like it. Or remember it, anyway."

"Jesus."

When I sucked in a breath, my bare breasts brushed against the fabric of his shirt. I tried to picture how I looked, sprawled back in the chair with my clothes cut open, and how he looked in…whatever he was wearing.

"Why are you still dressed?" I asked, trying to gain control. "When's this fuckfest going to commence?"

"Wondering how big my cock is? Do you want it, Chere?"

"Yes," I snapped.

"Too bad. You don't get my cock yet. You might not get it at all. You're kind of a bitch."

A bitch? That hurt my feelings, and clients didn't get to hurt my feelings. Clients were nothing, men to exploit. Cocks to service. Whatever. Fuck him. I inched my thighs together as far as I could and sat there, and tried to blank my expression so he wouldn't see he was getting to me. We were what, fifteen minutes into this scene? I felt wrung out already.

"Oh, no." He pushed my knees apart again. "You don't close those legs unless I tell you to. Answer *Yes, Sir.*"

"Yes, Sir." *You fucker.*

He slapped my cheek. Fucker *slapped me.* "Try again. Nicer this time," he barked.

I swallowed and leaned my head back. "Is this some kind of BDSM shit?"

"This is kinky shit, yes. I'm waiting."

"Aren't we supposed to negotiate first?"

"I'm waiting."

"Yes, Sir," I said, like a pussy. "But we're not supposed to do BDSM scenes, not without talking about things in advance."

"We're talking, baby. Otherwise you'd have a gag in your mouth by now."

The way he said it, I could tell he really, really wanted to put a gag in my mouth, which was *so* not what I wanted. The only BDSM I'd ever done with clients was the kind of BDSM where they're the bad boys and I'm the mistress in shiny latex, standing over them with a novelty whip. I didn't know how to do this kind of BDSM. I didn't know how to *not* be in charge.

I felt his body move in front of me. He took off one of my shoes, then the other. "All right, if you want to talk, let's talk," he said. "Ask me your questions."

"What are you going to do to me?" That was the number one thing.

"I'm going to fuck you, I promise. I know you want my cock. Patience, Chere."

He kept using my name, rubbing in the fact that he knew it while I didn't know his. Worse, he kept insulting me. What the fuck? I was Miss Kitty, whore extraordinaire, and he was paying dearly for the privilege of being with me. I wasn't used to being mocked by clients. I tried to think of some equally cutting response, but I didn't know where to aim. His confidence seemed all-consuming. If only he was ugly. If only he was toadlike, I could deal with him so much more easily. Maybe he was. I didn't fucking know!

"Can I please take this thing off my eyes and look at you?"

"No."

I could pretend he was ugly and toadlike, but somehow I knew he wasn't. He wouldn't talk and act this way if he wasn't beautiful as sin.

"What do you look like?" I pleaded.

He sighed, long and loud. "You're not getting what you want, Chere. You don't get to know what I look like. You don't get to know my name. You don't get anything but what I want to give you. Cock, yes. But first, a little pain."

"I don't like pain!"

"Good." I could hear the smile in his voice. "It's more exciting to me if you don't like it. But don't worry, I won't do anything to you that you can't bear."

My whine triggered answering laughter. He liked that I hated this. He wanted to give me *cock* and *pain*. Sicko. Henry was going to hear about this crazy fuck, and Mr. W wasn't ever going to date an escort in this town again.

"No one ever hurts you?" he asked. "None of your clients?"

He was stroking my leg again, and my pussy. *Ahhh*. Fuck. "No one hurts me like this," I said. "No one zip ties me to chairs and cuts apart my favorite outfit."

"Does anyone ever hurt your breasts?"

I jumped as he slapped first one and then the other, and pinched my nipples between vicious fingers. I tried to writhe away. "Oww! No. No one ever does that."

"I'm doing it."

"Fuck you." The expletive popped out, because my nipples *really* hurt.

"*Fuck you, Sir* sounds more polite."

"Oh, God, stop, please."

He stopped, but my nipples went on aching. He got up and started rummaging again. I hated that rummaging sound. I hated him.

No, that's a lie. I was excited. And scared shitless of what might come next.

"Let's try this," he said, moving closer to me. He grabbed my breasts, or more accurately, my nipples, pinching each one between his fingertips. It felt bad and good at the same time, thrilling and sexy and yet threatening as he pulled and tugged at them. He let go, and I felt a brush of fingertips. Then I felt the most excruciatingly acute pain, like hot metal skewers being poked into the tender tips of my breasts. While I flailed in my zip-tie bonds, he held me down and afflicted my other nipple with the same ungodly pain.

"What did you do to me?" I screeched. It felt like he'd pierced my nipples, which was so, so against the client rules. "Ow, fuck. *Oww.* Oh, God, am I bleeding?"

He chuckled. "I only put nipple clamps on you. You've never worn nipple clamps? Aren't you a prostitute?"

Oh yeah, I'd worn nipple clamps before—the sparkly, decorative ones that barely pinched. "It hurts. You put mega clamps on me. I'll have to go to the hospital."

"They're just clamps. I'll take them off in ten minutes."

"Ten minutes!"

"The pain will be more bearable by then. Of course, as soon as I take them off, you'll feel a totally different kind of pain, which is part of the fun."

Fuck you, fuck you, fuck you, motherfucker.

"I told you, Chere. I won't do anything you can't bear. Hey, that rhymes."

Motherfucker was rhyming while my nipples screamed in agony. Moving made it worse, so I sat as still as I could, rigid and trembling.

"God, that's beautiful," he said in a soft voice. "I'm a sadist, as you might have guessed. I like hurting women, but only as much as they can bear. I don't break them. Well, not very often."

Oh, that was comforting.

"Can't you make me feel good at the same time?" I asked. My pussy was wet as anything. It was clenching as hard as the damn nipple clamps. Where was his cock? I wanted him to put it in me and get himself off, because once the clients got off, the scene was usually over. *Please, God, don't tell me this guy plans to torture me for the whole two hours.*

I heard a zipper going down, clothes hitting the floor. *Thank you, God.* I felt his cock against my lips, and the tang of a candy-flavored condom. My hands made fists as I opened wide. And wider. Jesus. He had a big fucking cock.

"That's right," he said as I moaned at his entry. "What a professional. And a cock works great as a gag in a pinch," he added, tweaking one of my aching nipples.

In a pinch. Ha, perverted and funny.

He drove straight for the back of my throat. When I resisted, he grabbed my hair and made me take it anyway. I protested, making huffing noises when I came up for air.

"You're not allowed to kill me," I gasped.

"I'm not killing you."

"You shouldn't— We haven't negotiated anything. Not nipple clamps, not scissors, not deep throati—"

He shoved his cock back in before I could finish my sentence, and I choked and teared up behind my blindfold.

Okay, I could survive this. I'd sucked a lot of cocks, all sizes. I'd had a lot of men shove deep into my throat in the throes of passion. It happened all the time, but I wasn't usually blindfolded and bound.

Still, in some sick way I wanted to please him. I wanted to make it good for him, and I swear to God, I usually don't care that much. I mean, I care about getting the client off, because that means we're finished, but I don't usually *care*.

He didn't say anything, and I wasn't physically capable of saying anything. I felt powerless in a way I'd never experienced before. I got the feeling he wasn't fucking my face because it felt good for him, but because it felt scary for me. He yanked my hair when I tried to lean away from him, pulled it so hard I yelled, at which point he shoved his cock right back into my open mouth. He was so badass, so good at this. My throat hurt. My hair hurt. My nipples were killing me.

I wondered what he looked like. I wondered so hard.

I started to drool and imagined it dripping down onto my cut-open blouse. I couldn't stop the drooling any more than I could stop the tears leaking out of my eyes behind the leather mask.

When I was sure I couldn't bear for him to drive into my throat one more time, he pulled out. I felt his shoulders against my knees as he crouched to free my ankles. Snip, snip, goodbye zip ties. *Okay, fuck me now. Please be quick.*

But I knew he wouldn't be quick. He liked playing with women. He enjoyed tormenting them. I'd learned over the years to read clients like books. The title of W's book was *Take It, Bitch*.

He removed the clamps next, then grabbed my thighs, yanked my legs apart, and tilted me back in the chair. While my previously-numb nipples came alive with the biting pain of re-invigoration, he drove inside me balls deep.

And I can't say how, or why, but after he drove into me two or three times, I experienced the most powerful orgasm of my life. It was a shaking, twisting, sobbing, *protesting* orgasm, because there was no way I enjoyed this. There was no way that pain and pleasure could mix so exquisitely, while he filled me up with his rough, thick cock. No way. Oh God, *yessss*…

His mocking laughter barely registered as I gritted my teeth and rode out the aftershocks. I was lifted out of the chair and carried, still impaled, still orgasming, across the room. He pushed me back and I braced to hit the floor, but I landed on the bed. He came over me, driving my bound hands down into the mattress. I fought to escape him; my pussy felt too hot and sensitive to have him inside. But the more I fought him, the more powerfully he fucked me.

"I want you to come again," he said.

I shook my head. I was still recuperating from the previous orgasm, still trying to deny the scintillating pleasure lighting up every nerve.

"Yes," he said in his commanding voice. "Again. This isn't over until you do what I want."

"I can't come again."

"Why not? You like pain. You like force. You like getting your throat fucked."

"No!"

He was wrong. I didn't like those things. I was Miss Kitty. Meow. I liked being petted. I liked pretty things. I liked calm, sensual encounters where sex-starved men worshipped me and eased their cocks into me and contentedly got off.

Unlike them, he was intense. Demanding. His cock invaded me while his fingers played over my clit. I may have mentioned this earlier…he knew his way around a clit. He used the perfect touch, not too hard—

because I was still sensitive—but not too soft. I threw my head back and shook it back and forth. *Meow, motherfucker. This is not me.*

But that didn't matter, because I was going to come again. My pussy felt like a living, blooming thing, like it had been dead all these years and he'd just now brought it to life. He was the Resurrection Man. Or the Erection Man.

I writhed on the bed, trying to fight him, because when I fought him, it felt that much more exciting.

"Come on. Come again, damn it." He slapped me, a firm, stinging crack across my cheek. It hurt way more than the first time he'd slapped my face. It also made my second orgasm explode.

I think I cried *nooo*, but he said *yes*, and kept a grip on my shaking thighs. It occurred to me that I was experiencing the most powerful climax of my life, and I still had no idea who was inside me, or what he looked like, or why the hell he found it necessary to slap my face.

While I pondered this craziness, he cupped my cheeks, put his fingers right over the place he'd slapped me, and kissed me.

My pussy still pulsed around his cock, and now his lips were on mine and his tongue was in my mouth, and my hands were bound behind my back, and it was like he was inside me everywhere, making me feel more female and excited and sexual than I'd ever felt in my life. In my dark, blind world, his pleasure and scent transformed me. His rough kisses grounded me, but made me feel like I was flying at the same time. I didn't want the blindfold off anymore. I wanted it on. I wanted to hide and exist in this world forever.

I trembled while he came, because he fucked me so intensely. He didn't make any sound at all, just ground against me and pressed his cheek to mine. I felt completely possessed by his fucking, and strangely pleased that he came so hard.

Fuck. I lay still, breathless, satisfied, knowing there might be more, but not really caring. *Whatever. I'm yours. Whatever your name is, whatever you look like.*

"Please let me look at you," I whispered. More than anything in the world, I wanted to see him.

"No."

A minute later he pulled away, got up off the bed, leaving me alone in the center of it. I turned on my side and curled into a ball. I was still partly dressed, the top of me, anyway.

"Will you unbind my hands?" I asked.

"Yes. Just before I leave."

"Now, please."

"No, because the first thing you'll do is take off the mask so you can see me."

He was right. I would do that.

"Are you someone famous?" I asked. "Some famous politician, or movie star?"

"Yes."

The way he said *yes*, I knew he was lying again, yanking my chain, shoving my desire to know him back in my face.

"Whatever," I said bitterly. "I don't care. What does it matter? What does anything matter?"

"Are you PMSing? Shut up."

He was such an asshole, such a jerk. So good in bed. I hated him. Hate, hate, hate. I lay there honing my hate, hoping he wouldn't want anything else from me now that he'd come.

The bed dipped and he was back, lying behind me. He was dressed again, smelling of understated but yummy cologne. I felt his lips against my nape.

"How am I going to go home without a skirt?" I asked.

"Shut up."

"I can't just traipse naked through the W Hotel lobby and out onto the—"

His hand closed over my mouth, firm fingers muting me. Big hands. He was either a big person, or he seemed big because he was so aggressive and mean.

"You're mean," I whispered against his fingers.

He kissed my nape and my earlobes, and my shoulders, and my spine. His lips were warm and strong, and his face was smooth, just a hint of stubble. I hated him, but this was kind of pleasant after all the violence. His fingers massaged my hips and ass.

"You're beautiful," he said.

I couldn't say thank you, since one hand was still over my mouth, and I couldn't return the compliment, since I couldn't see him, but in my mind W was dark and seductively handsome. In the twilight of my orgasm, my whole body relaxed. I think I was half asleep by the time he leaned away and said, "I'm going."

Going...no. "I need clothes," I said.

"I'll send up clothes. Next time, bring something to change into. And you can have this room for the night, if you want to stay here."

"I don't."

"Fine. Whatever."

"And there's not going to be a 'next time.' Forget it. No way."

He made a soft, mocking sound. "Was it that bad for you?"

Was it? No. He was the bringer of violent and shimmering orgasms. But... "You cut up my favorite outfit."

"Jesus Christ." It was the first time he'd really raised his voice, and it startled me. "Your fucking outfit. I'll bring a replacement to our next session."

"You won't be able to find a replacement. And we're not having another session."

"I know where to find one, even if you look shitty in that color. Come on."

He hauled me off the bed and guided me across the room, and left me there. I heard a few more sounds while I stood, blind and shivering, trying to see his actions in my mind. Shoes on? Snapping a briefcase? The whisper of a necktie? I jumped when he touched my arm. His other hand wrapped around my neck as he held me against him.

"Listen, Chere. I like you. You're reckless and conflicted. Your body is perfect and your breasts are real. I want to see you again."

I leaned as far away from him as I could. "No."

"And next time," he continued, as if I hadn't spoken, "you will bring the eye mask, and extra clothes."

"I'm not going to see you again."

"The correct answer is *Yes, Sir*."

I stood very still with my lips clamped together. After a moment he put his hand against my cheek. He'd slapped that cheek—twice—but this was a caress. "Don't be an angry hooker," he said. "I adore you."

I felt metal against my wrists, and my hands were cut free.

"Don't touch that mask until you hear the door close," he said. "The fantasy's better, anyway."

What fantasy? He shouldn't flatter himself, but I stood where he left me and did as he instructed. I didn't move until I heard the door's latch click into place. My fingers reached up to the mask and then fumbled behind my head at the buckle. I wanted it off, but in some way I was afraid to take it off. I didn't know what I'd see. Shreds of my clothing? The walls drenched in blood?

No, none of that, just a clean and empty luxury hotel room. The bed was made and my shoes were arranged neatly beside it. My skirt and panties were gone. I pulled the two sides of my blouse closed. He could have just unbuttoned it. Asshole. At least my jacket was in one piece.

Jesus, what had just happened?

I went to the window and looked out from the eighth floor, like I could pick him out from the people below. Nope. I could pass him on the street tomorrow and I wouldn't know him, but he would know me. I found that idea horrifying.

I went into the bathroom and took a thirty minute shower, and washed all of W off me. Every slap, every kiss. By the time I got out and put on the robe, someone was knocking on the door. Thank God he'd come through with the clothes—a casual dress and scarf from a boutique across the street. The pale amber-beige looked perfect with my light brown eyes. I still had no panties. Fuck him. Good taste didn't make him any less of an asshole.

I got dressed, put on my shoes, and took one last look around the room at the W Hotel.

And for some reason, I made sure the mask was tucked in my bag before I left.

IN BETWEEN

I left the hotel and took a cab to my place in Tribeca. I needed my boyfriend. I needed normalcy and safety, and the knowledge that the date was really over. I needed home.

I didn't usually let clients rattle me, but on the way up to our loft on the third floor, I admitted to myself that I was rattled. Nothing terribly bad had happened. He'd hurt my nipples, yes. He'd slapped me. He'd called me an idiot. He'd also kissed me and given me insanely strong orgasms. My brain was officially exploded. And my pussy...

"Simon?"

I put down my keys. The loft was dark, but that didn't mean anything. Sometimes Simon painted in the dark. Other times, he waited weeks for the perfect light to work on a painting. Maybe he was out with some friends.

I hated when it was quiet like this.

"Simon?"

I walked through the living room, past the kitchen and the big cement table a friend had given us last year. Simon's studio was in the back, near the floor-to-ceiling windows. I found him sprawled on the low couch against the wall, a paintbrush still dangling from his fingers. A few fresh drips mixed with the history of drips on the rough concrete floor.

He was working on something huge, twenty feet long. All his works were huge, although some were huger than others. This one took up an entire wall. Dark ochre and aquamarine streaks mixed with black, a frenzy of heavy color on the canvas. It was striking, even if I didn't get it. I'd never gotten Simon's art, but I loved the artist.

I loved him enough to let him sleep. I watched him for long minutes, feeling my soul calm. He looked so innocent, like an angel. The first time I'd met him at a friend's party, that's what I thought. *He's an angel.* Long, wispy black hair, coal black eyes, an aquiline nose, and dark brows that had arched skyward when he looked at me. All he needed was wings. He'd touched my white-blonde hair while I stared at his night-black hair. We'd stayed up talking that entire first night, and spent the following day in bed.

When was the last time Simon and I had spent an entire day in bed? Life. It got away from you.

I tried to take the brush from his fingers without waking him, but he stirred and smiled at me.

"Baby, you're back."

"Don't wake up," I said.

He stretched and looked at me. Blinked. "You look pretty." He reached to touch my breasts, but they still hurt, and he was high. I nudged his hand away.

"Don't wake up," I said again. That had become our life, Simon not waking up. He said he needed the narcotics for his art, the pills, the coke, the syrup, whatever he was taking on any given day. I'd have to lecture him later, because he wouldn't remember anything I said to him now. *You can't change him,* my friends said. *You can't fix him. You have to wait until he hits rock bottom.* The thing was, most of those friends were also operating in a drug-fueled haze.

His eyes closed. I stood and left him, and dropped his paintbrush in the solution with the others.

I went into the bedroom and took off the dress W had given me, balled it up and tossed it on the floor. I hung up the jacket, even though the matching skirt had been destroyed. What did it say about me, that out of everything W did, cutting up the skirt seemed the worst offense?

I hadn't grown up with a lot of money, so I valued my belongings, especially my expensive belongings. I collapsed on the bed with a sigh, and scrolled through my contacts to Henry's number. I had to call three times before he picked up.

"Yes, love. What is it? How did your date go?"

"Shitty," I said.

"Hold on." I heard him speaking to someone, heard titters and cooing. His bed was always full of girls. If Simon was an angel, Henry was a God, or at least a minor deity. Golden bronze, beach tan, beach body, even though he was more businessman than Bahamas.

"All right. Tell me," he said when he got back on the line.

"He was an asshole."

"Aren't most of our clients assholes?"

"No. Some of them are nice. This one wasn't nice."

"He tips well. Jesus, Chere, what did you do for him? He left you a hell of a gratuity."

I waited. He waited. When he spoke he sounded kind, and concerned. "Did something happen? If I have to go after this fucker, I will."

He didn't mean going after him in a legal sense. He meant in a sense of calling his guys and making sure that W understood he'd behaved like an asshole. But that kind of action was reserved for extreme circumstances. W hadn't really damaged me, not any more than I could bear, as he'd promised.

"He was just weird," I said. "He wouldn't let me see him. He wouldn't tell me his name. It really bothered me."

"About that..."

"Have you seen him? What does he look like?"

"I don't know. He dated a few escorts through Prom Queen in Vegas, and they told me he was okay. Crazy about privacy, but okay. I'm sorry he was an asshole, and that the two of you weren't a good match."

"He was just...not my usual type of customer. I mean..."

Henry let a few moments pass before he prompted me. "What do you mean?"

"I mean that he was really dominant, really commanding."

"Maybe Nina would be a better match for him."

Nina was our resident pain-slut BDSM enthusiast. She'd probably love W. He'd probably love her.

"I guess I'll give him one more chance," I said. I didn't want him to date Nina, because then he'd be getting exactly what he wanted, and I didn't want him to get exactly what he wanted. Jerk. Plus he still had to replace my skirt, not that I believed he was really going to do that.

"So am I to understand it's okay for this client to schedule another date with you?"

"*This client*," I repeated with an edge in my voice. "What's so fucking special about 'this client,' that we can't use his name?"

"I only have a pseudonym. Do you want it?"

Gah. "No. Yes. Fuck it. Yes."

"E. E. Cumming."

"He's hilarious."

Henry made a soft sound. "He certainly seems to have captured your fancy."

I hated Henry sometimes, for the way he saw through me, the way he intuitively knew all his escorts and what made them tick. He was like an uncomfortably sexy father, only half the age.

"He hasn't captured my fancy," I said. "But he apparently tips well, and he's not boring."

"Speaking of boring, Mr. Linguard is hoping to see you next Tuesday night."

Mr. Linguard was incredibly boring and incredibly sweet. He was just what I needed after the W trauma. "Yes, book him. I'm looking forward to it."

"I'm sure he'll look forward to it too." I heard the tap-tap-tap of computer keys. Another date, another dollar. "Chere," he said when he finished, "are you absolutely certain you're okay with seeing Mr. Cumming again? Nina would be happy to take him."

I made some vague, ambivalent noise that Henry would recognize as a total front. "I already have his stupid blindfold, to protect his stupid privacy, so I might as well do the date."

"I imagine that blindfold requirement won't last forever. He'll probably reveal himself once he trusts you."

I snorted. "Why do I have to earn the 'honor' of looking on his magnificence? That's bullshit. He's the one paying me."

"I know. Don't let it get to you. It's probably just an ego thing."

Well, W had ego in spades. I hardly knew him, but I knew his ego went far beyond the usual size. Along with his cock.

I heard feminine voices in the background, and Henry's muffled reply. "Sorry, Chere," he said. "I have to go."

"Have fun." I hung up and buried my face in my hands. For the second time that night, I had to ask myself "What the fuck just happened?" I'd called Henry to complain that W was an abusive, asshole client, and instead I'd signed myself up for a second date. Only to spite him, I told myself. He would have liked Nina so much better. Fucker. He wasn't getting Nina. He was getting me.

2.

THE VICEROY SESSION

The Viceroy was one of my favorite hotels. So classy, so elegant. It felt wrong to show up there braless, in the casual amber-beige dress W had bought me. But if he was going to cut shit off me, it was going to be his own shit he'd purchased.

I mean, fuck, I shouldn't have even been here. I should have let Nina come instead and do her thing. I could have handed off the eye mask to her. Instead I was fastening it onto my own eyes and knocking on the door. We were high in the air, nineteenth floor. Would have been nice to actually see the view, instead of dark leather blackness. Unlike the first time, I didn't smile when he opened the door.

"Chere," he said. He sounded happy to see me, and gruff at the same time. How did he do that? He smelled the same as I remembered, with that enticing, understated cologne. He pulled me inside and shut the door, and pushed me back against it. Then he was kissing me, not a polite, welcome-back kiss, but a hard, commanding kiss that pushed my head back against the wood. My bag fell from my grasp and hit the floor. His fingers were on my jaw, my chin, my braless breasts.

"Nice dress," he murmured. "It looks good on you."

He trapped my wrists behind my back with one hand, and tugged the hemline up with the other. I wasn't wearing panties because I didn't want

27

him to have the joy of ripping them off again. But he seemed to find just as much joy in groping my bare pussy.

Thirty seconds into this date, my pussy was full of his fingers and my mouth was full of his tongue. I didn't normally kiss clients but he didn't leave me much choice. At least he was a good kisser. I could tell he'd brushed for me, or had a mint. I was pinned against the door by his big, and yes, tall body. I wanted to see him so badly. If I just yanked off the blindfold...

Ohh, damn. He'd found my clit.

I danced a little and pulled at my wrists where he held them. He stopped fondling me and gave a mocking laugh. "It's good to see you again. I didn't know if you'd agree to a second date."

I sagged against the door, hating how easily he worked me up. "I needed the money," I said.

He laughed louder this time, and his laugh sounded as cool and mean as my words. "You aren't here for the money. Not this time. You're here because you want me, you lying piece of shit. Don't be precious."

"Don't call me a piece of shit," I snapped back.

He pushed my dress higher and tugged it over my head, being careful not to dislodge the mask. As soon as I lowered my arms, my wrists were gathered behind my back. "No, not the—" I protested.

Zip ties. Grr.

"I don't trust you any farther than I can throw you," he said. "You get the zip ties for now."

"You're a freak. It doesn't have to be this way. I can do so many wonderful things with my hands." I drew out the word *sooo* to hint at endless, sensual possibilities.

His only response was another laugh. "I think your hands are wonderful bound behind your back. I'm the consumer in this relationship, and you're the product, and if I want to zip tie your ankles to your neck for the next four hours, I goddamn will."

Ugh, not a nice picture. "You only hired me for *two* hours," I said. "And I don't think that sounds very safe."

"I think it's time we shut you up. Get on your knees, Chere."

I felt extra naked as I obeyed, since my vision was obscured. I had no idea what the room looked like or if anyone besides W was there. What if he was taping this? What if he was streaming it live to five million people?

Maybe he was some porn kingpin. He certainly had money. The Viceroy wasn't cheap, and my services weren't cheap, and even the plain, casual dress he'd bought me wasn't cheap.

I heard him shed his clothes, heard the rip of a condom wrapper. I tried to call on Miss Kitty's glamour and equanimity as he shoved gracelessly into my mouth. His fingers molded around my scalp, not grasping, just holding me where he wanted me. It was so hard to give a civilized blowjob without your hands. I tried to control the depth of his thrusting. I moved my head and hummed against his length. I tried to make it classy.

He wasn't having classy.

"Don't try to be cute," he said. "I don't want your pretty whore tricks. I want to use you. I want your body to be mine. Do you understand?"

His fingers moved against my hair, my cheeks, my ears, manipulating me for his own pleasure. How could I not understand? My hands were bound behind my back and I couldn't see anything. His cock was my entire world, his smell and the smell of the fruity condom. It didn't belong, that happy, fruity condom smell. I wished it was just his smell. I wished there wasn't a rule about condoms.

I wished I wasn't having these thoughts, because holy hell. Bareback was dangerous. Bareback meant you were worthless, and Miss Kitty wasn't worthless.

I took him deeper, focusing on the blowjob, focusing on *my* job, which I'd worked damn hard at over the years. He was just a client, and I had to serve him for two hours. I couldn't let crazy thoughts start freaking me out. I took him deep in my throat until I gagged. I tried to be "his," which meant accepting his hard thrusts and letting the drool leak out of the corners of my mouth. I didn't use "whore tricks," and I was finally rewarded with his guttural bark and deep, thrusting sigh.

Did I dare hope that was it? That his frenzied nut in my mouth would be enough to satisfy him for this session? He took his time drawing away from me. "Stay there," he said, when I sat back on my heels. "Don't move. Don't get up."

Shit. I suspected the blowjob was a mere aperitif. It had been fifteen minutes, maybe, since I knocked on the door. One hour and forty-five minutes to go. I heard water running in the bathroom. Strangely, my freakiest customers were also my most fastidious. A moment later I heard him return, and felt his hand beneath my chin. He tipped my face up and swabbed the drool that was drying in the corners of my mouth and along my neck.

"Thank you," I said.

"You're welcome."

"Can I take off the mask?"

"No."

Argh. I shook my head like I could somehow dislodge the straps. He was off again, running water, clinking ice into a glass. What the hell was he doing? Why wouldn't he let me see him? Or see anything? But I knew why—because it kept me perpetually on edge.

When he grabbed my face again, I didn't feel it coming. He put a glass to my mouth and said, "Drink."

What was he holding against my lips? What did he want me to drink? Might be water, might be battery acid. It turned out to be something alcoholic. I choked and sucked in a breath.

"What is that?" I gasped.

"Scotch. Be civilized, for God's sake."

He tipped the glass up again and I drank, because my other option was to drool it all over the front of me after he'd just finished cleaning me up.

"I don't really like the taste of liquor," I said.

"I don't really like the taste of pussy, but we're all adults here. Stand up."

I tried to be graceful about it. I probably failed. "Where are you taking me?"

"Nowhere scary." His arms guided me forward until he sat me down on the bed. He pushed me back and I relaxed into the clean-smelling sheets. *Breathe in. Breathe out.* My mouth tasted like scotch now instead of the flavored condom. He kissed me again, open-mouthed. Why did he kiss me so much, when his main goal was to hurt me?

"W," I said against his lips. "You're so strange."

He pushed my legs open and fondled me. "I'll take that as a compliment." His fingers slid through my wetness, teasing my clit. "Chere," he said, mimicking my earlier statement, "you're so horny."

Yes, that was a fact. I was a horny, confused, scared call girl being groped by a person I still hadn't laid eyes on. I couldn't get comfortable. When I shifted and drew my legs together, he tsked and pushed them apart.

"Leave them open."

I sighed. "You make it very hard for me to do my job properly."

"What do you mean?"

"I mean that I'm supposed to be beautiful and alluring, and sexy. I can't do any of that when I'm trussed up like some hostage."

His lips grazed my ear. "I think you're most beautiful and alluring when you're trussed up like a hostage. Open your damn legs."

He accompanied this insistent command with a couple of stinging slaps to my inner thighs. I tried to roll away from the pain, only to have my hair grabbed and my body yanked against his.

"Stay where I put you. Be a good girl. I like good girls."

I gritted my teeth until he loosened his grasp on my hair. "So, are you one of those Master guys?" I asked. "Those BDSM Dominants with whips and chains and collars?"

"Sometimes."

"You have slaves?"

His lips brushed over my cheek and down my jaw. "Sometimes."

I shivered. I felt like his slave at the moment, although there were no whips, chains, or collars. My thighs still stung where he'd slapped me. "I'm not into that shit," I whispered.

"Noted."

"Why then?" I asked. "Why me? Why didn't you make arrangements to see a call girl who's into this?"

"The girls who are into this aren't as fun to play with. They aren't as fun to torment." He stroked my breasts and squeezed each nipple until I whined and pulled away from him.

"The thing is—" I began.

"The thing is, I fucking paid for you, and I want to play with you. I don't want to talk anymore about whether you're into this. I don't want any more complaining. I told you I wouldn't hurt you. I promise you'll always be able to walk out of our sessions with your body intact."

"That's so sexy. Leaving me intact."

His hand tightened in my hair. "Don't be sassy. I don't like sassy. Try being submissive."

"I told you, I'm not into—"

"And I told you I don't care. If you complain to me one more time, I'm going to punish you."

Holy crap. I should have passed him on to Nina, even with the huge gratuity from last time. "Do I have to call you Master?" I asked as submissively as I could.

"No. You wouldn't mean it. But I'd like you to listen to everything I say, and obey me without questioning and complaining."

"But what will you do to me?" That wasn't a complaint, was it? Just a question.

"No bad things today," he said. "Only good things. Well, we're working up to the scarier things, aren't we?"

"Are we?"

He didn't answer. I was lifted and turned over, his compliant toy. He arranged me so my ass was in the air and my shoulders were pressed down on the bed. "Ever been spanked, Chere?" he asked.

"Of course I've been spanked, many times."

"Hmm." There was a world of amusement in that *hmm*. "So I guess a little spanking won't bother you too much."

Smack. He cracked his hand down on my butt cheeks and it wasn't like any spanking I'd ever received. *Ohmygodohmygod.* I collapsed on the bed and used my bound hands to cover my posterior. "That fucking hurt. Are you crazy?"

"That sounds like a complaint."

"No—" I cried, but the punishment had commenced. This was no playful, sexy spanking, but a major beatdown on my ass. When I tried to crawl away—as any sane person would—he slid an arm around my waist to trap me in place. He spanked me with his other hand, alternating from cheek to cheek, each spank harder than the last.

Oh God, I couldn't be still. I yanked and jerked and fought him, but he was too strong. I added that to his list of attributes. *So strong. Hard spanker.*

"Quiet," he said, as my cries rose in volume. "You're in a hotel."

As the spanking continued, it bypassed stinging and throbbing and settled in the area of agony. I tried desperately to shield myself but his body was in the way. "Oh please," I whispered between yelps. "Oh please, stop."

"When you've had enough."

"Enough for what?" I started crying, I couldn't help it. It hurt too much and he wasn't allowing me time to process the pain. "Aren't you supposed to give me some word to make it stop?"

"A safe word?" He paused for a moment. "I know how much spanking you need, Chere. I won't give you any more than that."

"But—"

Smack, smack, smack. Back to the spanking, which wasn't a spanking at all, but freaking destruction. I kicked my legs and fought him as well as I could in my state of entrapment. There was nothing I could do to end it, no way to make it stop.

"Ow, *please*," I cried. I was literally bawling now, rivers of tears seeping from beneath my mask. "Please, you're hurting me."

"I know."

He knew. I wondered if he *really* knew. I wondered if he understood the power in those torture-slabs he called hands. My lips trembled with the effort not to scream. When he finally stopped, I waited in utter stillness, terrified he would start again. My ass felt like a thousand throbbing impressions of his fingers. His arm loosened around my waist as he caressed my butt.

"Now, Chere," he said quietly, "*now* you've been spanked."

"You hurt me!"

"I'm going to hurt you every time we get together. That's sex for me...hurting you, watching you squirm."

"That's sick."

"Don't judge."

Glib motherfucker. This wasn't funny. My ass hurt so much my legs were shaking. He stroked my throbbing cheeks a minute or two longer. He wouldn't let me lie down or relax. I had to kneel there with my ass in the air, waiting for more punishment. *Please, no more punishment.* I'd be submissive as hell if that's what he wanted, just no more spanking.

He put a hand on my back as if to settle me. His palm slid up and down my spine and I understood that he wanted me to stay where I was. *Yes, Master.* The bed dipped as he rolled off it. Rummaging noises.

Condom wrapper. He parted my sore cheeks and I was one big cringe under his fingers. A wild sob escaped.

"Don't cry," he said. "The whole point of that spanking was to get you ready for my cock." He slid the head up and down my slit. "You're so wet, Chere. You loved that spanking. It made you feel alive."

"No." I whispered my denial into the sheets, not wanting him to hear. Because it was a lie. I was so unbelievably wet, and my ass was so unbelievably sore. He jammed his fingers inside me, pistoned them in and out and rubbed my wetness up toward my ass.

"I don't even think you need lube," he murmured.

"I need lube!"

"Not yet."

He slid into my pussy. I didn't know if I was turned on, or my body was just so stimulated from the spanking, but it felt like heaven. Every inch felt like heaven. My hips bucked without intention, it just happened. I wanted more of him, all of him. He made a soft, satisfied noise and pulled out of me. "Feels good, doesn't it?"

"Yes." My voice sounded a bit desperate.

"You want more?"

"Yes."

"*Yes, Sir.* Be polite, Chere."

The last thing on my mind was manners, but I felt so empty, so needy that I complied. "Yes, Sir. Please fuck me."

And he did. He eased back into me, slowly, so I felt him everywhere. My breasts tingled, my ass clenched, my toes curled. Yes, it was like that. But I soon remembered that he was a sadist, because every time I got in that perfect rhythm, or found that perfect spot, he stopped, or moved, or twisted my nipples and unbalanced everything.

"Oh, please," I would whine or protest, and he would laugh.

I wanted to come so badly, but the teasing went on, accompanied by lots of filthy talk about what a whore I was, and all the depraved sex acts he planned to commit on my body. I'd almost come eight or nine times when he shifted his weight and teased the head of his cock over my asshole.

I cringed. I did anal, sure. I was great at anal, but I didn't usually do anal with sadists.

"Don't be too rough," I begged.

He seemed to take offense at that. He spanked my ass, *smack, smack,* each cheek, as hard as before. "Why don't you fucking trust me?" he asked.

"Because you hurt me!" The lingering fire in my ass cheeks was proof of that. "And because I can't see you, and you won't tell me your name."

"So little trust," he said. But he did use lube, smearing it in and around my asshole, which was good because he sported a pretty hefty girth. My legs shook. My whole body shook. It was partly because I was tired of holding this ass-in-the-air position, and partly because I was scared of the upcoming pain.

"Come here." He lay me down on my side, cradling me against the front of his body. My bound hands made fists between us, and his cock jutted through my legs until he reached down to point it at my ass.

I braced as he pushed forward. I couldn't help tensing up. He jammed his cock into my ass anyway, wedging the head inside. I moaned at the usual feeling of stretching and discomfort. Anal was sexy to me in theory, and I loved watching it in porn, but God, it hurt when you first got started.

"Please go slow," I gasped, leaning my head back against his chest.

"Hush."

And in that "hush" I heard *your ass is mine,* and *I'm going to do this, so deal with it,* and *you don't want another spanking, do you?*

He pressed deeper, assisted by the lube. My ass spasmed around him, trying to impede the invasion. He didn't stop until the entire length of his thick cock was buried balls-deep. I counted the inches. Remember, I still hadn't come.

I didn't expect to come now, because assfucking was sticky and painful and awkward, and anal thrusting didn't feel that good. A monster cock quickly became a minus when that monster cock was sliding in and out of your very sensitive asshole.

"You're so tight," he murmured against my ear. "I love fucking women in the ass. Since you sucked me off earlier, I'll be able to fuck your ass a long time. A long, long time."

That brought another moan from me, and a chuckle from him.

"Do you really not like it, or are you pretending not to like it to make me happy?" he asked.

"It's not that I don't like it," I said, which was true. "It's just that it doesn't feel very good."

"How masochistic of you, to want something that doesn't feel good."

I almost corrected him, reminded him that I didn't say I wanted it. I mean, he was the one who wanted it. If not for him, this wasn't happening right now. He could still be in my pussy, almost-but-not-quite making me come.

"You know why anal feels so good to me?" he went on in that mesmerizing whisper. "Because I have all the power in this. I could wreck your body right now if I wanted to. I could hurt you so bad. You're trembling and arching to me, and accepting all this because you don't want me to hurt you."

I let out a breath. Was his voice mesmerizing because of his words, or because he was sliding inside me again, prying me open, and yes, threatening me with the thick, hard weapon between his legs? "Please don't hurt me," I whimpered, and I think I did that to turn him on.

"I won't," he said, so gently, "as long as you're a good girl and let me do what I want."

We were on our sides, lying in bed, but there was nothing comfortable or relaxed about the way he drove into me. When I tried to push his body back with my hands, he yanked them high against my spine. My shoulders ached. My ass was stuffed full, and he seemed like he could go on another hour. When I tried to squirm away from the hard, repetitive thrusts, he reached around and spread his fingers across my pelvis. I was his hole to fuck. He wasn't letting me escape even an inch of his invasion.

It occurred to me that fighting him probably made him want to prolong it. If I surrendered and lay there—like a fuck hole—maybe he'd lose interest and finish faster. I stopped resisting and relaxed my tense muscles. Miss Kitty had become Miss Fuckhole. Okay, fine. I got paid plenty of money to be a fuckhole.

But as soon as I surrendered and stopped participating in my anal subjugation, he was ready with something new. More stimulation. Damn him, I didn't want it. The hand anchoring my pelvis slid down. One probing fingertip settled atop my clit, setting off a stuttering throb of sensation. I gasped. It felt so good. I wanted to come so badly, even now. All that unfulfilled tension from earlier was still there, aching and teeming.

"There's my girl," he said. I could hear the amusement in his voice, but I didn't care. I needed more touching, more stroking. He rationed it out to me, the lightest brushes, engineered to keep me simmering right at the edge. He teased my nipples, making me tremble and cry in frustration. This went on for an ungodly period of time. No one had ever fucked my ass—or kept me on the edge of orgasm—for half this long.

"Please let me come," I begged. He'd long since stripped me of my pride, another thing no client had ever done. No. Client. Ever. "Please, I can't bear this."

"You're bearing it," he said. "It's beautiful."

He licked behind my ear and tapped my clitoris again. It was torture. No, it was amazing. No, it was evil. He must have realized I'd really had enough, that I was about to check out in the very real sense of losing my sanity, because his thrusts quickened, and his fingers stayed on my clit. They played between my pussy lips, holding me open in the same way he held my soul open, via this sodomy session from hell. If he left me unsatisfied now, I would have disintegrated.

But he didn't leave me unsatisfied. He toyed with me and urged me on until we climaxed together. I didn't know what his orgasm was like, but mine was so intense that it was painful. The apex of it was literally painful, but once the pain softened into something I could process, *ohhh*. It felt really good. Throbbing, melting, singing, shuddering, super-extended orgasm good. And after the initial, incredible minute-long orgasm, there were still aftershocks that rippled inside me for seconds at a time. My spanked cheeks didn't hurt anymore. My reamed ass didn't hurt. Everything felt amazingly perfect.

His orgasm couldn't have been as good as mine, but he was silent and shuddery for a long time too. In fact, he stayed in my ass until he was almost completely soft, and even then, I could sense his reluctance to draw away. He got up and went to the bathroom. I didn't trust myself to walk so I stayed where I was. I couldn't clean up, anyway, until he released my hands.

He came back and I felt the bed dip. I was nudged onto my stomach. He slapped my ass again. "You're nice and red, Chere. You might have a few lingering bruises. A souvenir until you see me next time."

"If there's a next time."

He turned me back over and kissed me, tasting faintly of the scotch we'd had earlier. "Oh, there'll be a next time."

"Not if you don't stop blindfolding me. I can't stand it."

"I know you don't like it. I won't do that to you forever."

His fingers traced over my face. I wished I could do the same to him, just to know anything about him, but I couldn't. It frustrated me so bad.

"Are you okay?" he asked. "I've got to go soon."

"Go then," I said, turning my face away from his touch. "You pay for these sessions. You can leave any time."

He rose, and I felt bad I'd been so snippity to him after what we'd just shared, after the orgasm he'd just given me, which eclipsed even the orgasms he'd given me last week, which used to be the best orgasms of my life.

"I wish you'd tell me your name," I said. "Even just your first name."

"The E's stand for Edward and Estlin."

"You're not E.E. Cummings, and it's wrong that you use E.E. Cumming for your fake name. So wrong."

"He's one of my favorite poets. At least I left off the 's' so there wouldn't be any confusion."

"I bet you don't know one thing E.E. Cummings has written."

I jumped when he grabbed my hair. Shit, I never saw him coming. He yanked it once and tilted my head back, and kissed me hard this time, like a punishment. "You're a sassy little girl," he said against my lips. "If we weren't out of time, I'd punish you for that sass. Sex dolls should be seen and not heard."

Ugh, he was a disgusting pig. A sexy disgusting pig, which was so much worse.

"If you won't tell me your real name, at least let me see what you look like," I said. "If you won't let me see what you look like, I'm not coming back."

"I'll miss you."

That did it. His smug, self-satisfied "I'll miss you" had just driven the final nail into his coffin. I wasn't going to see him again. No. See how smug he was then. Asshole.

"You're not going to miss me," I said, "and I'm not coming back. Here's a tip. There are a lot of high-class whores in New York who specialize in BDSM. Maybe you should look into it."

"Shut your mouth and be quiet."

I clamped my lips shut, not because he told me to, but because he was an asshole not worthy of any more words. Ten minutes or more went by. I had no way of knowing if he was getting dressed, or primping, or just sitting there staring at me. I thought I heard a pen drop on the desk, and a rustle of paper.

"I brought you another skirt and blouse," he said. "You can take them when you leave."

I wondered what he'd done with my old skirt. I wondered why he told me to bring extra clothes when he hadn't cut my clothes off this time. I wondered why I cared.

He lifted me off the bed. I heard the rustles and noises and smells that were already so familiar to me in my enforced blindness, and the scissors against my wrists.

"You can stay here all night if you like," he said, slicing through the zip ties. "If you don't want to go home to your asshole boyfriend. But don't dare bring him here."

I stood a moment in shock, long enough for him to squeeze my hand and leave. The door lock engaged with a click. How could W have known I had a boyfriend? Maybe it was just an assumption. But then why had he called Simon an asshole? *He is an asshole, Chere, even if you won't admit it.*

No, W couldn't know about Simon. I stood there rubbing my wrists like an idiot before I finally reached up and unbuckled the mask. The first thing I saw was my bag on the table by the window. I'd dropped that bag by the door, so W had picked it up at some point. Had he gone through it? My phone screensaver was a photo of me and Simon. My *asshole boyfriend.*

Jesus Christ, he could have gone through everything in my phone. He might have pawed through my wallet. He might have all my credit card numbers, my phone numbers, my home address. I felt sick. I dug for my wallet and counted my money. But no, he wouldn't have stolen my fucking chump change. He had plenty of money.

No, he'd only stolen my privacy and peace of mind.

How dare he go through my bag and my wallet, and possibly all my phone contacts, when he wouldn't give me the first piece of information about himself?

I was so angry, I almost didn't notice the replacement skirt and blouse hanging on the back of the chair, or the note pinned to the plastic overlay, written in his rough, blocky hand.

Her heart breaks in a smile—and she is lust
Mine also, little painted poem of God.

I stared at it a long time before I placed it, and then my throat went tight. He knew at least one E.E. Cummings poem. It happened to be the one with the most power to make me cry.

IN BETWEEN

When I met Simon, I was working at a strip club. I believed I was a piece of shit. People treated me like a piece of shit. I worked with many, many pieces of shit, most of them my bosses. This felt normal to me, after being raised by a piece-of-shit mother, and being regularly abused by her piece-of-shit boyfriends.

But Simon was the first person in my life who refused to accept this piece-of-shit view of myself. We didn't have a lot in common, except that we were both very sensitive souls, and I thought, *finally, someone who understands me*. He came to see me at my strip club, even though it was gross and seedy. He supported me and tried to pump me up when I tore myself down. He talked me out of a dozen spirals, and then he gave me a copy of *A Chorus Girl* by E.E. Cummings, and brought me to his studio.

"Look," he said. And I hadn't had any idea what I was looking at. It was a huge, rough-edged canvas with scarlet blurs and pink splotches, and big swirls of paint. "It's you," he said when I didn't respond. "I painted this about you. About the poem. See?"

And God, I didn't see, but I changed during that moment of shock and confusion, because someone had *made a painting about me*. Not just any old someone, but a real, legitimate artist who had done a show and started a mailing list and whom followers and critics labeled as an up-and-comer.

41

If I was truly a worthless person, a piece of shit, he wouldn't have made a painting about me. That painting was acquired by the Louvre in Paris a few years later and hangs there to this day, in a great, white, airy, climate-controlled atrium. It was called *Heart-Lust*, and we became a couple, and I graduated from stripping to working for the most exclusive escort agency in the city, because I was too good for stripping. I was not a piece of shit.

Even if, most days, I felt like a piece of shit.

W couldn't have known any of this. Even if he snooped through my bag, even if he downloaded everything on my phone, he couldn't have known about that evening Simon pulled me into his studio and showed me that painting with a huge smile on his angelic face.

How happy W would be if he knew how much that snippet of poem messed with me, how long it had taken me to stop sobbing in the Viceroy hotel room. Fuck, fuck, fuck him.

I finally pulled myself together and headed home, red-eyed and exhausted. Simon wasn't at the loft, which was probably a blessing, since I didn't think I could have looked at him tonight without dying of grief. How had things changed so much between us? Why was he strung out on drugs now, and struggling to make art? Why wasn't I enough for him? What had happened, where had I fucked up?

I went to our bedroom and knelt beside the bed, and pulled out the decoupaged box from underneath. *The Chorus Girl* was in there, amongst the other sad, lingering detritus of our relationship. Simon had handwritten the whole poem for me in his arching, spidery hand, so different from W's square, bold lettering. There were pictures from our trip to Paris, and other trips we'd taken. Dried flowers. Show tickets. Invitations to weddings we'd attended, although the subject of marriage never came up between us, even after ten years.

I closed the box and leaned my head on the edge of the bed. Fuck. There was no love between the two of us anymore, only co-dependency. I needed to be in a relationship to prove I wasn't a piece of shit, and Simon... Simon needed a caretaker. He needed monitoring and money. He barely made art anymore, and drugs cost a lot. A fortune. An entire world.

I heard the hum of the elevator, heard Simon come in and bang the door shut. There was a time I would have run out there and flung myself into his arms. He would have kissed my temple and my hair and my lips.

He would have said, "Hello, gorgeous," and looked at me with his artist's eyes that were always bright and curious, and approving. He used to adore me. Now he adored the drugs more, and his artist's eyes were hazy and unfocused.

He puttered in the kitchen for a while and then retreated to his studio. I shoved the box back under the bed and stayed where I was, feeling too heavy to stand. Even after the thirty-minute shower, even after I put on my softest pair of yoga pants, my ass cheeks still hurt and I could still feel W on me. I wondered if he ever used drugs. I tried to imagine him slurring his words and twitching the way Simon did when he was really high. No. I couldn't imagine W giving up control in that way. Or maybe I didn't want to think about W not being in control.

I didn't like that W was so much in my thoughts, especially when he gave me nothing in return.

Oh, he gives you something, my conscience whispered. *Just not the something you want.*

I tried not to want anything from clients, except money. I tried not to get involved, but W made me feel involved. Since he wouldn't tell me his name, or let me see how he looked, I desperately wanted to know his name, and I was dying to see how he looked.

And the worst part of it was, he knew I felt that way. He enjoyed fucking with me. I didn't believe that he would eventually reveal himself to me, but part of me still wanted to meet him again just in case he did. Because never knowing the name and face of this man—that seemed an impossible burden to bear.

Speaking of impossible burdens to bear...

"Chere!" That was Simon's angry voice. He came into the bedroom, his hair disheveled, his shirt undone, revealing his chest but not his arms. He never let me see his arms. "Chere, I need money."

"For what?"

"For life," he spat back. "I know you just got back from a date. Don't be a bitch."

I drew back a little on the bed. "I don't get that money right away. Henry has it."

Henry had a lot of my money now, and deposited it in a secret account for me. It was his suggestion, since he knew about Simon's "problem."

"I won't get the money for this date until tomorrow," I said. "I only have sixty bucks."

"Well, I need it."

"Where's your money? When are you going to sell something?"

He was purposely tuning me out, looking around for my purse. "You went on a date two days ago. You have money."

"I need that money for rent. Jesus, Simon, you've got to stop this—"

He charged at me. I flinched. He saw my bag by the nightstand and grabbed it, and dug for my wallet like the junkie he was.

"I need to eat," I yelled. I pulled at the purse straps like an old lady being mugged. "You need to eat too. Let's go to dinner."

"I don't want fucking dinner. I need to work, I need to paint something."

"You need drugs."

He took my sixty dollars and threw the bag back at me. It was okay. I had money hidden everywhere. That's what the significant others of drug addicts did. They hid money. They maintained. They walked on eggshells.

"I need to work," he said, glaring at me. He didn't look like an angel anymore. He looked like a devil in withdrawal. "I'm going to get off the drugs, so you can stop looking at me that way. But it doesn't just happen like that." He snapped his fingers in my face, a sharp, bony click. "I need to build up some work first, so I can take a break and go into treatment. I need to have one more show, to make money, to keep the momentum going while I get clean. I have a career to think about. Why can't you understand that? Why don't you fucking give me some time to organize my shit?"

Because your career is dead in the water, and you're going to die if I give you any more time...

"I'm going to leave you," I said.

He laughed, knowing me for a liar. "Not if I leave you first."

He took my money and disappeared. The elevator hummed again. I wasn't invited anymore when he went out to do whatever he did. Party. Mingle. Sleep with other women. When I confronted him about his clinging art groupies, he silenced my complaints by pointing out that I slept with other men. Sometimes, in his rages, he called me a whore, and I thought, *I am a whore. Even if I'm classy and high-priced, and pretty on the outside, I'm still a whore.*

And he was a drug addict and a user, so I guess we deserved each other, for better or worse.

3.

THE PARK HYATT SESSION

I went back again for more, in the same fucking amber-beige dress. The Park Hyatt this time, across from Carnegie Hall, because I needed the money and W tipped twice as much as my other dates.

It was fine, I told myself. I could use this as an exercise to be hard and unreachable. I wouldn't let him get in my head or my heart this time. I would use him for money, turn the trick, and get out. I didn't even mind strapping on the damned black leather eye mask because I didn't want to know what he looked like. I didn't care anymore. Who fucking cared?

I knocked on the door and let him pull me inside. I held my bag against my chest as he kissed me, remembering his betrayal of trust last time. I hadn't brought anything this time, just extra clothes and some emergency money, and my phone, which was now locked with a passcode. He tugged it away from me in order to zip-tie my hands behind my back.

I let him bind me once again, because that was what he liked to do, and I was the prostitute he'd hired. I smelled his familiar smell, the cologne I knew by heart. If not for that smell, it could be anyone kissing me. I hardened my lips and my body. He could kiss me, but I wasn't kissing him back.

As soon as I stopped responding to him, he stopped pawing me and led me across the room. He turned me around and sat me on the bed.

"How did you like the poem?" he asked.

"What poem? The two lines you wrote last week?"

"You didn't plug them into a search engine?" he said acidly.

"I didn't have to, Mr. Cumming," I replied just as acidly. "Although I have to admit, it's the first time a client's ever written poetry for me."

"I've made it my mission to bring a little poetry back to the world." I flinched as his hand touched my cheek. "Back to your world anyway."

"Whatever floats your boat. I don't have much use for poetry in my line of work."

"Oh, you loved it. You memorized it by the second day. Repeat them, the words I wrote for you."

I wasn't in the mood for games. "You didn't write them for me," I said. "E.E. Cummings wrote them for some chorus girl he liked, and poetry memorization isn't one of the services I offer."

He opened my legs. I felt him stand between them, right against my front. "You'll do whatever I tell you to do, you fucking whore." He stuck his thumbs in my mouth, pried it open. "Speak."

I jerked my head away. "Fuck you. I'd rather suck you off."

"I don't want you to suck me off. I want you to repeat the words I wrote for you."

"I can't. I don't remember," I lied. "I didn't memorize them."

"Yes, you did. You still have the piece of paper under your pillow, or in some fucking scrapbook, don't you? You read it every day."

I hated his hubris, and the fact that he was right. I had looked at that piece of paper daily. "I only know the words because I knew that poem. I knew it before."

"No, you didn't. It's obscure, one of his earliest works."

I knew the whole damn poem by heart, and to irritate him, I recited it, word for word, up until the last two lines he'd written out for me. I wished I could have seen his face. Was he smiling? Did he find it funny? Was he irritated? Angry?

"That poem means something to you," he finally said.

I didn't answer. I refused to even acknowledge his speculative musing. If he wouldn't give me his name, he wasn't getting my story about that poem. Some hurts were best kept locked up in your heart.

"So, I'm pissed today," he went on, when my response wasn't forthcoming. "I wanted to see you two days ago, but you had an appointment with some other asshole."

"You're not the only client I see. Sorry."

He grasped my shoulders and shoved me back on the bed. He pulled off one of my shoes, then the other, and pushed up my skirt. I'd put on an old fashioned garter belt and beige stockings to match his classy beige dress. He ran his hands up the back seams.

"Trying to seduce me?" he asked.

I wasn't. It was only that I needed the power of feeling pretty. I needed to feel sleek and sexy like Miss Kitty.

So much for that. He had the clasps popped in a heartbeat, and the stockings down over my feet. Once he had them off, he knotted one around my ankle. I kicked at him, but not hard enough. He tied my ankle to the bottom of the hotel bed frame, and no matter how hard I pulled, I couldn't break away. I rolled across the bed, but he only grabbed my other ankle, knotted it with the other stocking, and bound it too. I flailed helplessly, and then I stopped because I figured I was only turning him on.

I stared into nothingness. It was utterly black behind my eye mask. For a while he didn't move and he didn't touch me. He could have been taking video. He could have left the room. I didn't know.

Then I felt the bed dip and felt his hands on my face. He put something into my mouth, a hard ball gag that depressed my tongue. I shook my head, making urgent, muffled noises that went unheeded. He hurt my hair when he fastened it behind my head. I didn't know what was worse, my hair pinched in the buckle, or my inability to shriek the way I wanted to.

"Sorry for the gag. Like I said, I'm feeling pissed today."

I couldn't respond to that statement even if I wanted to. He left and came back, and I heard the scissors, *snip, snip, snip.* The amber-beige dress was no more, cut to shreds, and I felt satisfied by that, because he'd bought it. The garter belt was snipped away too, though he could have easily unhooked it. But whatever. I had a drawer full of them. I didn't even like this one that much.

Then he started playing with my nipples, and I thought, *oh no. The clamps.* I mewled behind the gag, like that might help. My legs jerked, trying to break free, but the pain came anyway, the piercing, terrifying bite of his satanic nipple clamps. I pictured them, black and evil looking, my tender pink nipples smashed within their grip. When I struggled, the clamps hurt worse, so I lay still, panting. I shook my head in silent protest. *No, no, why are you doing this?*

I heard the clink of a buckle and the whisper of his belt being pulled from his pant loops. A second later, I felt the hot pain of leather, heard the whap of impact along my inner thigh. I jumped, the clamps jingled and tugged, my nipples screamed. I screamed. I gnawed on the gag and tried to pull my legs together, but the stockings bound me tight. I wasn't afraid of being killed anymore. He wasn't a killer, he was a sadist. I was afraid of being hurt, and hurt, and hurt, and not being able to stop him, or scream loud enough for anyone to hear.

"I have a proposition for you," he said, and then he whapped me on my other thigh. It wasn't unbearable pain, but it still felt awful. My nipples throbbed, my thighs burned. He placed the belt between my tied-open thighs, over my exposed and vulnerable pussy. "I know you can't talk right at this moment, but I want you to think about it. I want to pay you a weekly rate, and for that rate, I want you to stop seeing your other clients."

I shook my head. He brought the belt down against my pussy lips. *Whap.* I jerked my legs and surged up on the bed, only to be pressed back down again.

"You're not thinking about it," he said. "You're just thinking about the pain, which is okay. It's what I want you to think about right now."

He slapped my pussy with the belt again, the leather licking my sensitive lips. Then he moved back to my thighs, punishing me with the belt up and down the sensitive inner skin. When I was screaming behind the gag, when my legs trembled uncontrollably from the pain and heat, he moved back to slapping my pussy. It probably didn't sound that loud in the room. You probably couldn't have heard the impact from the hallway, but each blow made my whole body shake. The belt must have been worn, supple. It seemed to mold itself against my skin to hurt me more.

"Are you thinking about what I said?" he asked.

What had he said? A weekly rate. Ah, God, my pussy was so wet. Why was I wet? I was scared and suffering, in a world of pain.

"I don't want to see you every day," he said, continuing his earlier conversation. "That's not the point. But when I want you, I want you to fucking be available."

Whap.

"None of your other jackass clients know how to satisfy you. How to work you over."

Whap.

"But I do."

Whap.

What? He thought he was satisfying me right now? If I wasn't bound and gagged, I'd probably be calling the police.

He stopped. "Look at you," he said. "Look at you struggling, hurting. Are you pretending that gag is my cock in your mouth? You want me inside you?"

I shook my head, even though it made the clamps hurt worse. I shook my head hard, denying, protesting.

Lying.

He slapped my pussy again, this time with his hand. He shoved his fingers inside me and I could actually hear how wet I'd become.

"You're so juicy from having your pussy whipped, it's dripping onto the bed. You're making a fucking mess, you little pain slut. Next time, I'm going to bring harder clamps. You need it harder. You *want* it harder."

I shook my head again. Harder clamps would kill me, but part of me remembered how wet I'd gotten the moment he put them on. Maybe harder ones would only make me wetter.

Damn it, I hated myself. I hated being a liar. I wanted to come so bad. I wanted to come while he was flailing away at my pussy with his horrible, punishing belt. I wanted him to free my hands so I could open myself up, so he could bring the leather right down on my swollen clit.

"Please," I moaned behind the gag. "Please let me go. Please take off the clamps."

It sounded like nothing, a bunch of desperate whining. He slid the belt over my nipples, joggling the clamps, then trailed it down my trembling stomach and over my pussy. Then he slid it beneath me and pulled it up from the front and the back so I could feel the leather all along my slit. My pussy ached to be fucked. He moved the belt back and forth, and my hips bucked for more of the contact.

He chuckled. So humiliating. I felt his body close to mine, his bare skin. He must have undressed at some point. I felt the brush of his warm shoulder and his hard, muscular chest.

"When you're mine, only mine, we can do this all the time," he said. "I can gag you and hurt you and make you come and come and come until you can't stand it. We can fluid bond, and go bareback, and I'll come in you over and over, until my cum's dripping out of you like a fucking waterfall. I'd like that, Chere. You suit me perfectly, and I hate to share. I'll pay not to share you."

I shook my head, but clearly, at this point, I was only amusing him with my frantic, fake denials. He took off the clamps and I sucked air through the gag as my nipples flared in protest. His hands yanked my hips closer to the edge of the bed and his cock poked against my ass.

"When I'm pissed, I don't use as much lube," he said. "Good thing your pussy's so messy and drippy."

As if to demonstrate, he jammed his fingers in my pussy and gathered the copious wetness. I almost came right then, with his fingers rough inside me and his cock against my hole. Then he started pushing forward into my ass, and it hurt too much to come.

Oh, shit, it hurt. I fought him, but I couldn't really fight him. I couldn't draw away, or deny him, only squirm and toss on the bed. When he was fully seated inside me, he leaned his weight on me, and I wished I could see what he looked like, looming over me with his cock hard and deep in my ass.

I pictured dark eyes, a lover's gaze, even though he was brutal to me. He started to ride me with harsh, steady thrusts. I groaned behind the gag, hating this and loving it. When he drove especially deep, his pelvis ground against my clit and I ached for climax. Anal hurt, but it was a thrilling, hot kind of pain. I didn't want him to stop. My pussy clenched, still flowing with everything I felt for him.

He wanted me to himself.

He didn't want to share me with anyone else.

He pinched my still-tender nipples while he fucked my ass. I arched my back, and he made a pleased sound, a nonverbal cue, like a trainer rewarding a dumb animal. I was that dumb animal, blind, mute, strapped down, my asshole stuffed to the hilt, my nipples sore and sensitive. I tugged at my stocking bondage, but he obviously knew his knots, and nylon was impossible to break. Drool leaked from the corners of my gagged mouth as his pace quickened, along with his force. He hurt my nipples and toyed with my clit in equal measure, so the depth of my pain and degradation was matched by the height of my pleasure. The two of them got mixed up, these two powerful feelings, dread and bliss.

"You know why you like it in the ass?" he said. "Because that's what you deserve."

I did deserve it. I was a whore, a slut, an animal who couldn't stop myself from enjoying the perverted things he did. So much for being hard and unreachable. The only one hard and unreachable in our current scenario was him.

"You have one minute to come," he said as I endured his quickening thrusts. "One minute to come with my cock buried in your whore ass. You should have come already."

He fucked me harder, twisting my nipples. I panted behind the gag and spread my legs as far as I could, arching toward his pain and his pleasure, eager to take both of them to get what I wanted, which was relief. Or release. Maybe they were the same thing.

When I finally let go, I came hard, my ass clenching around his shaft in rhythmic pulsations. I vaguely remembered one of my fellow call girls bragging about anal orgasms, that her ass could come just like her pussy, and I remember thinking *bullshit*. But my ass was coming like hell, along with my pussy, and my clit, and my sore, aching nipples, all of it at once. I didn't make a sound. There was no energy left for sound, except maybe a rasping outlet of breath.

As for W, he made a sound like the one he'd made earlier, another animal-trainer cue, only more intense. He held my shoulders as he came, then his hands crept up to my neck and gripped me there. It made me clench him harder, everywhere, all over. I moaned, choking. *Don't hurt me anymore. I can't take anymore.*

He was gone in a flash. His hands gone from my neck, his cock gone from my ass. I was afraid he'd deserted me completely, but then I felt his weight dip the bed beside me. A moment later, his fingers ruffled my hair, touching, teasing. I fought the urge to turn my body toward him for more contact. I didn't want to need him. He was too rough, too cruel. I absolutely wasn't going to see him again.

He rose a moment later and went into the bathroom. I heard water. Not a shower, a bathtub. I drowsed to the sound of the bubbling water until he touched one of my ankles. *Snip, snip* through the stockings. Him and his damned scissors. The gag came off next. I opened and closed my mouth, waggled my tongue. My chin was coated with drool.

"Let's go take a bath," he said. "You're a fucking mess."

I let him lead me into the bathroom, not sure if he intended to bathe me or drown me.

"My arms ache," I said, my mouth still stiff and awkward. "Please unbind my wrists. I'm afraid to be in the water with my hands bound behind my back." No response. "I won't try to take off the blindfold, I promise. I don't care what you look like." Huge lie, but I really was scared.

I guess he heard enough fear in my voice—not the sexy kind of fear—to take pity on me. He cut off the zip ties but kept hold of one of my wrists. He guided me to the tub and helped me get in. Oh, God, it felt so warm, perfect temperature. He climbed in too, settling me in his lap. I leaned my head against his shoulder and thought I could fall asleep right here, cradled against his body with his muscles sliding under my skin. I was too tired to even care that I was blindfolded. My eyes closed behind the leather mask, and my body relaxed against his.

"Don't fall asleep," he said, and I perked up again. "We need to talk, remember?"

"Talk about what?"

He started washing me, using the Park Hyatt's fragrant soap, and a soft washcloth to sponge the drool from my chin and neck. "About an exclusive arrangement," he said.

"Why? Why do you want me to stop seeing other people?"

"So I can see you whenever I want. And because I want to fluid bond with you. Bareback."

"I'm not allowed to do that."

"Says who?"

"My boss."

"When you're with me, I'm your boss."

I shook my head. "I can't. I need to work at least four appointments a week."

"For what? For money? I'm offering you money." He named an amount that was four appointments worth of cash, plus extra. A lot of extra. It scared me. What would he demand for that kind of money?

"The thing is, I have a life," I said. "A home. A boyfriend. I can't be at your beck and call, no matter how much you pay me."

"I don't want you at my beck and call. I'd be reasonable. I just don't want you seeing other guys."

"Why?"

He ran a hand down between my breasts. "Because I don't like to share." He laughed softly. "Your fucking boyfriend. He puts up with your job?"

I wasn't going to talk to him about Simon, or my personal life. It was bad enough he was asking me to be exclusive. "I can't bareback with you, ever," I said.

"Okay, but you can stop seeing other people."

"Did you talk to Henry about this?"

"Yes, I've talked to Henry. He said it was up to you."

W was washing me so gently. I didn't think he was even washing me anymore, just stroking me. *Don't do this, Chere. Don't be swayed by how good he makes you feel. By this body, his scent, the rumble of his voice...*

"The thing is, you're not my only regular client," I said. "Those johns will move on when I'm not available. When you're finished with me, when you're finished doing...whatever this is we're doing together, I'll need to build up my client list all over again."

"You'll have enough money to coast for a while. And I don't think you'd have a whole lot of trouble finding new clients. You're a good lay."

His fingers delved between my legs. He stroked me until I couldn't hold back the noises, the need. His cock was hard, jutting up between us, and next thing I knew, I was sliding along the length of it, sloshing water back and forth in the tub.

"Are you on the pill?" he asked, stilling me with the tip of his cock against my entrance.

"Yes. I mean, no. I mean, you can't." I reached down to block him. I was on the pill, but he wasn't coming inside me without a rubber. No.

"I'm clean, Chere. I'm a very responsible person."

"How do you know *I'm* responsible?"

That laugh again. "Because you're too much of a bitch to be careless. I bet you don't even let the boyfriend in without a condom. If you really have a boyfriend."

There was a shift and a splash, and the sound of a condom wrapper, and then he was back again. I checked with my fingers and yes, he was sheathed. Yes, I was a bitch when it came to protection. Yes, since the drugs, I hadn't let Simon near me without a condom, although the truth was, we hadn't had sex for months.

"Be mine, Chere, just for a while." He surged into me. I was primed, even in the water. He teased my still-hurting breasts and filled me oh, so perfectly. "Be exclusive with me. It won't be that long. Just a few months. I'll probably get bored of you by then."

"You're an asshole."

"I never said I wasn't."

"I can hardly get up the motivation to see you from week to week, much less be exclusive with you," I said. "You're cruel and full of yourself. There's nothing about you I like."

He manipulated my clit, just to prove me a liar. My hips bucked, rebelling, arching for more. "Nothing you like, huh?" he said in that bemused tone of his.

"And I don't know anything about you. You act like your personal information is some holy grail that no mere mortal can look upon."

"You know my name."

"Your fake name."

A pause, just long enough for me to realize how cranky and pathetic I sounded.

"You like me that much, huh?" he said, pressing me down on his cock. "You're crazy about me."

"No."

"You are. You want to know all about me. It's killing you that you don't know my name, my favorite color, my birthday—"

"I don't want to know anything about you." Jesus, if only he wasn't such a good fuck, even now, in a bathtub, when I was pissed at him for being a jerk. "You know, if you want to build up an exclusive arrangement with an escort, zip ties and blindfolds aren't the way to go about it. Or hard anal, tied to a bed."

"You love hard anal, tied to a bed."

"I don't."

"Admit that you do, or I will take you back, tie you down again, and prove you wrong."

I was silent a moment. He said, "Okay," and started to get up, cock inside me and everything.

I grabbed his shoulders in a panic. "No. Please. Okay, I admit it." I couldn't go through that again.

"You fucking idiot," he said. That was his only answer to my capitulation. That, and renewed bathtub intercourse. He hit my G-spot like magic. I hated him for it. I hated him for making me feel good when he was such an asshole.

"I hate you," I said.

"You don't, but I don't mind if you pretend."

"I'm not pretending," I said with more fire.

"I like design, Chere. I like chocolate cake. What do you like?"

I committed these small and pointless details about him to memory, and hated myself for it. "You're giving me tidbits of information about you, what, as some form of apology for being an asshole?"

He ignored my vitriol. "What do you like, Chere?" he asked in a tone that demanded an answer.

"Seeing people who are fucking me." That was my answer, and I felt like crying, and I still hated myself. "I like seeing the person whose cock is inside me. I know that sounds crazy and unreasonable."

His fingers tightened on my arms. I waited for him to drown me, or throw me out of the tub, but he did neither. Instead he said, "If you want to date me without the blindfold, you have to be mine. Exclusive."

Fuck. I wanted to be angry. I wanted to throw *him* out of the tub, but he felt so good inside me. He reached down to massage my clit.

"You can see me, starshine. You can see all of me. Just agree not to see anyone else for a while."

Oh God, the temptation. I really wanted to know what he looked like. I couldn't bear to never know, to never see him. "Fine," I said in a huff. "I'll be exclusive with you for a few months. Will you take off the blindfold now?" I wanted to see him so badly.

He gripped my wrists. "No, next time. Next date."

"Why next date? Why not now?"

"Because I said so. When I set up our next date, Henry will tell you which hotel, and what time to be in the lobby. If you recognize me when I come in, we'll have our date. If you don't recognize me, too bad. No date, no money, no tip. No seeing what I look like."

"How am I supposed to recognize you? Magic?"

He took my wrists and pulled my hands up, and flattened them against his cheeks. "Feel me. Learn me. You'll be able to recognize me."

Oh, God, I was touching his face. It felt so sudden, so intimate. I tried to think how he looked from the contours I felt. His cock was still inside me—I knew his cock. I knew it well. But everything else, I was feeling for the first time. He moved inside me, fucking me as I raped his face with my sense of touch.

Stubble. I knew there would be stubble. Soft eyebrows, taut cheekbones, a masculine nose, not too pointy, not too prominent. At least I didn't think so.

I traced his lips next. They felt firm and rough, and warm under my fingers. He opened his mouth and bit me, just above the knuckle. I laughed and felt his cock buck inside me. I'd never recognize him, but this was wonderful. I reached up to explore his scalp, and the texture of his hair. It was short, a little prickly. Cropped close on the sides, but a little longer on top. Much longer near the front.

"What color is your hair?" I whispered.

"That's cheating," he whispered back. "Are you going to come or not? The water's getting cold."

He made me come about thirty seconds later, because he knew how to do that, and the whole time I groped his face, trying to picture him.

"Talk to Henry," he said as he drained the water from the tub. "Tell him you agree to be exclusive. And find me next time we meet. You know enough by now to pick me out of a crowd."

I didn't think I did, but perhaps I'd recognize him by some internal lust-meter. How could I not recognize the man who'd given me so many orgasms? I'd give it a try. At least I wouldn't have to wear this damn eye mask anymore.

He threw a towel over my shoulder, and we dried off. Afterward, he led me back into the room. "Sit," he said, and I sat when he forced me down, trusting a chair would be there. "Did you bring extra clothes?" he asked.

"Yes."

"*Yes, Sir.* Use your damn manners."

"Yes, Sir, I brought extra clothes." I hoped I didn't sound too sassy. He put a hand on my back and shoved me forward in the chair. Oh, Jesus.

"Be still," he said. "Don't move."

I felt a weird, tingling sensation on my back, from shoulder blade to shoulder blade. I finally realized he was writing on me. Too much to hope for, that it wasn't permanent marker.

"What do you do, that you have so much money?" I asked while he scrawled across my back.

I didn't think he'd answer, but he said, "Design."

"What do you design?"

"None of your business."

High fashion? Web design? What kind of designer made enough money for Park Hyatt call-girl sessions?

"I thought you might be an Ivy League English professor, with all the poetry," I joked.

He did a flourish with the marker against my lower back. "Poetry is just another form of design." I heard him cap it and zip his briefcase, and then begin to dress. My hands were free. I could have unbuckled the blindfold and looked at him before he could stop me. I could have finally seen what he looked like, and satisfied my curiosity. Of course, I also would have lost his trust, and possibly the ability to see him again. My whore hands stayed curled in my lap.

"There's a pool here," he said. I heard the whispery sound of him sliding on his shoes. "Did you bring a bathing suit?"

"No."

"Next time, bring a bathing suit. Will you stay here tonight?"

"I don't know."

"You can if you want. I won't come back and bother you."

It was almost sweet, how he wanted me to stay in these ritzy hotel rooms after he left me. Like he wanted to spoil me. More likely, he knew I'd think about him the entire time I was here. While I was on the bed, I'd think about him. While I was in the bathroom, I'd look at the tub and remember his skin against mine, and the smell of the soap, and the soft, scratchy loveliness of his hair. If I wasn't so chicken, I could know the color of that hair.

I would know the color of that hair, next time. Did that mean he trusted me now? I got a sickly, nervous feeling in my stomach at the idea of him revealing himself. Mere eye contact would feel like a crazy-scary level of intimacy after the way we'd begun.

He stroked my back and tugged a handful of my hair. "Goodbye, Chere. You can get up when you hear the door close."

"Bye," I said.

I heard his footfalls across the room, heard the door open and close. I wondered if he still felt pissed, or if he felt better now. My feelings had run the gamut since I arrived.

I took off the blindfold and stuck it in my bag, even though I knew I wouldn't need it again. I tried to wrestle the halves of my stockings off the bedframe, but I couldn't undo the knot. Oh well. I was sure the staff had seen everything in this kind of hotel. I collected the pieces of my dress and garter belt—he hadn't taken them with him this time. I tried not to read anything into that. *He's weird, don't try to understand him.*

And it was weird that it took that long to remember I had poetry on my back. I went into the bathroom and twisted around to try to read it in the mirror. No dice. I had to use my camera timer to take a photo. I swiped at the screen to enlarge the black words written on my skin.

Oh drink me up
That I may be
Within your cup
Like a mystery

I didn't know if it was a whole poem or part of a poem, written by him or someone else. I typed the words into my phone's search engine and got the answer: *Mystery* by D.H. Lawrence. *I lift to you my bowl of kisses/And through the temple's blue recesses/Cry out to you in wild caresses.*

I had cried out at his wild caresses, that was for sure. Well, as much as I could cry out when he gagged me. I touched my wrists, remembering the feeling of the zip ties, and then I touched the insides of my thighs, studying the pale pink marks from his belt. Talk about mystery...why the hell was I getting hot and bothered remembering that beating? Fuck me. Fuck, fuck, fuck. *Oh, drink me up...*

I sprawled back on the rumpled bed, masturbating and reading the words over and over, searching for meaning, or maybe the answer to a question I didn't know how to ask. When I finished with a shuddering orgasm, I stood and crossed to the window to look out at the city. W always picked the higher floors with the best views. Beautiful, so beautiful.

Maybe I would stay here tonight and gaze out at the vibrant cluster of New York City's lights. This room was so white and clean and bright, nothing like the loft I shared with Simon. Our loft was dark and claustrophobic, with no view at all.

IN BETWEEN

I met with Henry a couple days later, at a quiet, private cafe in midtown. The first thing he did, after air-kissing both of my cheeks, was look into my eyes with deep concern. "How are you, Chere?" he asked.

"I'm fine."

"Talk to me about this exclusive arrangement with Mr. Cumming. Two dates ago, you were calling me to complain about him. You said he was an asshole."

"He is an asshole."

He waved to the waitress, and when Henry waved, women always came running. When she scurried over, he asked for a seltzer, then turned his attention back to me. "You know, you don't have to be exclusive just because he asked you to."

"I know. But I'll make more money by being exclusive, right?" I didn't want to admit the real reason I agreed...so I could see what the asshole looked like. "Not just more money, but less work."

"Less work now. More work later, when you have to build up your client list again."

"That's where you come in. You always find more perverts to send me. I assume that's not going to change."

Henry smiled at me, his friendly, handsome smile with his white, handsome teeth. "I've got your back, love. I'll always have your back." He turned to the waitress and gave her the same drop-dead smile as she handed him his drink. "Thank you, Jessica," he said, reading her name off her tag. "I appreciate it."

Jessica practically curtsied as she backed away from the table. Ridiculous, his effect on women. I was glad he was my agent and not my boyfriend, not that Simon didn't turn a certain type of woman weak at the knees. But Simon was artsy-beautiful. Henry was beautiful-beautiful.

"One to two times a week," he said, turning back to me. "That's your contractual duty. And those are two-hour sessions, not overnights. It's a great arrangement, Chere. If you're willing..." He shrugged. "Why not?"

Oh, there were so many why nots, but I wasn't going to share them with Henry. I sipped my Irish coffee and looked out at the street, at people hurrying to appointments or jobs or lovers. "Do you know what he does for a living?" I asked.

"No."

"Where he lives?"

He spread his hands. "New York, some of the time. I don't know any more than that. I told you, I don't even know his real name. He pays me from a business account."

"What kind of business?"

"Taunt, Incorporated. It's a dummy account, as the name suggests."

I blew out a breath and rested my head on my hand. "It's so weird. Most of them are proud of what they do. Most of them want me to know who they are, how rich and powerful they are, even the ones who want me to spank them and make them stand in the corner."

Henry leaned closer to me. "Why does it matter so much to you? You're not supposed to know anything aside from the client's first name, and you know why."

Agency rules, so we wouldn't be tempted to contact clients outside of work. Bad for business. Bad for security. Bad for commissions.

"That's not why I want to find out more about him," I said. "I'd never cut you out after all you've done for me."

"I know. But that's not the only issue."

He stared at me hard. We could have whole conversations without talking. *Clients are clients. The relationship ends when they walk out the door. Don't think of them as anything more than a business transaction. Don't try to get too close to them.*

Don't ever, ever fall in love.

"It's because he's so different from the rest of them," I said. "A mystery. I've dated him three times and I still don't know what he looks like. But now, I guess I'll get to see what he looks like. A perk of going exclusive."

"I'm *dying* to know what he looks like," he said, taking a swig of his drink. "You have to call me right after your date. I hope he's not a gorilla."

"He might be."

Henry laughed. He used to be a very successful gigolo. His laugh made women's vaginas wet. Not mine, of course. Henry was my boss. A sexy boss, but still.

"If you find out his real name at some point, will you tell me?" I asked. "I won't tell him you told me."

"He'll tell you himself one day, if he wants to. Otherwise, don't worry about it. I extra-checked that there wasn't something deeper going on with him. He's safe. His privacy..."

He paused.

"What? What do you know about him?" I begged. "Just tell me. Give me one fucking scrap. I'm the one who has to date him, and in three dates, I've had his cock up my ass twice. Not a small cock either. Spill it."

He held up a finger. "I'll tell you this one thing. His desire for privacy isn't based on necessity. He's not a public figure or a celebrity. He's not in hiding, or running from the law. He's not a secret agent."

I thought to myself that he would make a pretty good secret agent. He was great at torture. "Darn," I joked. "So he's not dangerous at all?"

"He's not dangerous at all," Henry confirmed. "And that's all I'm telling you about the mysterious Mr. Cumming."

I shot him a side-eye. "But...do you know more?"

"Even if I did, I wouldn't tell you."

"You're an asshole sometimes."

"That's probably true, but you need me if you're going to work. And as you know, this dude's not going to stick around forever. All men get tired of the thing they have, and want some new thing. He'll eventually move on, and take his money and his secrecy with him, and oh, how we'll miss it." He reached out to stroke my arm. "So string him along for as long as you can. You're making a lot of bank right now. Don't fret about who he is, or why he's the way he is. Just be sexy, pretty Miss Kitty. Meow."

"He knows my real name is Chere."

Henry's eyes widened. "I never told him."

"I told him. I don't know why." I confessed it to Henry because he might eventually find out, and it was against agency rules to share our real names. "He asked me in such a demanding, scary way. It blurted out of my mouth. I'm sorry."

"You didn't tell him your last name?"

"No."

"Or anything else about yourself? Where you live? Simon's name?"

"No. Of course not." I didn't mention that W probably had all that information from looking at my phone. Henry was the one who had okayed the blindfold. I also chose not to mention the bondage. That wasn't allowed either, except with established clients and Henry's express permission. This whole conversation was making me feel sneaky and defensive. I'd never broken any of Henry's rules before now.

"He hated the name Miss Kitty," I said, as an excuse. "He hates fake stuff."

Henry's expression lost some of its warmth as his gaze bore into me. "Everything between the two of you needs to be fake. The escort-client relationship is fake. Don't ever forget that, love."

It was a warning.

"I won't," I said. "I swear I won't."

* * * * *

I returned home to find Simon in a tempestuous mood. He was painting, which was good. He didn't like what he was painting, which was bad. He was on some kind of stimulating drug, which was worse.

"Where were you?" he asked as he stabbed at the canvas with his brush.

"Meeting with Henry."

"You weren't with one of your men?" He flipped some of his hair over his shoulder, getting paint on his shirt with the jerky movement. "Tell me about your last one. Was he any good?"

We used to do this. I used to tell him about my clients to amuse him. I didn't do it anymore because he was rarely amused. More often, he used it as an excuse to lose his shit and fight with me.

"My last client was very boring," I lied.

"Oh, yeah? You didn't come home that night."

"You don't come home every night either."

He smiled like that was funny, but it wasn't a nice smile. I felt the warning systems go off. *Tread carefully, Chere.*

"But hey," I said to soothe him, "here's some good news. Henry's giving me a raise, so I can see less clients and still make the same money."

I wasn't going to tell Simon I was going exclusive with one person, not in his current, edgy mood. But he'd wonder why I wasn't going on as many dates, so I lied. I lied to Simon all the time these days. The lies felt more comfortable than telling him the truth.

"Less dates for the same money?" Simon said. *Stab, stab, stab,* still stabbing at his canvas. "Why don't you keep seeing the same number of guys and just make more?"

Why don't you make more? I thought to myself. *Why does your art suck? Why are you blowing our savings on drugs? Why can't things be the way they used to be?*

"Or are you losing clients?" he said, turning to me with an accusatory stare.

He was worried about the money. He knew his comfortable drug-addict existence was dependent on my career. If I stopped escorting, he wouldn't have the money he needed for narcotics and partying with his lemming-artist friends.

"My work is going fine," I said coolly. I wondered if he read my tone, the tone that said *Unlike yours.*

Apparently he did, because he came at me, stalked across the studio, his dripping brush pointed at me like a weapon. He jabbed the brush toward my face, his features screwed into a furious mask. I was terrified he'd try to take out my eyes. I told him to fuck off, and pushed him away. The brush flew across the room and then he was attacking me, slapping me, pushing me down on the floor. I rolled away from him and ran, but he caught me before I got to the door. I hit, I punched, I kicked, but he was stronger, and whatever he was on made him stronger still.

"What's wrong with you?" I shrieked, although I knew what was wrong with him. "Let go of me. Let go!"

"You cunt. You bitch. You think you're so much better than me."

"No, I don't!"

"I talked to Boris White. Boris White, you fucking cunt. I'm going to do a show next month, so fuck you."

"Let go of me."

I screamed *no* and *stop*, and pushed at him, but when he wigged out like this, there wasn't any way to calm him. *You asked for this*, I thought. *You set him off.* As quickly as he'd attacked me, he was gone and I was gone, running out the door, not looking behind me. I ran into the guest room and slammed the door and threw the lock. This was my safe room. It had a dead bolt, because Simon had these druggie freak outs now and again.

A moment later he was back, banging on the door like a maniac.

"Don't lock me out!" he yelled.

"Go away!"

He started kicking the door so hard I was afraid the frame would give way. I stood with my back against it and prayed for it to hold.

He finally stopped kicking, and I slept and cried, and slept and cried some more, and waited for whatever he'd ingested to wear off. Whatever he'd taken, it had made him into *that* person. Not Simon, but that monster who was erratic, heartless, terrifying.

I had to leave him.

I knew I had to leave Simon, but after a decade together and so much history, how did that leaving start? How did you forget all the memories and cut those ties? And what would happen to him when I was gone?

I stroked my face where he'd slapped it, and wondered if there'd be bruises. My mother had always had bruises. Her partners always slapped her around, and I had always thought to myself, *not me. I'll never put up with that when I'm in a relationship.*

But I did put up with it, and I hated myself for it. In some sick, twisted way, I believed that I deserved his abuse, and I probably looked just like my mother had looked when her men were hitting her. She used to cry for me to help her, but I always ran away because I didn't want to be hurt too.

She asked for this, I would tell myself, but the sounds were awful, and I'd hide under my pillows, pressing them to my ears. In the darkness, her image would be burned in my mind, her cowering, her pained expressions. She always looked resigned and guilty, just waiting for it to end.

4.

THE EMPIRE SESSION

I arrived at the Empire Hotel lobby a few minutes early. No eye mask today, which was great, but I was still a wreck. At some point, W was going to come strolling through those doors, and I was supposed to recognize him and follow him to the elevators. He seemed to think it would be easy. I wasn't so sure.

I found a place with a good view of the entrance, and sat in my call-girl skirt and blouse with my legs pressed together. Ice blue linen today, with an ivory top and pearls. Designer bag and shoes, and freshly blown out hair. I'd worked so hard to look nice, to reward him for trusting me. If I didn't recognize him, it would all be for nothing. I'd just sit in the lobby and wait, and eventually have to go home.

For some reason, I imagined him with dark hair, and olive skin. The machismo thing, I guess. I figured he'd be older, old enough to know what he wanted, and old enough to be really good in bed. When I closed my eyes, I saw someone tall, muscular but not too built, with glossy black hair and dark eyes. But at two minutes after seven, someone walked through the door, 40ish, tallish, with blond-burnished hair and a natural tan, and I thought, *that's him*. I can't say how I knew. The way he walked, the way he carried himself, the way he wore that crisp white shirt and dark red tie. The way he didn't look around the lobby. He headed toward the elevators and I surged to my feet.

But then I paused. Was it him? He didn't look the way I'd expected him to look, and he didn't seem like he was waiting for someone. He seemed like he was in a hurry to go upstairs. If he was W, wouldn't he turn to see if I was following him?

I glanced back at the lobby, frozen. No one else could be him. Maybe he wasn't here yet. But Jesus, the elevator was there and he was getting on it. I ran in my tight pencil skirt and heels. There were six other people on the elevator. I caught the man's eyes. Nothing, only the same detached appreciation I was getting from the guy next to me, and the other guy who asked me what floor.

What floor? I didn't know what floor.

"You already got it," I said, because six different floor buttons were lit up.

If the blond man was W, he would have said so by now, wouldn't he? No. He'd make me sweat all the way up. He'd punish me for pausing in the lobby, for not being sure. I straightened my shoulders as the elevator rose. Passengers got out one after the other. By the end, it was just me and the blond man. I didn't look at him. My cheeks flamed hot with embarrassment and fear. I felt attracted to him, even though I wasn't sure it was him. He definitely wasn't dark and Mediterranean. No. Blond, a *natural* blond, unlike me.

The elevator stopped at the final floor. He looked at me and gestured for me to go before him. I got nothing from that look. No recognition, no approval. Nothing. Shit. I'd fucked up. It wasn't him. I got out and lingered, feeling stupid as he headed down the hallway. I followed forlornly behind him, hoping he'd turn and laugh, and give me a thumbs up, and say, "You did it, you found me."

But he didn't do that. He keyed open a hotel room door, and turned to look at me. "Can I help you with somethin', darlin'?"

The accent was pure Texas. He looked like a Texan, like a cowboy, with sky blue eyes, and that rugged, solid body, that gold, shining hair and that real, natural tan, the kind you only got from being outside. Damn it. Was it W? Was he fucking with me? I couldn't shake the feeling that it was him. By this time, I'd been standing and staring way too long.

He tilted his head, studying me. "Would you like to come in? Have a drink?"

Still the Texas accent, but it was exactly the way W would say it. And he wouldn't invite me into the room if it wasn't him. A complete stranger wouldn't invite some random woman into his hotel room.

I decided it had to be him, and that he was just fucking with me. I believed it was him, up until the point the door shut, and he clapped a broad hand over my mouth and nose. He spun me around and thunked my head against the wall at the same time the lock clicked into place. This man, this polite Texas cowboy, stared at me with murder in his eyes.

"Didn't anyone ever teach you not to talk to strangers?" he taunted.

I stared back at him, disordered thoughts tumbling through my head as he worked to suffocate the life out of me. His accent made me sick, because it wasn't W's accent and I should have known it wasn't him, and W was in this hotel somewhere right now thinking what an idiot I was. And I was an idiot. An idiot who was about to get murdered. Blood rushed in my ears as I clawed at him, struggling to break away.

"You don't want to leave yet, do you?" he drawled. "We're just gettin' started."

The edges of my world started to go black. I didn't think about W, or Simon, or anyone as darkness overtook me. I just thought, *really? This is how my life is going to end?*

When I woke again, I was lying face down on the floor. My skirt was pulled up around my waist and my panties were gone. I tried to swallow and choked on a mouthful of fabric, and realized my panties were in my mouth. I scrabbled at my lips but he was tightening a rope around my head so I couldn't spit them out. I pulled at the makeshift gag, screaming, but all that came out was a hacking, muffled sound.

I turned onto my side and then flopped onto my back, gasping for air. He stood over me with a bright, maniacal smile. *Oh shit, oh shit, he's going to fucking kill me.* His tie was off, his shirt undone. Had I ripped open all the buttons when I fought him? I kicked at him, losing my stilettos, but he just laughed and hauled me off the floor, and threw me on the bed.

Shit, shit, shit. Now that I was this close to him, I realized he didn't smell right. I couldn't smell W's cologne. It wasn't him, and I was locked in a hotel room with a sociopathic stranger. I shoved at him as I sent a frantic look around the room, seeking some weapon, *any* weapon, within reach. Nothing. There was nothing.

I tried to scurry off the bed, only to be dragged back where he'd originally thrown me. As he held me down by the neck, I noticed the ends of his red tie fall on the covers beside me, and realized that was what he'd used to gag me. Red for emergency. Red for blood. Red, red, red. *It's not him. It's not fucking him.*

"Let me go. Let me go!" I flailed at him, to no avail. My words were garbled nonsense behind the gag he'd improvised. I wanted to fight, but I was helpless and held down, with my own panties impeding my breath. My lips hurt, and my throat hurt from useless, muffled screaming. My whole body was one big, terrified heartbeat, throbbing *help me, help me, help me, help me.* But no one was going to help me.

"Listen, sweetheart," he growled in his country twang. He knelt over me, pressing me into the bed while I tossed beneath his body weight. "Listen to me." When I didn't listen, he pinched my nose shut so I couldn't breathe. I whipped my head from side to side, punching, whacking at him. He grabbed my wrists and yanked them over my head.

"Fight all you want," he said. "This only ends one way."

One way? What way? Rape? Dismemberment? Death?

Maybe he'd be satisfied with rape. Maybe I'd get lucky, but probably not. I'd seen too much of him by this point. I'd stared into his cold smiling face long enough now to work up a pretty accurate description for the police. He'd never let me go.

When I left stripping to start escorting, one of the other girls had told me I'd get myself killed, that half the johns in New York were murderers. I could still remember her shrill voice, and the way I'd laughed at her warnings. Now I wish I'd listened.

I screwed my eyes shut, unable to look at him anymore. I didn't want to see the man who was going to snuff out my life. I tried to keep fighting him, but I was running out of energy. He was so much bigger and so much stronger, and when he covered my nose, I felt so close to death. If I was some superhero woman I might have come up with a brilliant plan to save myself, but I wasn't a superhero, so I just lay there choking and shaking in terror, trying to block out what was happening to me.

He knelt on my thighs. I could hear him undoing his pants. "Don't move. Don't fucking move," he growled. I obeyed, because I didn't want him to choke me again. I turned my thoughts inward, away from the hands and hips and cock shoving between my legs. The rape part barely registered. Of course it hurt, and it was terrifying and awful, but not as terrifying and awful as knowing he was probably going to suffocate me when he finished. I started to weep, moaning against the panties in my mouth.

He made a disgusted sound. "Crying like a fucking baby. Shut the fuck up."

He ripped my blouse open, yanked down my bra and grasped my breasts as he thrust into me. It hurt so bad. My skirt was still up around my waist, a bundle of fabric between his hips and mine. In the midst of a hard thrust, he jerked the string of costume pearls and broke it. Pearls scattered everywhere. Cheap jewelry. I was going to die wearing cheap jewelry with my skirt up to my waist and my panties in my mouth. *No. You can't die. You have to fight him.* I scratched frantically at his arms as he tugged off my blouse and bra and tossed them across the room. I screamed through the gag, praying someone passing by in the hall might hear me.

But no one came to my rescue, and he didn't let me escape. He held me down by the arms and drove into me without mercy, until my frantic cries broke from the force of his thrusts. Oh, God, what happened when he finished? What happened when he came? Was that the moment he would kill me? All I could think was *fight, Chere, fight,* even though the fighting wasn't getting me anywhere. Tears ran down my cheeks into my nose, into my ears.

He pulled out of me and I fought like hell to get away, to escape his grip. He only grasped me harder and forced me over onto my stomach. When I tried to head butt him, he held my face down into the covers. I couldn't breathe. I was going to die. The edges of my vision went black again and I thought, *this is it. So fast. So soon.*

But no, I woke again from a virulent, scarlet-tinged dream I couldn't remember. He was pounding into me from behind now, his cock thick and hard and painful. I tried to crawl away, to escape this violence, but he just dragged me back and made me submit. There was a ticking in my brain. Maybe it was the last remaining seconds of my life counting down.

I wondered where W was, if he'd left the hotel yet. I wondered how he would feel when Henry told him what had happened to me. He'd feel guilty. He'd blame himself. And Simon... Oh, Simon. He'd go off the deep end, go totally batshit and overdose on some drug.

No, I couldn't die like this. It was wrong. It was horrible and wrong and impossible. I fought with all my strength, kicking, bucking, jerking my shoulders back and forth to try to dislodge his weight.

"Yeah, baby, fight me," he chanted, fucking me harder. "The more you fight me, the harder I'm going to come. I'm going to come so fucking hard."

I could feel pearls rolling around on the bed beneath me, under my breasts, under my cheek. I felt him jerk inside me, felt his fingers tighten on my shoulders as he came in a series of stuttering thrusts. I waited to feel those fingers close around my neck. Would he suffocate me like this, with my face in the sheets, or would he turn me over and watch my eyes as he choked the life out of me? I thought he'd probably want to watch me die, but he didn't turn me over. He groaned instead, and collapsed on top of me.

Oh shit, there were the fingers on my neck. Holy shit. I was so scared. I didn't want to die. I gave a long, low moan of agonized denial. This blond man was going to be my killer, and I didn't want that. I hadn't planned to die like this. It was so sordid, so violent.

"No, please," I begged with the last of my breath, as his fingers tightened around my windpipe and cut off my air.

Then they loosened. The man kissed the back of my neck and laughed softly against my ear.

And I knew that laugh. It was W's laugh.

I felt so many feelings in that moment. I felt such an explosion of angst and disbelief that I literally couldn't cope. I couldn't think or react. I felt rage, I felt humiliation, I felt confusion, I felt relief, I felt sadness. But mostly I felt rage. I started trembling, uncontrollable trembling that made the bed shake. He lifted me a little. The pearls rolled under me, pooling into groups on the sheets.

"Wait a minute. Hold on," he said. He worked at the gag, unknotting the tie. As soon as I could, I spit out my panties and turned around and punched him in the face. He deflected my fist, but I punched him again, punched him as many times as I could before he grabbed my hands and stopped me.

He laughed and tried to catch my gaze. "Stop, Chere. Jesus. It was just for fun." The Texas accent was gone. W was back, laughing at me, laughing at all the horrible things he'd just done. "Don't be mad. It was fucking hot."

"Hot for who?" I shouted. "I didn't know it was you!"

"You weren't supposed to know. That would have ruined all the fun."

Fun? *Fun?* I tried to hit him again and then I thought, *why expend the energy? Why am I still here?* I'd gotten to see W, which was the only reason I'd come here. I'd learned that he was a handsome, smiling, blond psycho, and that was pretty much all I wanted to know about him.

I hated him. I despised him. I pushed past him, staggering away from the bed and pulling down my skirt. "I need my clothes. I need my clothes." I saw my bra and blouse on the floor, but I felt too numb to bend and pick them up.

He studied me with his brows drawn together, and his lips pursed in a line. "It's okay," he said. He wasn't laughing anymore. He reached out to me with the same hand he'd used to suffocate me. "It was just a kinky game. If it upsets you this much, I won't do anything like it again."

"Stay away from me." I was afraid to take my eyes off him. I still didn't *know*. What if he wasn't W? What if he was? My mind was officially broken. "I don't know you," I said. "I want to leave."

He reached for me again, and now he looked worried. "Chere, come here, please. It's me. I wouldn't know your name if it wasn't me. I'm not fucking with you now. The game's over. I'm sorry, I took it too far."

He kept calling it a *game*, which I didn't understand. You couldn't scare someone that bad and call it a "game." I couldn't stop shaking. The danger was over, but the adrenaline was still coursing through my veins with nowhere to go.

This wasn't a stranger. This man wasn't going to kill me. He wasn't going to snuff out my life and cram me under the bed, and fuck off back to Texas, but for ten whole minutes I'd believed that would be my fate, and my mind couldn't seem to grasp the fact that this had all been W's idea of "hot" and "fun."

"I'm sorry," he said. "I'm really fucking sorry. I didn't think you'd freak out this bad. I thought you'd realize it was me."

"How?" I started bawling, loud, awful bawling in the silent room. "You choked me and raped me. I thought you were going to kill me when you finished. How was I supposed to realize it was you?"

"You know my body. You know what my cock feels like. I even used a condom." He held it up in his hand like he deserved a medal.

"I don't think about those kinds of things when someone *is raping me.*" My voice rose to a shriek and broke, and I knew I had to stop talking to him, or I wouldn't be able to figure out how to get dressed again, how to breathe and talk and leave. He threw away the condom and watched me struggle with my blouse. I couldn't put it on. I was shaking too bad.

"Shit," he said.

He came toward me and I held up a hand to ward him off, but he still came. He yanked the comforter off the bed and wrapped it around me, and sat with me on the edge of the bed. He held me tight and nuzzled his lips against my ear.

"Okay, baby. Take deep breaths. Try to calm down."

I couldn't calm down. I turned my face into his neck because I needed shelter, even if that shelter had to come from him. He ran a hand up and down my back and told me everything was okay now, but I couldn't stop shivering.

"I thought I was going to die," I repeated, over and over. "I thought I was going to die."

"I'm sorry, Chere. I'm really sorry."

He didn't make any more excuses. There were no excuses. He'd fucked up. At least when Simon attacked me there was a reason, an explanation. W had done this thing for *fun.*

I cried and cried, because he was awful and what had just happened was awful. The fact that he was soothing me now was awful, but he made me curl and rest against him until there were no more tears.

"Better?" he asked, tilting my face up to his.

No, nothing was better, but fuck, now that I could look at him, he was so fucking handsome. He was so much sexier, so much more beautiful than I'd ever imagined behind my blindfold, even if he was gold instead of dark.

It didn't matter. I still hated him. "I'm not better," I said stiffly.

"What can I do? How can I make it up to you? How can I make you feel better? I didn't hurt you, did I? I mean, your body? I was careful not to hurt you, even if it didn't feel that way."

In hindsight, I realized that. When he hit me, he hadn't hit me hard. When he deflected my kicking and scratching, he hadn't retaliated. When he manhandled me, he hadn't injured me. But he'd scared me to death, which was the worst injury of all.

"I wish you hadn't done this," I said. "You ruined everything between us."

He looked into my eyes, and then he shook his head. "There's nothing between us to ruin. You didn't trust me to begin with. You don't trust me now."

He could be so harsh. Such an asshole. "I trust you less now than I trusted you before," I said.

"You shouldn't. You know what I look like now. That's trust, isn't it? I'm not horrible. You thought I'd be horribly ugly, didn't you?"

"You're horribly ugly because you're mean. You're a psycho."

I watched the faint smile fade from his lips. "I go too far sometimes," he admitted. "I do everything too big, too far. It's my worst fault. You know what your worst fault is?"

I gave him a withering look. "Continuing to see you?"

"No. Your worst fault is not trusting yourself. Not believing in yourself. You knew it was me. You knew in the lobby. You knew in the elevator. You knew when we stood there looking at each other in the hall." His quiet voice accused me. Everything he said was true. "You knew in your heart that it was me, but you doubted yourself. Not only did you doubt, but you didn't speak up. If you'd turned to me and said, 'I know it's you' I would have nodded and said you were right. I mean, I still would have stuck your panties in your mouth and raped you, but I would have admitted it was me."

"I couldn't say anything," I reminded him. "Your hand was over my mouth. You made me pass out."

"That was extremely hot, by the way."

"I hate you. I should press charges."

He didn't look afraid when I said this. He looked approving. "Yes, you should, but you won't. That not-trusting-yourself thing again. Is it enough for me to say that I won't ever fuck with you that bad again? On the bright side, now I know how far is too far."

"First thing," I said, sticking a finger under his nose. "There is no bright side to what you just did to me. Second thing, you *don't* know how far is too far. What you did was way, way past what I'm okay with. What anyone would be okay with. Especially me."

76

"All right. Let's talk about that."

"No, I'm leaving."

He took my hand when I tried to get up. "Did you bring a bathing suit?" he asked. "I told you to bring a bathing suit."

Of course I'd brought my bathing suit. I enjoyed following his directions, to a point. "I brought one, but it doesn't matter, because I'm leaving," I told him. Our time wasn't up, but I didn't care.

"The pool here is really beautiful. Peaceful. When's the last time you went swimming?"

I looked into his eyes, his handsome, intent blue eyes, and said, "I don't want you to touch me ever again."

I saw a flicker of disappointment. Regret. He let go of my hand. "Will you go swimming with me if I promise not to touch you?"

His promises meant nothing to me. Less than nothing.

On the other hand, I hadn't been swimming in a long, long time.

IN BETWEEN

Now that I was calmer, and not in fear of being murdered, I was able to study the man across from me in the azure blue pool. He was handsome as fucking sin.

So far he'd kept his promise. He hadn't touched me. I needed distance and he seemed to understand that. Even in the elevator, we'd stood on opposite sides, facing the front.

The Empire Hotel's pool was beautiful and peaceful, situated high above the cacophony of the city. The sun was setting and the air was thin and pink, like my bikini. Breezes blew across the patio enclosure. The pool was small, but the sky was big, and no one else was here. W swam laps like a fucking Olympian, perfect form, back and forth, muscular arms slicing through the water. I bobbed in the corner because I could only dog paddle.

It had been a hard week for me. Between Simon's attack and W's quasi rape, I felt battered. Not my body. My body was used to indignities. It was my soul and my emotions that felt battered. I'd looked forward to this date all week. I'd looked forward to finally finding out what W looked like. I'd tried to look all pretty and feminine and special for this first real meeting. I wonder how special I'd looked while I was sobbing, choking on my panty-and-necktie gag.

I turned away from him and stared up at the sky. What did a pink sunset mean? Good tidings, or bad? I needed some good tidings. I felt miserable enough to drown.

No, no drowning. There was something healing about water, perhaps because it washes things away, or because it embraces you and makes you buoyant. W swam over and leaned on the edge of the pool near me. Not touching. *Don't touch me.* I still felt confused by his Anglo-Saxon blondness, when I'd expected him to be a dark Mediterranean lover.

He didn't say anything to me, just stared at my breasts. He was winded from the billion laps he'd just banged out. I tried not to notice the drips of water traveling down his sculpted chest, or his rippling arm muscles.

"How old are you?" I asked.

"None of your business."

Any other personal questions were sure to get the same response.

"I thought you would have dark hair," I said, because it still flustered me.

"I don't have dark hair," he said. "I have blond hair."

"Are you from Texas?"

"No. But the accent's not that hard." He sighed. "I'm sorry I fucked with you. You're fun to fuck with. You're so earnest."

Earnest? Never heard that before. Sweet, sexy, feline, seductive? Yes. Earnest? No.

His eyes left my face and traveled to my shoulder. "What happened to you? I didn't do that."

There was a lingering bruise from when Simon had socked me on the collarbone. I covered it with my hand.

"What happened?" he asked again.

"None of your business," I replied, borrowing his earlier phrase. "So, I guess there's no more mystery between us."

"Huh?"

"The poetry from last time. It was *Mystery* by D.H. Lawrence."

"Your Googling skills are impressive. And there's still mystery between us. What do you know about me? Besides how I look?"

I thought a moment. I could pretty much list the rest of what I knew on one hand.

1. Good swimmer
2. Rich
3. Private
4. Pervert
5. Psycho

"Are you still going to see me after today?" he asked.

I wanted to say no. I should have said no, but instead I said nothing at all, because I was undecided.

"I'll give you more poetry," he said. "You'll be swimming in rhymes and metaphors. Speaking of swimming, why don't you swim? Why are you hugging the wall?"

So I won't hug you. Because I want to hate you, but now you're being kind and charming and polite and I want to hug you and grope your muscles.

"I'm not a big swimmer," I muttered. "But the water feels good."

"I'd like to kiss you." He didn't move closer to me, or grab me. He kept his distance. "We haven't kissed yet today."

"I don't know why you want to kiss me when you won't even tell me your name. It's stupid."

"It's not stupid. Not to me."

"Do you have a horrible name?"

"No, I have a normal name."

"Mortimer? Herman? Gaylord?"

"Normal."

"Wilbur? Barnabus?"

"Keep guessing. You're pretty far off."

A hot young stud strolled onto the pool deck. Another escort, probably. His Speedos were about twenty times tighter than W's navy swim trunks. I gave Young Stud the once-over just to yank W's chain. When I looked back at him, I realized he knew my intention, and that it amused him. Ugh. Why did I bother trying to ruffle him? He was unruffle-able.

"Can I kiss you?" he asked. And I knew what he really meant was, *Are we okay again?* because his eyes were saying *I'm sorry* and his lips were saying *let me kiss it better.*

I didn't answer, I just swam over into his arms, because that's where I wanted to be, for better or worse. He caught me against him and lifted me in the water, and fastened his lips onto mine. The young stud made a faint sound of disgust, but I didn't care.

W tugged at my hair, demanding my attention as his lips recaptured mine. His kisses mended my soul, at least a little. He might not tell me his name, but he kissed me like a lover every single time.

"Do you want to go back down to the room?" he said when we parted.

"Maybe."

"I probably owe you an orgasm."

I glared at him. He owed me a lot more than an orgasm after what he'd done, but an orgasm would work for starters.

"All right, then," I said, moving my arms under the water. "Yes."

5.

THE EMPIRE SESSION, TAKE TWO

We didn't kiss in the elevator. We didn't hold hands, and things felt uneasy again. Then some toothpick-slim chick with a plastic surgery face and size triple-G fake tits got on at the eighteenth floor and W glanced over at me like, *what is this shit?*

It felt nice to share that secret joke with him. She eyeballed him and I wanted to smack her. But who wouldn't eyeball him? He was shirtless, a towel slung over his shoulders. His trunks rode low on his hips, revealing not just his six pack but the tease of iliac furrows on either side, and a trail of gold-blond fur that doubtless continued all the way down to his cock.

He preened under her appreciative gaze—again, who wouldn't?—but when we reached our floor, I was the one he led off the elevator. Sorry, unnaturally plastic bitch. I was the one he wanted, I was the one who got those abs and those iliac furrows, even if my D cups looked miniscule next to her massive GGGs.

"Don't ever do that to your body," he said as we walked to the room. "Just don't."

"I might have to, if I want to keep working. When women get older—"

He turned to me with a silencing glare. "Don't talk to me about your work. For the time being, your only work is being my whore. Your only customer is me, and I don't ever want you to look like that woman. End of conversation."

Oh, right. Our exclusive thing. I shut my trap while he keyed open the door. When we got inside, he let me take off my swim suit, then he picked up my panties. They were still in a ball on the bed where I'd spit them out.

"Open up," he said.

I would have argued, but his expression told me it would be pointless. This was what I'd missed seeing those first few dates: his intent, commanding expression, the taut lips, the arched brow. He was great at it. I opened my mouth.

He jammed the panties in and grabbed his tie and gagged me every bit as roughly as he'd done it the first time. I played along, because I could see he had a plan, and it was my job to make it work for him. I moaned and pushed back at him so he'd grab my wrists and force me to comply.

Amazing, that he could hold me so forcefully and not bruise me, but I was starting to understand how he did it. It was a trick of movement and firmness, and the area of his body. A big hand could grip you firmly and make it feel really painful, when what you were really feeling was the real estate of that hand on your skin. Understanding it didn't make it any less thrilling.

He pushed me back on the bed. I wanted to hide my face. I thought the gag probably made me look ugly, but when I attempted to turn away he yanked me back and made me look at him. He knelt over me and collected my hands, and placed them over my head.

"You leave your hands there," he said. "Don't even think about moving them."

The threat in his voice had my thighs inching closed. He made an irritated sound and forced them open, wider this time.

"Don't you dare close your legs, or I'll tear your ass up. This pussy is mine." He grasped my mons and shoved a couple fingers inside me. I was just out of the pool, so I was wet, but not that wet, and it hurt a little.

And I liked it.

I was freaking scared of him "tearing my ass up," but I liked being scared about it, and holding my legs open so he wouldn't do that to me. That was when I realized he was changing me, changing my sexual preferences and what I was willing to put up with. If I wasn't wet a few seconds ago, I was wet as a river now.

"No," I moaned through the gag, and he knew I meant yes. I was rewarded with another finger inside me, a rough piston in and out. I had to fight the instinct to close my legs again, to escape the discomfort.

"Don't dare," he said. "Don't dare try to stop me. Your body is mine, your mouth, your ass, your tits, your cunt, everything that makes you my sex doll. Isn't that right?"

I nodded. Oh, yes, I was his sex doll. What else could I be, with my mouth full of my panties, my hands above my head in surrender, my whole body exposed and aching for him? I wanted his cock. I wanted him to use me. He kicked off his trunks and he was so hard, so thick. All this time I'd only felt it, not seen it. Even earlier, I was too scared to look at his cock, but now I saw it in all its jutting, masculine glory, framed by a heavy set of balls. If I wasn't gagged, I would have begged for it. *Please put it inside me.* But with W, I never got what I asked for, only what he wanted.

He knelt at the edge of the bed and pulled me toward him. He slid his fingers back inside me and lowered his mouth to my pussy. Oh, sweet Jesus. He used his thumbs to hold me open, and dragged his tongue along my pussy to my clit. He prodded it, caressed it, stimulated it while my hips went wild.

I panted behind the gag. It felt too good, too intense. I reached down, I couldn't help it. I pushed on his shoulders and the pleasure went away, replaced by stern admonishment.

"What did I tell you? You fucking listen to my instructions or you will know pain."

He held my wrists over my head with one hand, and smacked the underside of my ass with the other. And by "smacked the underside of my ass," I mean destroyed my ass. Eight hard, stinging spanks, one after the other, all on one cheek as I wailed past the panties in my mouth. He let go of my hands and no words were necessary. His expression and my throbbing ass cheek were message enough. I curled my fingers into my hair so I wouldn't fuck up again, and I opened my legs the way he'd told me.

"That's better," he said. "You're here to obey me, and please me. Do your fucking job."

Yes, Sir. I couldn't say it, I was gagged, but the words echoed in my head. *Yes, Sir, Yes, Sir, whatever you like, Sir.* I was his sex doll, and I existed to serve him. There was something freeing about that idea, something comforting. Even though his mouth was tormenting me beyond bearing, I was going to lie there and take it because that was what he wanted.

But *ohh, God.* Now it wasn't just the fingers probing my pussy, and his tongue teasing my clit, it was the lingering heat where he'd spanked me. I bucked my hips up into his mouth, opening my legs even wider, like some crazed yoga maven. I didn't do yoga. Maybe I'd better start. My whole body felt like a rubber band connected to the place where he licked and sucked me. I was tensing in pleasure, and I felt like I was about to snap.

The first orgasm arrived before I was ready. I didn't have time to brace against its power. My hands yanked at my own hair and my legs flailed. I think I might have kicked him. He didn't stop and I thought, *oh God, he has to stop or I'll die.*

"Stop fighting," he said, massaging inside me. "Stop fighting it. Get out of your mind."

I didn't think I'd be able to "get out of my mind" but I tried. I stopped thinking about my body's exhaustion, and how wrung out I felt, and started thinking about pleasure expanding and billowing beyond the climax I'd already felt.

And when that happened, I stopped thinking at all. His fingers were wreaking havoc along my walls, inciting every nerve, and his tongue pushed and sucked my flesh. His mouth pressed, his teeth bit me. My muscles trembled from holding open for him, at the same time my body worked toward an even higher peak.

When the second orgasm came, I shouted into my wadded-up panties. I shouted *now* and *no* and *yes.* He held me down when I tried to buck away from him. The rippling contractions went on and on for what seemed like five minutes, each more excruciatingly wonderful than the last.

I had literally gone out of my mind. I lost track of him, what he was doing, what he was saying. The gag came off, the panties came out, and his cock was shoved into my mouth instead. I sucked like the satisfied, obedient sex doll I was. My pussy was still clenching, still buzzing with bliss. My hands lay open over my head as his balls whacked against my chin. Not one gag reflex as he surged over and over into my throat. Who needed breathing? Who needed personal space? Not this girl. Even the cherry flavor of the latex tasted good.

He didn't finish in my throat. He pulled away and flipped me over, and rammed into me from behind. His knees held mine open, and his hands gripped my wrists on either side of my head. Fuck if I didn't come again, the rubber band finally snapping as he bucked his hips against mine. He came with a grunt, his fingers clamping hard around my wrists. Maybe, that time, he would leave a bruise. I didn't mind.

He collapsed on top of me. I was dead, literally dead. My pussy was dead. My body was dead. Death by orgasm, my grisly fate.

But no, I wasn't dead. If I was dead, I wouldn't have felt his lips against my shoulder, and his breath against my ear.

"You're mine, Chere," he said quietly. "And I can make you feel good, or I can make you feel bad."

That's what he said, but all I really absorbed was "I can make you *feel.*" Just today, he had made me feel terrified, and relieved, and anxious, and jealous, and comforted, and right now, content. I realized that was why I kept coming back for these sessions. That was why I wanted so badly to see his face, because I needed to see the person who finally, *finally* forced me to feel something authentic.

How long since I'd felt such intense emotion? To be a prostitute, you had to deaden your feelings. To live with an addict, to love an addict, you had to deaden your feelings. I'd been stuffing down my emotions for so long that it felt like a dangerous thing to let them out. I didn't weep the way I wanted to. I didn't let my body convulse into sobs, but tears trailed down my cheeks and fell onto the comforter, turning it a darker hue.

My tears didn't seem to bother W. He turned me over and pulled me into his arms, and swiped them away without comment, even when they kept coming. Most johns didn't want anything to do with you once they'd gotten off. Ninety-nine percent of johns didn't want to hold you afterward, especially if you were crying.

W, obviously, wasn't like most johns.

Do not develop feelings for him, Chere. Don't even. I mean, what the fuck?

I slowly emerged from my emotional breakdown orgasmic stupor and realized we were way, way over time. Almost an hour over time. Careless, to get lost in him. Let one session slide, and he would expect more things to slide. It would get messed up and awkward and screwed.

I didn't have to say anything to him. He was an experienced escort consumer. He knew as soon as I sat up that it was time for him to go. I went into the bathroom, limping over the occasional stray pearl. It was fun to go to Orgasm Land with W, but it was time to return to the real world, where I was an escort and he was my customer. A poorly behaved customer, sometimes.

And then...sometimes...

He was dressed when I came out. Shirt and pants, no tie. I was pretty sure I'd ruined it when I tried to chew through it. It was in the plastic laundry service bag, along with his wet trunks.

He turned over a sheet of paper on the table and started writing. "I'll pay you for the extra time," he said.

"You don't have to. We're not supposed to go over. Henry will blame me."

He turned to me with a derisive expression. "What's he going to do? Fire you?"

"He'll make me feel guilty," I said, which was the truth. "But he wouldn't fire me. It's my choice whether to work for him or not."

W rolled his eyes and looked back at what he was writing. "I'll leave an extra big tip then," he finally said. "You earned it this time."

He didn't say that with any special emotion, but my throat went tight. This had been a tough session. It was nice to hear him acknowledge all I'd gone through to get him off. He folded up whatever he'd written and brought it over, and held it out to me.

"Are we okay?" he asked. "Are you okay?"

I nodded and took the paper. "Poetry?"

"Yes. Maybe a little bit of an apology."

I thought back to the previous poems, quickly scrawled, or written on my back. He wasn't copying this shit from his phone, or from a book. He was writing it from memory.

"How many poems are in your head?" I asked.

He didn't answer. He just placed a hand on either side of my head, kissed me on the forehead, and walked out the door.

IN BETWEEN

I stayed at the Empire that night, because I had too much crap to work through in my mind. I couldn't risk going home and finding Simon in one of his moods. I couldn't deal with his shit on top of mine.

I lay instead with W's poetry on the pillow beside me.

I'd rather have the dream of you
With faint stars glowing
I'd rather have the want of you
The rich, elusive taunt of you

God, he never gave me enough. His snippets never made sense, never explained anything. What did this mean, that he didn't want me? That he only wanted the "dream" of me? I didn't know whether to be flattered or insulted. His poems never made me feel good, only confused.

Speaking of confused, why had I decided to stay here at the Empire, and sleep on this bed where W had done such horrible things to me?

But he hadn't done them, not really. The Texas stranger had done them. Somehow the two of them had become separate in my head, which was fucked up, because they were the same person, and I should have been furious with that person. I should have stayed angry longer. The first time Simon hit me, I stayed angry for days, and then the rationalization started. Was I doing the same thing here? Rationalizing W's behavior because I didn't want to let him go?

But unlike Simon, W was in control that whole scene. He didn't attack me with true intent, with malice to cause harm, so it didn't count. When Simon attacked me, he did it to hurt me. When W attacked me, he used a condom and didn't leave bruises. It wasn't the same.

Was it? Fuck me. I didn't know.

I was sore the next morning, my heart from emotion and my body from too much orgasming. Light streamed through the hotel curtains, and housekeeping tapped at the door. I got up and dragged home, and let myself into the loft. I heard voices from Simon's studio, his voice and another girl's. Someone was smoking.

Rachel.

Rachel was an old friend of Simon's from Florida. She had a sultry voice and a model's body, and rainbow-colored highlights on the tips of her dark hair. She chain-smoked in our loft and hung all over Simon at every opportunity because they were *friends.*

The door to the studio was half open. I peeked in, saw Simon with his brush and canvas, looking animated for once. Rachel was on the couch, sprawled on her back with a cigarette dangling from her fingers. She wasn't wearing a shirt or bra, but that wasn't unusual for Rachel, who thought the rules of the decency didn't apply to her. Her father was some Miami billionaire so Rachel didn't work, didn't do anything that didn't feel good to her.

Simon and I had argued many times about Rachel. I knew she was the one who had gotten him into drugs, and I hated her for it. He went to a few rich, artsy, hippie festivals with her, and all of a sudden, he was getting high because it made the art "better," like it was some noble sacrifice he was making. Rachel told me to relax, that Simon wasn't half as bad as some of the people she knew.

Was that supposed to make everything okay? Ugh, I hated her. During one of our arguments, I accused Simon of sleeping with her behind my back. He sneered at me. "One, you sleep with tons of guys. Two, there's more to life than sex. I know that's hard for you to understand, considering what you do for a living. And three, we grew up together. I mean, ugh. Incest. She's like my fucking sister."

But he wasn't looking at her like a sister right now.

That smile of his used to be for me. That intent gaze, that expression of inspiration. I pushed the door open and stalked in. "Hey, Simon. Hey, Rachel."

"Chere!" Simon exclaimed, like he was happy to see me. He was always happy with Rachel around. Rachel gave me a bitch look, and waved at me like that somehow erased the bitchiness.

"Look." Simon gestured to the rainbow colored canvas before him. It reminded me of her hair. "What do you think? Rachel finally agreed to model for me."

I used to model for you. I used to inspire you. Not to be nasty, but the pieces you painted of me sold for a lot of money. This one looked like a piece of carnival art. I supposed it was for his upcoming show, if it even happened. I had my doubts.

"It looks great," I said with fake enthusiasm. I looked from the canvas to Rachel, and then back at the canvas. I never understood why he needed models, when nothing he created ever looked like any of those models. I never understood why he needed the drugs, when his own talent and imagination used to be enough.

"Well, I'll leave you to it," I said.

"Hey, where were you last night?" he called out when I was almost to the door.

I turned. "At the Empire Hotel. The client said I could stay if I wanted, and it had a nice view."

Rachel tittered, even though I didn't think I'd said anything amusing. I could have said more, like that I felt more relaxed when I stayed at a hotel. That the lack of clutter and cigarette smoke and color-vomit canvases helped me sleep better.

"I'm tired," I said. "I'll see you later."

I went into our bedroom. The bed was still made. It was very possible that Simon and Rachel had been up all night, partying, club-crawling, dancing, and then coming home to make "art." Our clothes were piling up in the corner. I needed to do laundry. Later. I'd face that later.

I took out W's poetry instead, and searched the first couple of lines on my phone. *Choice*, by Angela Morgan, a little known American poet born in the late 19th century.

Her work was wistful, kind of sad. I smoothed out the paper, studying his writing, trying to remember the expression on his face when he put down the pen. Was he insinuating something about me by choosing this poem? Or him? Or neither of us?

Did I want "the want of him"? The "rich elusive taunt of him"? I was afraid I did. Our date was over but he still occupied far too many of my thoughts.

He'd said it was "a little bit of an apology," but I didn't see the apology. I pored over commentary about the poem, its theme of obsession and unrequited love, as if that might explain something, or help me understand him. It didn't.

I wondered if he knew all these poems by heart, or if he only memorized snippets that were meaningful to him. I tried to picture W in love. In unrequited love. I tried to picture him sitting and memorizing poetry.

No. I couldn't see it at all.

6.

THE GANSEVOORT SESSION

I knew W better now. I knew his face, if not his name, so I felt a little more relaxed as I walked from Times Square to the Gansevoort Hotel on Park Avenue. It had been a week since our last date, a wonderful, relaxing week with no other clients, thanks to our exclusive arrangement. He was literally paying me not to see other men.

It felt nice to be wanted that way.

It felt so nice that I'd dressed up for him. I'd bought my outfit with his tastes in mind: a classy little black dress with a matching garter belt and stockings, and gorgeous black velvet stilettos. I thought it was pretty safe to spend the money, since he hadn't cut anything off me in a while. We'd had a pretty bad scene last time around, but we managed to salvage things between us. I had looked into his eyes and seen a man there, a man who cared about me, for all his rough edges.

Now that we were exclusive, I imagined a comfortable closeness developing between us. Well, not comfortable. Sex with W would never be *comfortable*, but I imagined us moving to something more...intimate. Or affectionate. I imagined longer, more playful sessions, culminating in even better orgasms, for him, for me, for both of us. Now that we were exclusive, I could focus all my energy and attention on him.

And he deserved it. Thanks to him, I had free time now to nap, to primp, to go shopping, to wander around Central Park and bask in the sun. Thanks to him, I didn't have to accept dates with men I didn't like that much.

There was only one date—him—and I actually found myself looking forward to seeing him, because he had *chosen me*. He liked me enough to *want me to himself*. I didn't even have to put on the simpering, airheaded Miss Kitty act, because W was the first client in ten years who didn't want to sleep with Miss Kitty. He wanted to sleep with *me*. Chere. He'd yanked my name out of me within the first minute, and he still used it every session.

The fact that I didn't know his name didn't deter me in these escalating fantasies. I traipsed into the Gansevoort Hotel fully believing that our exclusive arrangement meant that he cared about me. I should have known better after all my years in the business.

I took the elevator upstairs to the room number Henry texted me. I knew something was off as soon as W opened the door. He didn't smile at me in welcome, didn't take me in his arms and kiss my forehead the way I pictured. He frowned down at his phone and pointed me to the bed. I sat on the edge of it and awaited instructions. I'm not sure he even noticed what I was wearing. If he did, he didn't seem to care.

Whatever, Chere. Don't be vain. Don't worry about it.

The brightly colored, modern room decor made my head hurt. I studied him instead, trying to figure out his mood. In a way I still felt blindfolded. I mean, I recognized his golden blond hair, his piercing blue eyes, his fine body and sculpted features, but that was all I understood about him. I looked out the window, at the view of the Empire State Building.

"I've never been at this Gansevoort before," I said. "Only the one in the Meatpacking District."

He didn't answer, just threw his phone down beside the room key and went to the table to pick up a drink. He wasn't drunk—he seemed too sharp and irate to be drunk—but he was still drinking, and he didn't offer any to me. When he turned around, I crossed my legs and did my best to look enticing.

"I was glad you finally called Henry," I said. "Have you had a busy week?"

"Yes. Not that it's any of your business."

His gaze traveled up my legs. No smile. No kisses. I would have put on the blindfold again, if he would have kissed me. Maybe he was already getting bored with me. Maybe we already knew too much about each other to suit his tastes.

He finally came over and stood in front of me. I smiled, even if he didn't.

"Now that you have me to yourself, I thought you'd take advantage of me more often," I flirted.

His scowl deepened. "Stop talking and open your fucking mouth."

He unzipped with one hand and held my head with the other. As for me, I kept my lips clamped shut. He was supposed to wear a condom.

"Fucking bitch. I said open your mouth."

He pushed me back on the bed. My arms flew up, but he wasn't coming at me. He was taking off his clothes and ripping open a condom.

"With what I pay you, you should at least suck me off without a condom," he said. "What the fuck kind of diseases do you think I have?"

"I don't know. It's company policy—"

"Shut the fuck up about company policy. Take off that fucking piece-of-shit dress and open your fucking legs."

I didn't know if this was more kinky games, or if he hated me, or if he was only acting like he hated me. I didn't dare get up off the bed. I just twisted where I lay to unzip the dress I'd bought for him, which he'd so coldly dismissed as a *piece of shit*. I didn't expect to get a better reception for the garter belt and stockings.

"Do you want me to take these off too?" I asked.

He climbed onto the bed between my legs and shoved my hands away from my body, and forced them over my head. He stuck his cock in me like he was sticking it in some inanimate hole. That was the level of warmth I received from my "exclusive" client. I blinked my eyes, determined not to look upset. It was really hard. He wasn't raping me this time—he had my consent—but somehow it felt worse than being raped.

While he drilled me with absolute detachment, he fumbled at the garter belt clasps, and the tops of my stockings.

"You don't have to wear all this shit," he said. "All I care about is what's between your legs."

I tried to help him, only to have my hands pushed away.

"What the fuck did I tell you?" Two smacks on the cheek, hard enough to hurt me. I put my hands back over my head and let him struggle with the clasps. Asshole.

When he couldn't get them open, he tore the stockings free instead, then unhooked the belt from my waist and flung it across the room. The pushup bra was next, unhooked and discarded like it was something disgusting. I guess I should have been grateful he didn't use the scissors in his current mood.

"Are you acting like this because I wouldn't blow you without a condom?" I said. "You're being a dick."

Some mayhem flashed in his gaze, to complement his cruel expression. "At least I'm not a whore."

I didn't know what kind of sick scene this was supposed to be, if I was supposed to go all meek and limp while he abused me. It wasn't happening. I slapped him way harder than he'd slapped me, and it felt good to hurt him. I drew back my hand to slap him again but he arrested it midswing.

"Don't fucking dare," he said, taking me with steady thrusts. "You're not in charge here. I dish it out, you take it."

"I never agreed to that."

"You take my money, I take your body. That's our contract." His fingers dug into my wrists, and the more I fought him, the harder he fucked me. "You're so wet," he mocked. "If you didn't like this, you wouldn't be here. You've had ample chances to say goodbye to me."

"Chances I should have taken."

"Simmer the fuck down or you'll be sorry."

I didn't know how I could possibly feel more sorry than I felt at that moment. I felt hated and abused, and mocked. I wanted him off me, and I wanted to hurt him. I wasn't getting anywhere trying to knee him in the groin. Women doubtless tried to do that all the time. I did manage to pry my wrist free and smack him again, square in the face.

"What the fuck is wrong with you?" he growled. He used force and body weight to manhandle me onto my stomach. "You're a stubborn little bitch, you know that?"

"Get off me. Get off!" He was holding me down with all his weight. I could hardly breathe, but I used the breath I had to try to buck him off me. A moment later, he hooked his right arm around my neck.

"Stop fighting," he said. When he clenched his muscles, blood roared in my brain.

You're the one who needs to stop, I wanted to cry. *You need to stop being mean. You need to stop hurting me.* I could feel his cock hard and thick between my legs. My vision blurred, from tears or panic, or lack of blood flow.

"Don't kill me," I whispered.

"I'm not going to kill you. I'm trying to get you under control." His arm loosened but stayed where it was, a hug and a threat. His weight crushed me, and his rough voice rumbled in my ear. "I know you're all pouty and hurt because you didn't get enough attention, because I didn't fawn over your pretty dress and your fucking lingerie. You're not getting what you want, are you?"

"I want you to get off me!"

"And I want you to let me fuck you without all the feelings and drama." His voice was sharp as a sword, stabbing through me. "You're nothing to me," he said. "You're my prostitute. You don't get kisses and compliments unless I feel like giving them to you. You don't get to look pretty. I don't want you to look pretty. I want you to open your mouth when I tell you to open your mouth, and open your legs when I tell you to open your legs. Do you understand?"

I managed to yell "I hate you" before he tightened his arm around my neck again. I pressed back into his chest, trying not to pass out. I understood what he was saying. I understood that he was paying me, and that I was his whore, and that this was his show, but I didn't see why he had to be so obnoxious about it. One of my shoes dropped to the floor with a thunk. I kicked off the other one, not caring where it landed.

He spread my legs wider with his knees, and shoved a hand between my thighs, gathering moisture from my pussy. I was so wet, and I was afraid it was because I liked this. I didn't want him to be right.

"Now," he said, "you're going to take it in the ass where it hurts, instead of your wet pussy where you want me, or your whore mouth where you could have had me."

I shook my head no, but I knew he didn't care. He was already pushing inside me, using only the slickness he'd gathered from my pussy. I groaned and squirmed but his knees had me open so wide, splayed on the bed. One of his hands trapped my wrists under my stomach, and the other, of course, was still wrapped around my neck.

He gave a long, low sigh, made a guttural, animal sound of pleasure as I trembled under him. My ass hurt, pried open once again by his oversized cock. But there was nothing I could do. I was literally held down from top to bottom, and from inside where he impaled me.

"I know you don't want this, but it feels so good to me," he said. "You're so tight, and it feels like fucking heaven when you fight me."

I didn't want to fight, not when he'd enjoy it, but when he started moving in me, it was like I had no choice. Fight or die. Fight, or admit that I liked being held down and brutalized this way. I clenched around him and he growled.

"That's right. Do I hurt inside you? That's what I want. You don't get what you want. That's how this works. You don't get to come today, bad girl. You're just gonna lay underneath me and get fucked, and fucked, and fucked." He punctuated each word with a balls-deep thrust.

"Please stop," I said. "I don't like this. It doesn't feel good."

"That doesn't matter, does it? If you don't get to come?"

His scent surrounded me, the scent I had come to equate with W and sex and terror. I dreamed about the smell of him, sometimes, in sex-soaked reveries and nightmares. I hated that he would probably find that funny, or pathetic. I dreamed way too often about the feeling of him fucking me and hurting me.

When all the fight went out of me, when I'd been fucked just that long and hard, he finally released my wrists. He unwrapped his arm from my neck and used it to brace himself over me. I didn't want him over me. I wanted him closer to me. I needed comforting. I needed to be touched and given pleasure as he reamed out my ass, so I slid my hand down and fingered my pussy. I was still so wet.

"Don't you dare make yourself come," he said. "Not today."

"I want to," I whined.

"No. I'll beat you into next week if you make yourself come after I told you not to."

I didn't hear what he was saying, or maybe I did and I just didn't want to believe him. I was so hot by now, so wrought up with anger and lust. His pounding thrusts had driven my clit against the bed over and over, and I felt like a big, seething volcano of need.

"Don't," he said once more, but he didn't pull my hand away, and I couldn't stop rubbing my clit. I wanted to come with him inside me, while I felt so full and used. I could feel him start to come. I heard it in his breathing and I sensed it in his jerking thrusts. I thought he wouldn't notice if I climaxed at the same time, if I was really, really quiet. Oh God, it felt like heaven when I let the orgasm come. I clenched around his cock, gritting my teeth to stay silent. Everything inside me clenched and vibrated, and if I could have, I would have cried out with pleasure.

W pulled out of my ass while I was still pulsing through aftershocks. I didn't care. I'd already floated away. I might as well have been wearing my blindfold, I was so lost in my little world. My hand curved over my pussy, petting it, soothing it.

"You don't understand yet, do you?"

Uh-oh. He sounded angry. His fingers wove into the hair at my nape, and he wrenched my head to the side.

"Don't hurt me anymore," I said. "Leave me alone."

"What the fuck did I tell you?"

"Not to come. Not today." I yowled as he pulled my hair harder. I was starting to regret that orgasm I'd stolen, shattering as it was. "I'm sorry. Please, I'm sorry, I couldn't help it."

He got up off the bed, grabbed his pants and pulled the belt from the loops while I ran toward the door. He caught me and shoved my face against the wall.

"Please don't," I cried, as he yanked my wrists behind my back. He cinched them together with the belt, and dragged me toward the bed with the tail. When I resisted, he wrapped an arm around my waist and carried me. I kicked and wriggled, but his arm was like a steel band. I wasn't escaping him.

There was an orchid in a medium-sized pot by the window, staked to a long bamboo rod for stability. With his free hand, he yanked the rod out of the pot as we passed it. The bamboo was at least as thick as my finger.

He threw me face down over the edge of the bed, so my ass was in the air. I tried to yell *no*, and *help*, but he solved that problem by pressing my face into the covers until I stopped.

"Are you done fighting me?" he asked. "Because we can go again."

"Fuck yo—" I tried to yell, at which time my face was shoved into the covers harder. This time he held me there until I ran out of breath, and I had to kick and struggle to be released.

"I told you very clearly not to come, didn't I?" he said. "And you did it anyway. Stop fighting, because you earned this punishment."

He yanked my hands up and braced his knee on the small of my back. The bamboo rod landed with a thud across my ass cheeks. *Owwww. Ohmygod.* My legs kicked up as a sizzling line of heat exploded across my flesh. Before I could come to terms with the agony, another stroke landed above it, and a third stroke below. He stifled my howl of pain in the blankets, pulling my hair again. No, no way, the orgasm wasn't worth this. If I knew I'd be getting this, I wouldn't have done it.

Thwack. Thwack. Thwack. Thwack. The throbbing lines of torment built on top of one another, as he whacked a lattice of hell from the top of my ass to just above my knees. The blows came one after the other, and the only thing that kept me bent over the bed was his kneecap wedged into my back. I scratched at his leg, whenever he gave the belt enough slack for me to do it. "Please, stop," I gasped.

"Beginning to regret that orgasm now?"

"Yes! I'm sorry. Please, I'm sorry."

"Next time I say no orgasm..." He gave me the hardest whack yet, so hard I couldn't even find the breath to scream. "Then I mean no orgasm. I'm not into games, Chere. Remember that next time."

He left off, went back over to the orchid and jammed the bamboo rod into its former place. I watched this with a kind of traumatized wonder. No one would ever guess, looking at that potted flower and stake, that it had been used to cause someone so much pain.

"Oh, the tears," he said, throwing up his arms. He went back to the table and downed the rest of his drink. I took the opportunity to finally curl up into that ball. My hands struggled within his belt.

"Let me go," I sobbed. "Undo my wrists."

"In a minute." He came to lie beside me, and stroked a hand up and down my back. "You need to calm down first."

"I can't. My ass hurts. And you're not supposed to mark me! My other clients—"

But I wasn't seeing any other clients. Now I understood why. It wasn't because I was special, or because he couldn't get enough of me. It was so he could leave all the marks he wanted on me without ruining some other man's date.

"Stop crying," he said. "You're the biggest fucking baby." He turned me to face him and looked at me a moment. I must have appeared a mess. I must have looked like I wanted to murder him, but that didn't seem to matter. He tugged me closer and kissed each of my cheeks, slowly, lingering over the moisture of my tears.

After that, he finally reached behind me to undo his belt. He had to lean over my body to work the buckle. His cock was flaccid now, and his skin slightly damp with sweat, a post-sex man, not a monster. I had to restrain myself from seeking comfort in the curve of his neck.

"Finally," I said, when he released me.

He ignored my irritated exhortation, pulled my hands in front of me, and inspected my wrists. They were red, but the skin wasn't broken. He lifted them and placed my palms against his stubble-roughened cheeks.

He stared at me, and I stared back at him. What did he want? Why did he think it was okay to go from flat-out rape and torture to these post-sex gazing sessions? These gentle caresses lying beside each other on the bed?

"Something's wrong with you." I spread my fingers over his cheek where I'd slapped him earlier. "You're a horrible person."

He didn't flinch, didn't frown. He only covered my hands with his. "I know I'm a horrible person. Do you want those kisses now?"

Damn him. Yes, I wanted them, and I hated myself for wanting them, because he wasn't nice. He was horrible. *I know you're all pouty and hurt because you didn't get enough attention, because I didn't fawn all over your pretty dress and your fucking lingerie.* It was all true, and I hated that he said things like that to my face, that he called me on all my faults and insecurities. He made me feel awful.

And then he held me and kissed me like this.

His fingers eased along my neck, gentling me, collecting me as his lips played over mine. When I responded to his caresses, he pulled me closer and upped the violence, nipping me, biting my lower lip.

I opened my hands on his chest, needing this closeness and connection, even though I knew it for a lie. He was so handsome, so sexy,

100

and he could sweep me away so easily if he wanted to. It wasn't fair. Every session, he tormented me and tied me into emotional knots, and then kissed and caressed me afterward, like that took away everything he'd done to me. It didn't.

His kisses weren't sweet, or passionate. They were lies. I turned my head away so his lips ended up on my cheek. I closed my hands and drew them away from his chest.

"What?" he said.

"I don't want to kiss you."

"I'm paying you, and I want to kiss you."

"You're mean to me." I hated how childish and whiny I sounded. He made me feel childish and whiny and ridiculous and desperate for his small gifts of affection.

"I don't understand you," he said with mock annoyance. "Last week you were mad because I raped you. Now you're mad because I choked you, beat you, and sodomized you. I don't know how to make you happy."

"This isn't a joke. It's not funny."

"No, it's not funny. It's sexy. You enjoyed everything we did today."

I moved to get up and he pulled me back down. I fought, hitting out at him, but as usual he was one step ahead of me, deflecting and trapping my hands.

"You need to stop hitting me," he said in a stern tone. "I mean it. I'm paying you. Show some respect."

I gazed into his eyes, trying to see the humor, the irony. Trying to understand. "Are you for real right now?"

"I'm very real, and I'm very honest. Why won't you be honest and admit that you like these scenes we do together? The world won't end because you lose yourself in a little rough sex. I don't hurt you. I don't *really* hurt you," he qualified, when I gave him a look.

"You hurt me every time."

"Sexy games. I'm a sadist. It's what I like." He touched my cheeks, dragged my face up to his. "And I like you because you fight me," he murmured against my lips. "Even when you submit, you fight me. That's a hard thing to find. Do you know how happy I was when I found you, Chere? After our first session at the W, I went home and masturbated so hard I almost injured myself, and then I called your pimp and set up our next date. I couldn't wait to see you again. You made me so happy that day. You make me so fucking happy every time you struggle and fight me."

I gazed into his intent blue eyes. His sadistic blue eyes.

"What's the reality?" I asked. "The way you hate on me when we have sex—"

"I don't hate on you."

"Or this now, this kindness and sweetness? What's the reality between us?"

"There's no reality between us. You know that."

I turned away from him in a huff. He turned me back to him and this time he didn't look sweet.

"Okay, here's the reality," he said. "You excite me. You push the right buttons for me. But you need to remember something, starshine: you work for me. I don't want to deal with any of your girly, emotional shit. *Do you like me or do you hate me?* Who the fuck cares? I pay you so I don't have to deal with that."

"By 'girly, emotional shit,' do you mean crying when you're anally raping me?"

He leaned his head on his hand, like I was so misguided and unreasonable, and had to be set straight. "You weren't crying from the assfucking," he said. "You were crying because you dressed up for me, and I didn't care. Because I don't want you to dress up for me. That's not our dynamic. I'm not your lover or your boyfriend or your best pal or anything like that, and I never will be. Please remember all this, so we don't have to go over it again."

Oh, I was going to remember every word. I was going to remember that he was a megalomaniac and an asshole, and that I shouldn't have warm and fuzzy feelings for him. Maybe I'd read a little too much into his kindness at the end of our last session. He was probably just being nice so I wouldn't call the police.

"I think you're giving yourself a bit too much credit," I said coolly. "I was a prostitute for a good decade before you came along, and I'll still be turning tricks when you're no longer my client. You don't mean as much to me as you think. I dressed up to please you *as a client*. I'm friendly and conversational because *most clients like that*. Please remember all this, so we don't have to go over it again."

Ha. I mentally dropped the mic, but he didn't react to my sassy comeback. He was staring at my lips.

"I'm paying you a lot of money for your exclusive service. I want oral without condoms," he said.

"I can't. That's against company policy."

"So is exclusivity. Anything can be bought." His head was still propped on one hand. The other hand traced lazy trails up and down my thigh, occasionally meandering over a sensitive welt. "What do you want in exchange for full access to your warm, wet mouth?"

"Your name," I said. "Your real name."

Irritation twisted his features. He gave me a look.

I shrugged. "I'd need an STD test, and that would have your name on it."

"You don't need an STD test. For fuck's sake, I'm as concerned about protection as you are. I'm clean."

"If you're so concerned about protection, why do you want to have oral without condoms?"

"Because I know you're clean, and I'm clean."

I glared at him. It was the principle of the thing.

"Okay, fine," he said in exasperation. "I'll show you a clean test, but it's not going to have my information on it. Your pimp promised me privacy."

"Weekly tests, if you want to keep doing it."

He rolled his eyes. "Jesus, Chere. I'm only sleeping with you at the moment."

"Why should I believe that?"

"Because I'm too self-centered to bother with lies." His fingers moved up my side and caught my right nipple, and pinched it. "That's all you want? A clean bill of health? What kind of whore are you? Name a price," he prompted. "Something reasonable."

It felt unbearably icky to haggle with him, to talk about money and what I would do for him for money. I felt like a scrabbling stripper again, willing to gyrate my ass as hard as necessary to make the next rent check.

He waited. I waited. I wasn't going to name a number and he wasn't either. The truth was, he was already paying me too much.

"Bring me some test results," I finally said. "And we can go without."

"Swallowing too, right? No spitting, or I'll lose my fucking shit with you."

"And how would that be different from any other session?" I blinked at him, once, twice. "If you want me to swallow your cum, then you'll just have to force me to do it, won't you?"

He pinched my nipple again, so hard I pushed him away, which only resulted in a grasping struggle. Of course I lost. He laid over me, still pinching me, still hurting me. "You little flirt."

I wasn't the flirt. He was. He was stroking me, kissing me, flirting with me when he was the one who'd just lectured me about client-escort boundaries.

He stood up then and went into the bathroom, and turned on the shower. He'd gotten what he wanted—oral without condoms, pending his test results. No need to lie beside me and pretend to be nice anymore.

"Are you coming in?" he yelled over the water.

Hell no, I wasn't "coming in." Boundaries, you asshole. I'd shower after he was gone, because if I went in there now and got in the shower with him, he'd start kissing me and being lovey-dovey and I'd fall for it hook, line, and sinker, which would only give him the chance to mock me again.

I must have fallen asleep to the sound of the shower. By the time I woke, the room was dark and silent. Empty.

I sat up, feeling grungy and unsettled. He'd left the key for me on the table. He always left the key so I could stay if I wanted, but I was looking for something else. My poetry. Why hadn't he left me any poetry?

I was disappointed enough to turn and look at my back in the mirror. When I didn't find any words, I inspected my entire body, as if I wouldn't have woken up while he was writing on me. No. Nothing. Nothing but a bunch of ugly bamboo welts.

Well, this had certainly been an ego-bashing session. I thought he'd at least leave me with some poetry, something he'd picked out especially for this fucked-up moment between us, but he hadn't, and I was left feeling small and ridiculous again. Ugh.

I took a long shower and tried to summon the glamorous, sexy Miss Kitty from the depths of my despair. Men paid a lot of money to spend time with me, to sleep with me. I had clients who paid just to take me out to dinner and have conversation. I was worth something besides fucking.

I was kind and caring. I cared for Simon, who was a mess, and I didn't complain about it.

I tried to build myself up, tried to avoid pitching into a depressive spiral. I felt a little better once I dried my hair and put my dress back on. It was a gorgeous dress, and it looked good on me. If W didn't like it, he could go fuck himself. Someone would like it. I decided that I needed to be around people tonight, happy, uncomplicated people who didn't know me as Miss Kitty, or Chere, or anybody.

I wasn't a huge drinker, but tonight, I was going to the Gansevoort bar.

IN BETWEEN

The Gansevoort's rooftop bar wasn't the scene it was in its heyday, but it was classy and elegant, and a really nice place to chill out under the night sky. Patrons crowded the tables, but it didn't feel suffocating, and the sultry, jazzy music created a laid-back vibe. There were plenty of dark places and alcoves to hide in if you felt like it, but I sat at the main bar. I needed to be seen. I wanted to be admired. W was right about that, he was just too mean and sadistic about throwing it in my face.

The bartender smiled at me as he handed over my Old Fashioned. See, a friendly smile. That was all I needed. I felt some taut misery within me begin to uncoil. I knew in my heart that I was more than an escort. I was more than a "whore," as W was so fond of saying. He didn't know how much those careless comments poked at my tender spots. Or...wait. He probably did, which was exactly why he said them.

The dirty, depressing truth was that I hated escorting. The money was good, sure, but the work was so soul-deadening. So many of my clients annoyed me or disgusted me, and I felt disgusted by myself when I played along with their fantasies and desires. The whole thing was just so fake. I didn't feel okay about my life. I didn't feel authentic when I was playing that damn Miss Kitty role, because that wasn't me.

And W was the one who'd made me face these truths, with his blatant disdain for my Miss Kitty persona and my profession. W was to blame for ninety-five percent of my unsettled feelings at the moment, which freaking made me mad. It's not like I could quit and do something else. I had no degrees, no qualifications, no way to do any other job that would pay me enough to support Simon. I had to keep escorting until he made it through this rough patch, but maybe, just maybe, he was on the other side of it. He'd started painting with more energy and inspiration, getting ready for his show at Boris White's gallery.

If Simon could straighten out his shit, get cleaned up and start making money again, then I'd feel more secure about killing Miss Kitty. I could go back to school, study fashion or art or design, and start a new career where things could be beautiful rather than squalid. W had told me he worked in design. If the two of us could have talked, really talked like friends, I might have asked him about design careers. But no, that wasn't happening because he wasn't my friend.

Ugh. I didn't want to dwell on the distancing lecture he'd delivered down in the hotel room. I didn't want to get all depressed again. *Take a drink, lift your chin, be normal.* I looked around at the other bar patrons. What did they do at their jobs? This was New York City, the land of endless opportunities. If I was going to find a real job, I'd have to get on the ball soon. I was pushing thirty, for God's sake.

I took a big swig of my drink, wanting to quiet my stresses and regrets, wanting to quiet every thought and feeling. Hell, I wanted to get so wasted I could barely stumble back to my hotel room. I was just signaling the bartender for another Old Fashioned when the man next to me turned around and looked at me. His generous mouth tilted up in a smile.

"An Old Fashioned girl, huh?" He studied me more closely. "Wait, do I know you?"

I always freaked out when men asked, "Do I know you?" because my first thought was always, *is he a former client?* But on closer inspection, I knew he wasn't. I would have remembered those eyes. They were big and expressive, and looked brown at first, until he leaned closer and I realized they were a very, very dark hazel that looked nice with his curly black hair. He wasn't model-gorgeous, or hyper-masculine like W, but he was attractive in a friendly kind of way.

I needed friendly, so I smiled and said, "I don't think I know you. Maybe we live in the same neighborhood or something."

"Lower Manhattan? Tribeca?"

After playing twenty questions, we figured out that we did live pretty close to each other.

"So what are you doing here?" he asked. "Cocktail after work?"

I almost choked on my drink. Yes, this was essentially a cocktail after work, but I wasn't going to tell him that. "I was supposed to meet a friend here," I said, "but she flaked out on me." Already with the lies. I gestured down at my get-up. "I came out anyway since I was already dressed."

"Why waste a great dress?" he agreed, giving my outfit the appreciative once-over that W had so angrily withheld.

Ah, he was charming. He had a bit of a Mediterranean look, the way I pictured W before I met him. Actually, he looked a lot like Simon—*yes, Simon, remember him, Chere? Your boyfriend?*—but I could tell this guy was nothing like Simon. He wasn't artsy and haunted by demons and complicated. He was clean-cut and well-adjusted, a businessman probably. An ad account exec or something. Maybe a lawyer, for the prosecution, not the defense.

"Are *you* having a cocktail after work?" I asked, indicating his dark suit and patterned tie.

"Yes. Well, I'm celebrating with some people from work. We nailed down a huge account today, closed out the books—"

He interrupted himself, jabbing a finger in the air.

"And I'm not going to talk about work, because it's boring, and I'm an accountant, and I try to forget it when I'm in a situation like this."

"When you're on the roof of the Gansevoort?" I joked.

"No. When I'm talking to a beautiful woman who's not looking over my shoulder and planning her exit strategy."

"You know, I can plan exit strategies without looking over your shoulder. I mean, with eye contact and everything." I held his gaze and smiled. "Some of us are that good."

He gripped his chest, the universal gesture for *you wound me*. I took the opportunity to check for a ring. Was it possible he was just a normal single guy having a celebratory drink with some coworkers?

A couple of them sidled up, right on cue. He introduced them to me. One was Vince, an older dude with a comb over—the absolute visual of an accountant—and the other was Randy. And they were nice, and all of this was so nice, and I felt like I could have wrapped myself up in this nice normalcy and lived like this for the rest of my life.

"Vince and Randy were great," I said, after his coworkers left us. "But I don't know your name."

He seemed so pleased that I'd asked. "It's Tony. Tony Pavone."

No secrecy, no mind games, just the offer of his name. I wanted to kiss him for it. *Tony* and *Pavone* rhymed, and he was Italian, and he signaled the bartender casually, not like an asshole, and ordered me another drink. "What's your name?" he asked.

"Chere." *Chere, who shouldn't be talking to you, because she has a drugged-out, failed artist boyfriend, and bamboo welts all over the backs of her thighs.* "Chere Rouzier."

"And what do you do for a living, Chere Rouzier? Nothing so boring as accounting, I hope."

"I'm a...consultant. Physical therapy. Physical therapy consultant." I had no idea if such a thing existed. I headed off any further questioning by saying, "But we shouldn't talk about work. I need a night where I don't think about work."

The bartender brought my drink and Tony held up his glass as if to make a toast. We clinked and gulped, and he was so perfectly normal I wanted to cry.

"My friend is a bitch," I blurted, meaning W. "And work is a bitch sometimes, you know?"

"Oh, I know. I could tell you some stories. But I won't." He grinned at me. "Because we're not talking about work. Let's talk about not working. What do you like to do for fun? What would you do all the time, if you didn't have any other responsibilities in the world?"

I thought it was really weird, and really crazy, that I couldn't think of anything. I was so consumed with my work world, and Simon's world, and Simon's problems, and my dreams of W. What was my world? What did I like to do?

"I like to watch movies," I said. "I know that's boring."

"It's not boring. What kinds of movies do you like?"

I named some of my faves, and he came back with some of his faves. He told me he also enjoyed photography, and model airplanes, and making stuff work. He said he got into accounting because he liked everything to be in order. I wondered what he would have made of my life, if I had actually told him the truth about my life. Which I hadn't.

I was a liar, and I didn't belong here sharing this lovely conversation with him.

When he offered me another drink, I declined. I didn't want to get any drunker, because it would only end one way, with an invitation back to his apartment, and I didn't want our hour of pleasant and friendly conversation to go down that road.

"It's been wonderful talking to you," I said, "but I'd better go. Early appointments tomorrow."

"Is that your exit strategy?" he said, smiling. Oh, that smile.

"No, it's the truth." *No, it's a lie. I've told you so many lies.*

"Well, you know, we live close. Maybe I can take you out to dinner sometime."

No was on the tip of my tongue. Regrets, and my polite decline, but he was already scrawling his number on the back of a business card. *Anthony Pavone, Brooker and Associates, P.C.*

I took the card from him and jammed it down in a pocket inside my bag. That's when I noticed the piece of paper with GANSEVOORT PARK AVENUE at the top, and lines of W's handwriting.

He'd left me a poem after all.

I shoved W's paper deeper into the pocket and smiled up at Tony. Maybe I would go to dinner with him sometime, just to do something nice for myself. I was so grateful he'd talked to me, and been kind to me after all of W's fuckery. He'd never know how much I'd needed it this particular evening.

We said our goodbyes, and I went back down to the room. I needed to dig out W's poem and read it before I headed home, even if it blew up my fragile happiness. I thought about throwing it away instead, but I knew I wouldn't be able to do that. I lay back on the bed and braced myself, and accepted the risk of his words.

She walks in beauty, like the night
Of cloudless climes and starry skies
And all that's best of dark and bright
Meet in her aspect and her eyes.

For what it's worth, Chere, he added in a post script, *you're more beautiful than any of that shit you put on.*

IN BETWEEN AGAIN

I knew it was stupid, and I knew it was selfish, but I called Tony a couple days later. We picked a place to meet for dinner, and "not talk about work."

I never would have done it, except that Simon and I had argued about Rachel again, and he called me a jealous bitch, and knocked me down when I wouldn't give him enough money, and I thought, if he can have Rachel in his life, then maybe I can have Tony in my life, just for a friend. If you want to know the truth, I was thinking about really crazy stuff, like getting a real job, and leaving Simon for someone steady and kind like Tony. Maybe it could be one of those friends-to-lovers things, and everything in my life would change.

I tried not to think about W and our exclusive thing, or the fact that he'd called me beautiful, or that he wrote me poetry. I didn't think about anything except that he would be sorry when I quit, because then he'd have to find some other escort to blindfold and torment. If he asked me why I quit, I'd say, *because you never told me your name.* But really, it was everything. I was tired of selling my body, and tired of doing a job I didn't like.

So I went to meet Tony with all these ideals and hopes in my heart. I dressed up for him, a cute pink sweater and skirt, but not Miss Kitty pink. Just casual, friendly summer pink. Tony greeted me with a gracious

111

compliment and a kiss on the cheek. He'd suggested a tapas place and I thought, *of course, a place for sharing. All of this is fine.*

"What do you like to eat?" he asked. "Let's get, like, twenty things."

"That sounds perfect."

We got margaritas and ordered a few dishes to start, fish tacos and watercress salad and some calamari thing. There were tiny beef sliders and crusty bread with tomato and olive tapenade. In hindsight, I was doing too much drinking and not enough eating, and he...he was asking so many questions. He genuinely wanted to know about me, and it was flattering, but it was difficult too, because I had to lie about so many things. And lying and drinking don't go together well.

He finally caught me in a lie, because I'd told him I was born in New York when I'd really been born in New Orleans, and I said something about growing up in the south and blew that all to hell. I was so tipsy and nervous I started making up this extended story about my childhood and some step-family I knew I'd never remember, and I looked into his warm, deep hazel eyes and thought, *why can't I just be me? Why can't I tell the truth? Why am I making up lie after lie?*

Because if we were going to have a future, as friends, or maybe something more, we needed to start out with honesty, and move forward with honesty. I put down my margarita and stared at the tangle of fried calamari, and it looked to me like the disgusting tangle of my lies.

"I'm going to say something really honest," I blurted out. "Because you deserve honesty."

He smiled, and I knew I was doing the right thing, because he was a very on-the-surface person. An accountant, who liked everything to be in order.

"So..." I lost my nerve a little bit. "Don't judge me. Please."

He shook his head. "I never judge."

"I know we're just having a friendly dinner here, and God, I'm having a great time, but I think you should know that I have a boyfriend."

His smile faded. His eyes narrowed a little bit, but then he shrugged. "Okay."

"I didn't know... I wasn't sure if this was supposed to be a date or just a casual get together."

"I guess it can be whatever you want." Still, he looked unhappy, which maybe was a good thing. It meant he was interested in me as more than a friend. "What kind of boyfriend are we talking about?" he asked. "Long distance?"

"Kind of long distance." I spread my fingers, forcing myself not to take another gulp of the margarita. "In the sense that we've grown apart. Things are really not good between us. In fact, they're really, really bad."

"Oh. I'm sorry."

Tony was so nice. He settled so smoothly into the role of concerned friend.

"How long have you been together?" he asked.

"Ten years." I couldn't believe it had been that long. "He's an artist. He's gotten into drugs and everything. He's gotten really...flakey."

Tony listened to all this, sitting still, staring down at his plate. He felt sorry for me.

"Drugs," he finally said. "God, addiction's tough. That's got to be hard on a relationship."

"I don't use them myself." It sounded like he thought maybe I did, and I wanted to set him straight. "I hate drugs. I hate what they've done to him, to us, to our relationship."

"Is he at the stage yet where he's willing to seek help?"

"No. But I feel like *I* need help. Like I need to let him go, but I can't let go." He looked so sympathetic, so kind, that all my shit came pouring out. "That night at the Gansevoort, when you came up and talked to me, I really needed someone to be nice to me, you know? I needed someone to be friendly and considerate. I haven't had that in a while."

He shifted pieces of the calamari around with his fork. "If you haven't had that in a while, then it's definitely time to let that relationship go."

He was so right. His voice sounded deeper, almost reproachful. I didn't blame him for disapproving.

"I'm sorry if you feel like I'm here on false pretenses, or to lead you along," I said. "I should have told you the night we met that I was in a relationship. I just didn't know how to explain everything. It's complicated. I'm in that stage where I don't know what we are, or what to do."

"Can I ask you something?" He put down his fork and looked at me. "Does he know you're here having dinner with me?"

"He's passed out back at our apartment," I said. "It happens a lot."

113

"Is he the one you were supposed to meet that night at the Gansevoort?"

"No, I was there because..." *No. Don't say it.* But you couldn't build a future without truth. As for why I thought Tony and I had a future, I didn't know. "I was meeting a client there," I said.

"Physical therapy? It was almost midnight."

"The physical therapy I do is... Well, not the kind of physical therapy you think. I'm an escort."

There was a silence. He cracked a smile. "Oh, okay. You're joking."

"Not joking," I said quietly.

"You're an escort?" His opinion of me rearranged itself, went plunging downward. I saw it happen in real time. "You mean, like, a *prostitute* escort?

"I'm not a street hooker. I'm not even a hundred-dollar-an-hour kind of deal." Like I could put a positive spin on my job. "I work for the best agency in New York. Big spenders. It's very classy."

"Like, Heidi Fleiss classy?"

"Better than Heidi Fleiss. I make a lot of money," I said, hoping, praying, wishing that he wouldn't stand up and stalk away from the table. "It's very lucrative."

"And illegal," he said, frowning again.

"Not really. The dates are what the client pays for. Not the sex."

"Although you usually have sex with them."

"Not always." I shrugged. "Some of them just want dinner conversation, or a travel companion. Some of them want a pretty woman to take to the company party."

He'd turned a little pale under his olive Mediterranean complexion, but he didn't stalk off. After a moment, he picked up his drink and smiled. "So, I'm lucky then, I guess. I've had drinks with you, and now dinner, pretty much for free. I mean, for the cost of a meal." He waved a hand at all the dishes. His lips were curved like he was smiling, but the warmth had left his gaze.

"I don't even know why I started doing it," I said. "I'm saving money to get out of the business, to go back to school. That's my ultimate plan."

"So it's just temporary."

"Yes, absolutely. A temporary thing." That wasn't a lie.

He blinked rapidly for a moment while I clasped my hands together under the table. "How does that work with your boyfriend, and your job?" he asked.

"Well, this is hard to explain, but it's really just business. The men I see in those hotels are just customers, you know? It's a transaction."

"A transaction that pays well," he said with another smile.

"Yes. I make way more than I should."

"So that night at the Gansevoort, you had just seen a client? Or you were waiting to see a client?"

I looked down at my lap. I didn't want to talk about any more of the details. I just wanted to be real with him, and I wanted him to accept me, at least as a friend.

"I'd just seen a client," I admitted. "Honestly, I couldn't even tell you the guy's name."

I sensed he wanted to ask more questions, but he was too classy to do it. I imagine he wanted to know what I'd done with W that night, all the lurid details, because even the classiest guys were obsessed with sex. At least I knew Tony wasn't an undercover cop. He would've whipped out the badge by now. He would have been reading me my rights.

And in some way, that would have been a relief.

"I'm sorry I lied to you," I said. "I'm sorry I wasn't myself, but I think you're great, and you helped me that night, and I thought you deserved to know the truth."

"Thank you for telling me the truth." He let out a breath. "This is kind of anticlimactic, but after all the margaritas, I've got to hit the restroom. I'll be right back."

"Okay."

And I knew from the way he stood up that he wouldn't be right back. That he wasn't coming back.

He didn't come back, although I waited almost half an hour, nursing my drink and picking at the food left on the plates. I would have felt sad if I didn't feel so humiliated and numb. I took out my wallet to throw down the money for the check, but then I realized Simon had taken all my cash. My wallet was fucking empty. One of my credit cards was missing too. Shit.

I paid with a different card, a secret one Simon didn't know about, that I kept hidden in a different pocket in my bag, then I stormed home planning to rip him a new one. But when I got there, he was super high and super messed up.

"Where have you been?" he asked. "Where the fuck have you been?"

His eyes were wet, his clothes covered in paint. He'd been in the middle of working when the drugs took him to a bad place.

I made him some coffee and sat with him on the floor of his studio. I let him talk because he needed to talk, and because that way, I didn't have to admit I'd been out with someone else. He talked about his art and his upcoming show, and the way nobody wanted him to succeed. Anxiety and paranoia didn't mix with whatever downer he was on. He felt heavy and listless in my arms.

"I just want you to be happy," I said. "If the art doesn't work out, you can do something else."

"It's got to work out. It worked before. I'm going to make a comeback. Trends come and go, but real talent never goes out of style."

I stroked his hair. It felt greasy. He didn't smell the way he used to, all fresh and masculine. He smelled stale. "I want you to get better," I said softly. I hoped he was too down at the moment to fly into a rage.

He didn't. He started crying again instead. "I'm sorry I'm like this," he murmured against my neck. "Addiction is really hard when you have children. I feel like I'm letting them down."

"Simon," I said wearily. "We don't have children."

"My paintings are my children. These paintings are my babies. They're suffering because I don't have my shit together. And then I feel bad, and I do more drugs because I'm so tired of feeling bad."

"I know."

"I'm going to die pretty soon," he said, clutching at me.

"No. Don't say that."

"I'll die if I can't beat this. I don't want to die, Chere. I went to a meeting. I wanted to stay sober and I went to a meeting but I found out Baxter died." Baxter, one of his art world friends. "I couldn't believe it," he said. "I just talked to him last week."

"You have to stop using drugs, or you'll end up like Baxter. You have to keep going to meetings, and get sober."

"I'm trying!"

There was the rage. I held him tighter, trying to head it off. "It's okay. Don't worry about it right now."

"I'm afraid." He wrapped his long, paint-stained fingers in my sleeve, turned around and gave me a clumsy embrace, a kiss. "Don't leave me. Please, I'll change. Please help me."

"I will. I'll help."

"Don't leave me. Don't go away. I needed you tonight and you weren't here."

I was still angry about the money, the money he probably used to get high like this, but I felt guilty too. What was worse? Stealing, or cheating on your partner? I held him in my arms and rocked him, and rested my cheek against his. "I'm sorry," I whispered. *I'm sorry I was out with someone else.*

Even if that someone else was nicer, and better adjusted, and richer than Simon, in the end, that someone else hadn't wanted me. That someone else walked out on me without saying goodbye because I was just that horrible in his eyes.

But Simon wanted me, and Simon accepted me. All these fucked up things that were happening to me—they were the universe's way of punishing me for making plans to desert Simon. I decided I wasn't going to let W, or Tony, or anyone mess me up like this again.

7.

THE STANDARD SESSION

I tried to pull my shit together when W scheduled a session for that weekend. He told Henry he wanted to meet me at The Standard, a hotel in the Meatpacking District known for its floor-to-ceiling windows and unobstructed views.

Voyeurs congregated outside at night, to watch the exhibitionists have sex with the curtains thrown open and the lights on. I hoped that wasn't what W had in mind. The Standard was for people who wanted to be seen, and I wasn't in the right frame of mind for exposure. I wasn't in the right frame of mind for W and his shenanigans either, but a job was a job.

And I was a whore, as he was so fond of saying. So I straightened my dress—nothing fancy, I was done dressing up for him—and knocked on the door.

He opened it and motioned me in. He looked handsomely businesslike, in summer slacks and a button up, with a light blue tie. He didn't look irritated like last time, and I let out a breath I hadn't realized I was holding.

"Take off your clothes," he said by way of greeting. "Take off everything and sit on the bed."

I stripped and sat where he indicated. It was seven in the evening, our usual meeting time, and summer sun still streamed in the windows. I felt like I was under a spotlight, but at least it was too bright for anyone to be peeping in from outside.

"How have you been?" he asked, peering down at me.

"All right."

He handed over a paper. A clean STD test, with all his identifying information redacted, as promised. Stupid, so stupid. I shrugged. "Fine. Oral only, though."

His eyes narrowed as he studied me. When I ducked my chin, he raised it again and scrutinized me in the evening light. His voice, when he spoke, was low and even. "What happened to you?"

I hesitated a second too long. "Nothing happened to me."

His fingers tightened on my chin. "You look guilty. You look beaten." His eyes moved over my body, but all the bruises were on the inside. "What happened to you?" he said, giving my face a little shake. "What the fuck did he do to you?"

I tried to push his hand away. "Nothing. I don't know what you're talking about."

"Sit on your hands and open your fucking mouth."

He unzipped himself with jerky movements, drawing out his cock. My head was pulled into position while my hands curled into fists beneath my thighs. I hated being treated like this, but my rebellious body still responded to the passion and violence of being forced. My nipples hardened and ached, and a pulse bloomed between my legs. His cock was granite-hard, and yet it felt smooth and warm in my mouth without the latex barrier. It had been so long since I'd sucked a bare cock.

I lifted my hands to caress his length, to make it sexy and civilized, but of course he wasn't interested in my efforts. He jammed my face on his cock until I choked.

"I told you to sit on your hands, bitch. I don't want your hands. I want the wet, hot, lying little hole in your face. Just suck me."

I glared up at him, taking him deep, gagging myself on his length. *Like this, you asshole?* He undid his tie and yanked my arms behind my back, and cinched them together above my elbows.

That made it easier somehow, this force and degradation. I was tied up, and W had taught me there was solace in surrender. I grunted as he used my hair to pull me off the bed and onto my knees.

I'd given many blowjobs in my life, but those blowjobs were different. Those men allowed me control. W allowed me zero control over my balance, my swallowing, even the angle of my throat. He shoved his cock in as far as he liked, and withdrew when he felt like it.

"Please," I choked when he let me come up for air. "Why are you like this?"

"Why are you a liar?"

He plunged back in again and drove deep, in, out, in, out. Tears squeezed from my eyes and my scalp hurt where he held my hair bunched in his fist. I cycled between wanting to breathe, and trying not to gag up puke.

"Stop with the retching," he scolded. "Don't be a drama queen. Just blow me. That's your job, you whore. Suck me off until I manage to empty myself in your worthless little throat."

I knew this was his thing. The insults, the humiliation, the roughness. I knew he'd hold me afterward and make me feel better again, but that didn't help me handle this now. I gagged hard and really almost vomited. He pulled away and slapped my face.

"I said cut it out. Look at me."

As soon as I looked up at him, he slapped my face again. I was fucking over it. I tried to crawl away on my knees, tried to lunge myself away from him even as he tightened his grip in my hair. Big mistake. Nothing thrilled him more than a fight. That was the whole point of this. If I'd just gone limp and collapsed on the floor, he would have walked away and abandoned everything. But I couldn't not fight, and he couldn't resist controlling me, and I was choking and spitting and gagging with both his hands on my head now. My chest was covered in drool.

I made crying sounds in my throat, and I did start collapsing, because you can only get hammered so many times in the throat before you can't take it anymore. He merely lifted me up again and made me continue. He was so good at this force, this terror. If he'd been wearing a condom, I probably would have broken it with my teeth by now, and choked on the latex when I accidentally sucked it into my mouth.

See, Chere, be grateful you aren't literally dying.

No, I was just emotionally dying, because he was using me so brutally, and I couldn't breathe, and I couldn't be sexy, and I had no control.

"Look at me," he barked. "Look up at me."

I stared up as well as I could through the tears and the trauma. His hard blue gaze riveted onto mine as if to say *I own you. I own this hole in your face. Deal with it.* I tried to shake my head, but I think that only turned him on more.

"Jesus Christ," he growled, low and rasping. "Jesus fucking Christ."

I sucked. I shuddered. I hunched forward and stared up at him, begging for that cum, because I wanted this to be over. I felt his fingers tighten and tremble against my scalp, and I braced as he thrust in me hard, over and over. He finally came in my throat, too far back to taste. All I tasted was him, his skin and his scent and his heat.

His fingers loosened, but I didn't dare move. When he finally withdrew, I swallowed convulsively and took halting breaths. He let me go and I crumpled to the floor.

"No. We're not done. Sit up."

I couldn't. I didn't want to, but he reached down and grabbed the tie that bound my arms behind my back, and forced me to sit up again.

"What did he do to you?" he asked, standing over me. His cock still glistened with my saliva.

"What? Who?"

"Your boyfriend. Tell me the fucking truth, Chere."

"Nothing. It wasn't..." I clamped my lips shut. Too late.

"It wasn't your boyfriend? How interesting." He yanked the tie tighter when I tried to turn away. "Who?"

"No one."

"We're supposed to be exclusive," he barked.

"We only went to dinner!"

The fury in his face hardened to disgust. "Fucking liar."

"It's not a lie."

He walked away from me, zipped up his pants and stalked across the room like he couldn't stand to be near me. I wiped my face on the edge of the bed and tugged at the tie holding my elbows. I hoped to ruin it, like I'd ruined the last one.

"Cheating on your boyfriend?" he asked from the window.

"It wasn't a date. He didn't even stay for the whole dinner."

"A client?" He turned back to me, his brow dangerously arched. "Taking a little work on the side?"

"He wasn't a client! He was just someone I met, nothing to do with work."

"What's his name? What's this fucker's name?"

My lips trembled in indignation. "I'm not telling you."

He came at me and I shied away, panicked. I tried to get to my feet and failed. He ignored my flailing, lifted me and set me forcefully on the edge of the bed.

"I'm not telling you his name," I insisted, doubling down. What could he do to me that was worse than the violent blowjob? "It doesn't matter anyway, because nothing happened. I met this guy, okay? He was friendly and nice, and he lived close to me, so we went to dinner. As soon as he learned what I do for a living, he said he had to go to the bathroom and he never came back. He ditched me there in the restaurant and left me with the bill. Does that make you happy? Once he found out the truth about me, that I was an escort—"

"The truth about you?" W scoffed, interrupting my tearful tirade. "There's no truth about you, Chere. Just girly, emotional shit, and a bunch of lies holding it all together."

I turned my face away from him. "Please close the window. My eyes..."

"Is the sun bothering you? Too much exposure? How about some darkness?"

He yanked the drapes closed with a snap. In the dim light bleeding from beneath the edges, he seemed a menacing shadow standing over me.

"Better?" he asked.

He walked away again. I felt relief, but at the same time I was afraid of the dark, and the darkness in him.

"What do you care about any of this?" I asked, raising my voice. "You said last time that you didn't care about me at all, that we're just escort and client. So why do you care if I lie? Why do you care what I do when we're not together?"

He stripped off his clothes, his shirt and pants thrown across the same chair as my dress. "I care because I just had my bare dick in your mouth. I care because I'm paying you to be exclusive with me. Do you understand what that means? No one else, Chere. No one gets a shot at your pussy but me."

I scoffed at that ridiculous assertion. "As you pointed out earlier, I have a boyfriend."

"Your boyfriend?" He gave a mocking laugh. "That fucked-up, narcotic-addicted failed artist you live with? If he can get it up with the amount of chemicals in his system, I'd be amazed."

Fucked-up. Narcotic-addicted. Failed artist. I stared in shock at his dark silhouette. "How could you know all those things?"

"You think I don't investigate the whore I'm sleeping with? You got your fucking STD test. I'm allowed to get my information too."

"You had me investigated? You had people spy on me? Is that even legal?"

"It's as legal as prostitution." The darkness hid his expression, but his voice dripped with contempt. "Are you going to file a police report? Because I can file those too."

"You're an asshole," I said in a fury. "You get to investigate me, but I don't get to know anything about you, not even your name? That's not fair."

"You know what's not fair? Paying for a whore to be exclusive to you—"

"I'm an escort, not a whore," I yelled, as he went around turning on lights.

"And then finding out your exclusive whore is going to dinner with some fucking jackass."

I blinked as the bright bedside lamps illuminated his irritated expression. "Nothing happened."

"You think he didn't want to get into your panties, Chere? Men only want one thing from women who look like you."

"Shut up."

"If you think otherwise, you're a fucking idiot."

"Shut up!"

"I'm not going to shut up," he said, pointing a finger at me. "You didn't only break our agreement. You also cheated on your shitty-ass loser boyfriend." He went to his briefcase and unzipped it. "And why? What came out of it, but a lot of fucking hurt?"

"My life and my boyfriend are none of your business."

"Maybe not. But I have you for another hour and fifteen minutes, and you've been a bad girl. A lying, conniving, two-timing bad girl." He came at me with a pair of black clamps. "You have no integrity. That sucks. But maybe I can teach you the error of your ways."

"What are you going to do?" I asked, shrinking back.

He took one of my tethered arms and held up the first of the intricate looking clamps, and worked it open and closed a few times in front of my eyes.

"No," I said. "Please. No."

I tried to get up but he had me by the arm. When I started fighting in earnest, he pushed me back on the bed and straddled my hips. My arms were crushed behind my back and my legs weren't going anywhere. I watched helplessly as he tugged at my right nipple and opened the clamp's jaw.

I didn't scream when he applied it. It hurt too much for a scream. The sharp, biting pain went beyond screaming right to gasping for breath.

"Take it off," I said shrilly.

"Hush."

I bucked and flailed under him, but he was heavy and he had me pinned, and the second clamp went on, more painful than the first. When I cried out, he tugged the chain so they cinched even tighter, and jammed it up between my teeth.

"Bite this," he ordered.

"No." The pain was worse when I moved, so I'd gone still. My nipples felt like they were being gnawed off.

My refusal to cooperate earned me a slap to one of my aching breasts. "Bite the fucking chain. Keep it in your mouth. Otherwise I'll keep hold of the chain, and you won't like that."

I snarled at him—and I'd never snarled at anyone in my life. The pain was that bad. But I opened my teeth and let him shove the cold metal chain between them.

"Good girl," he said in a silky voice, staring down at me with elegant severity. I hated that my body responded to the approval in his gaze. Even through the pain and the helplessness, I felt some fleeting stab of joy. Which was quickly replaced by a fleeting stab of pain as I lifted my chin.

I dropped it back down and stared as he rose from the bed and returned to his briefcase. He reached inside and drew out a braided whip. It was only about the length of his forearm, but it looked sturdy enough to fuck me up.

I shook my head and moaned at the resulting nipple torture as he approached the bed. He grabbed my legs when I tried to kick him, and wrapped an arm around them, yanking them in the air. This, of course, left all my ass and pussy exposed, as well as the backs of my thighs. The marks from the bamboo rod had faded, but I remembered the pain.

"Don't," I begged through the chain. "Don't. Don't." It sounded like *duh, duh, duh*, which was appropriate, because only a very stupid person would keep returning, week after week, to be tortured by this madman.

"Don't lose your shit," he said, looking down at me. "I can only leave those clamps on you for ten minutes or so before you start to suffer permanent damage. Your beating will be over before then."

As he said it, he brought the whip down across the area where my ass met my thighs. I don't know why it still shocked me every time, how much he could hurt me. My entire body arched in a panic. I jerked my hips and tried to escape his grip on my legs, but I only ended up hurting my nipples. Before I could come to terms with the slicing agony of the first stroke, he drew his arm back and hit me again, and again.

I started to keen against the chain, pathetic crying even as I fought to escape. He took such lazy pleasure in torturing me. He could have hit me harder, yes. He could have sliced me to ribbons, until I was a bloody mess, but he wasn't a psychopath. No, just a pervert. He wanted my squirming and my panicked sounds and he knew this was how to get them. He wanted my features contorted in agony and my legs straining against his grip, and so he toyed with me, pausing between strokes, alternating hard ones and less hard ones. There were no soft ones with an implement like that.

After a couple dozen blows, I knew I couldn't take it anymore. I spit out the chain and tried to explain it to him. *No, oh, no, you can't, no more, no more, no more, please, please.* His response was to tug the chain until I screeched, and shove it back between my lips. I decided I'd better not do that again. How much longer until ten minutes? I felt the tip of the whip prod against my pussy.

"No," I whined against the metal links.

"Yes. You need it, bad girl."

He started flicking the whip's tip right along the center of my pussy. I cried. I bawled. *No, no, no.* It hurt so bad, and I was so wet, and I hated him for reducing me to this groaning, terrified, needy creature. As I fought and strained, he started alternating his method of depravity. First I'd feel the hot, hard licks across the backs of my thighs, and then the *thwack* on my pussy.

"Do you want the clamps off?" he asked. "Listen to me." I could barely focus through the haze of my agony. "Do you want the clamps off?"

I nodded frantically. *Yes, yes, please, off!*

He put my legs down, spread them wide, and forced me back with his hands when I tried to sit up.

"Don't," he said in his evil voice. "Don't you dare move. Don't you dare get up. Keep your legs open for me. Show me how bad you've been, how badly you deserve to be punished."

My arms ached from being tied behind me. My nipples felt like they were going to fall off, and my pussy and thighs throbbed from the damn whip, but I lay back, my eyes locked on his, and opened my legs, baring myself to whatever horrible thing he might do next. My chest rose and fell in frantic pants, and a noise leached out of me, a warbling, fearsome sound I couldn't control.

"Jesus," he whispered, staring down at me. "You're magnificent like this."

I expected him to whip my pussy the way he'd done earlier. I lay there waiting for him to whip it to shreds, but instead he reached out and started to stroke me. I was *so wet*. I think that's why he did it, to show me how wet I was.

He fucked me with one finger, two fingers, three fingers, and it hurt and felt good, two feelings at once. He half knelt, down on one knee, and shoved my legs so wide open that my muscles strained. His fingers dug into my inner thighs, each fingertip a point of domination. As soon as his tongue touched my clit, I knew his goal was to make me die.

I thought he would be rough, like his fingers were rough, and his whip was rough, but he ate me out with the delicacy of an expert. He used the perfect pressure, the perfect teasing variation of taps and strokes and fluttering caresses. I wasn't groaning and crying from pain now, but from pleasure.

Without stopping, he reached up and undid the nipple clamps. They hung, forgotten, from my mouth. I was too distracted to spit out the chain. Blood rushed to my poor, blood-deprived nipples, resulting in a burning frenzy of feeling. All it meant to me was more of his power, more of his torture. More of him.

His fingers rested on the whip welts, intentionally, I was sure. I hurt and I burned, and his tongue was miraculous. He was a silent, intent predator and I was the prey animal tossing in his grasp. Dying, slowly but surely. My hips jerked in time with his tongue and then the orgasm broke wide, making me tremble with a complete loss of control. The bliss of it felt sharp as a whip stroke. The chain slithered from my lips as I gasped through my open mouth. The death throes, escaping through the lying hole in my head.

I didn't move. I couldn't. He left and put on a condom, and came back to the bed. He pulled up my limp body and turned me over, and arranged me face down. The tie binding my arms made a nice handle for him to grasp.

He thrust inside me, and even as wet as I was, he felt big and scary. He pounded into me, jerking me back against him. I was still sensitive from the orgasm, not to mention the whip. My nipples hurt from scraping across the comforter, soft and luxurious though it was. The bedside lamps seemed like spotlights, intensifying every humiliation.

Ow, ow, ow. I'd had my pleasure. This excruciating finale was *his* pleasure. He fucked me and fucked me and fucked me until I chafed, until I started to go dry, and then he finished with even more force than he'd started with.

Somewhere in the middle, I'd started crying. There was a big wet stain under my face, smeared with makeup, foundation and eye shadow and mascara. I blinked down at the stain as he untied my arms. He was still inside me, even now that he'd come. I had this thought that maybe my body would never be mine again.

I had another thought: he wanted me, literally. He wanted my body *to be his*. Not only had he insisted on an exclusive arrangement, and stalked my personal life. He was also methodically and intentionally ruining me for other men by making sure they could never be as perverted, as passionate, as forceful as he was. He was devouring me with his desire, his charisma. He was taking from me until he had all of me and I had nothing left.

And he gave me none of himself in return.

"Get out of me," I said when he finished, using my limp arms to push myself up.

"Stop." He grasped my hips with enough force to still me, and pushed himself deeper. "Stay there."

"Get out of me," I said more loudly.

He slapped my ass. Hard. "Don't fucking order me around. I'll get out of you when I fucking feel like it."

Escorting wasn't supposed to be like this. It wasn't supposed to be violent and antagonistic.

"I'm not seeing you again," I said, and this time I meant it.

His fingers moved a little on my hips. "Did you learn anything just now?" he asked. "Anything at all?"

"I learned that we hate each other, and that you're a stalker."

He made a gruff noise that sounded like disagreement and pulled out of me, and got up off the bed. He went in the bathroom and started the shower. I stayed where I was, too heavy with self-loathing and depression to ever move again.

"Chere," he yelled, when I didn't join him. I couldn't do it. I couldn't spend any more time with him right now.

I heard him get in the shower, heard the change in the patter of the water. I got up and dressed in record time. My eyes fell on his briefcase. *What was his name? What did he do?*

If I went digging through his briefcase, and he caught me, what would he do to me? I was afraid to find out.

Anyway, I knew he wouldn't leave any identifying information in there. If there was anything in that briefcase I could use, he wouldn't have left me unattended with it. His wallet was with his clothes in the bathroom. That might have provided some identifying information, and I could probably go in there and grab it before he could stop me, but then I'd be no better than him. A dishonest, aggressive stalker. I wasn't sure I cared about his name anymore. I didn't want to care. I didn't want to see him again.

I made sure I had all my shit, and then I whipped open the curtains with the same snapping flourish he'd used to draw them closed.

"Chere," he yelled from the bathroom. "Get your ass in here."

The water shut off and I ran for the door. I didn't check to see if our session had timed out. If he didn't want to pay me because I left early, he didn't have to.

Sometimes running like hell was more important than money. Sometimes saving yourself was more important than sticking around for the payout, and this qualified as one of those times.

IN BETWEEN

The whole way home, I looked over my shoulder, like W might be coming after me. He wasn't, of course. He might be angry, but he'd have to hash things out with Henry, not me. I wasn't seeing him again. I'd let Henry straighten everything out.

When I let myself into the loft, it was almost a relief to find Simon passed out, snoring, on the couch. I couldn't handle a blowup tonight, or some drug-fueled drama. He'd probably be a mess later though, when he woke up. I'd sleep in the spare room, with the door locked.

What had happened to me, that I was sleeping behind locked doors? Why was this my life now? *Because you're weak, and a loser. Why don't you change?*

Maybe walking out on W was a start. Maybe it was the first step in figuring out my shit. Getting Simon under control was the second part, but that wasn't all me. He had to get to the point of wanting to change too. Maybe this upcoming show would do it. I hoped so. I hoped so desperately hard.

I tiptoed through the living room and kitchen, past my snoring partner, into his artist's studio. I looked at all his works-in-progress while I had the time and privacy to do it. I wondered if they were good enough to bring him back, to revitalize his career. The thing was, they looked crappier than his earlier works. Sprawling, messy, unfocused.

I was so tired. I needed a shower. I stood under the hot water, but it didn't wash away the soreness of my nipples or the welts on the backs of my legs. My pussy was still wet and my jaw was still sore from the blowjob, and I didn't even get any poetry or kisses to make it better. That was my fault, but first steps required sacrifice. Getting better required sacrifice. I stayed in that shower and washed W off my skin until the water started to run cold, and I still didn't feel like I'd gotten rid of him.

I ate a little bit of leftover Chinese from the refrigerator, and I would have made coffee, but I was afraid the smell would wake up Simon. I grabbed a bottle of water and a self-help book about codependency, and went to hunker down in my locked room.

It's Your Life: Recognizing and Overcoming Codependency. I'd been trying to get through the book forever, but it wasn't helping much. It wasn't giving me any practical steps, just warning signs to look for, which I absolutely recognized by now, and goals to strive for, which still seemed so far out of reach as to be ridiculous. There was a whole section missing out of the middle, namely explicit instructions on how to reach those goals.

It is unhealthy to rely on other people for happiness.

It's better to have no love than to have dishonest love.

It is okay to be alone.

Fuck you, dumbass author. You don't know. You don't understand my struggles and my problems, or anything about my life. I closed the book and rested my cheek against the cover, emblazoned with bold primary colors to compel me to take action.

I tried to think about Simon and how to help him, rather than enable him, but my mind kept drifting to my date with W instead. There was something so sad and unfinished about us, some lack of understanding that had probably doomed us from the start. I didn't understand how he could make me feel sexy and wonderful, and so horribly devastated at the same time. He'd given me more than any other client, and yet refused to give me anything at all.

I had to walk away. I had to stop thinking about his passion and energy, and all the attractive things about him, and remember all the ways he made me hurt.

It is unhealthy to rely on other people for poetry.

It's better to have no love than to have violent love.

It is okay to save yourself.

My phone buzzed, displaying a number I didn't recognize. It wasn't unusual in my business. I answered with a noncommittal "Hello?"

"Chere?"

Oh God. It was W. It shocked me that he would call. I couldn't believe he'd reveal something so personal as his phone number.

"Chere?" he said again, when I didn't answer.

"How did you get my number?"

I heard him take a breath. "Does that really matter?"

Fuck. Fuck. Fuck. Hang up on him. I did not hang up.

"What do you want?" I asked.

"You didn't wait for me to say goodbye." He sounded angry. Stern. *Bad whore, leaving without saying goodbye.*

"I had to go." That was the simple truth. I had to get out of there.

"You didn't wait for me to try to make things better."

"You can't make things better when they're that fucked up."

He was silent a moment. Then: "I don't think we're that fucked up." Another pause. "I try to make things better afterward. I didn't want you to leave."

"I'm sorry. I felt like I had to leave."

"Why?"

It felt strange to talk to him on the phone, to talk to him in a situation where he couldn't hurt me. At least not physically.

"Why did you leave?" he prompted. "Because I hurt your feelings? Because I hurt your body?"

He didn't say it mockingly, or I would have hung up. "Yes," I said. "To both of them."

"You didn't give me a chance to hold you afterward. I think that's important. I worried about you after you left."

I tried to picture him in the Standard, worrying, pacing back and forth in front of the big glass window with all the voyeurs outside. I couldn't imagine it. I couldn't imagine him caring, but he'd called me. Henry would never have given him my number. He must have gotten it the day he went through my bag.

"I'm fine," I said sullenly. "I was just reading."

"You're at home?"

"Yes." Ugh, I shouldn't have told him that. It was none of his business. None of this was any of his business. "I'm not supposed to talk to clients outside of our sessions," I told him. "We're supposed to go through Henry. I can't talk to you."

"Don't hang up."

I cradled the phone against my ear and waited.

"I like being with you," he said.

I closed my eyes. There was something in his voice I'd never heard before, some longing or tenderness. It ripped my heart to shreds. My throat constricted in despair.

"I can't talk to you." I had to force the words out. My voice trembled. "I have to go."

"Are you crying?"

"Phone calls aren't allowed."

"I don't give a fuck what's allowed."

Goodbye, tenderness. Hello, scary person I didn't want in my life anymore. I wiped my eyes put the phone down on the bed.

"Chere?" I could still hear him. I swallowed hard and steadied my voice as well as I could.

"I have to go. I'm sorry, but I can't see you anymore. I have to...change something."

I pushed the button on the screen to end the call. Goodbye. So easy, one finger could do it. Even so, I felt a terrible loss. The sobs I'd held inside broke free, ugly and desolate sounding. I buried my head in the covers, wary of waking Simon. I couldn't stem the tide of grief.

My chest ached with pent up emotion, with all the weird hopes and inspirations W had spurred in me. All of it was hopeless because we couldn't be together. Tony's rejection had hurt me. W's continued rejection would eventually kill me, and I couldn't even understand why.

I flung the codependency book across the room. I hated him for doing this. I hated that he messed me up this way. *It is okay to save yourself. It is okay to protect yourself.*

Five minutes after I hung up on him, the phone rang again. I looked at the number and sent it to voice mail. Twice more he called. Finally, I answered.

"Don't hang up," he said, and this time it was less of an order and more of a plea.

"Why are you doing this? Why are you calling me?"

"To be sure you're okay."

"I'm okay," I said, and I was bawling.

"You don't sound okay. What happened today, Chere? Things were okay between us. I mean, they weren't great, but you seemed to get something out of our sessions before. Today you seemed hollow. Upset."

"You hurt me! You called me a liar, and said all kinds of other terrible things."

"I also said you were magnificent, and I meant it."

"It doesn't matter. It doesn't take away everything else."

He was quiet a moment. I wondered where he was, what his place looked like. Was he lying on a couch? In a bed? Did he have a wife in the next room? Kids? A dog?

"I'm sorry about that guy," he finally said. "That jackass who left you at the restaurant."

"Yeah, well, he didn't approve of my career."

"I think you're great at your career. That's what I would have told you if you'd stuck around. It was a hot fucking scene today. I thoroughly enjoyed myself."

I didn't say anything. I didn't have any words.

"Chere?" he asked after a moment. "Are you still there?"

"I'm not going to do escorting much longer," I said. "I'm already thinking how to get out of it. It's not making me happy."

"It's not making you happy, or *I'm* not making you happy?"

I sighed. "This isn't about you. There's so much more fucked-up shit in my life, shit that has nothing to do with you."

"Like what?"

I rubbed my eyes. All this time he held me at arms' length, and now he wanted to have a therapy session? I heard a thump from the living room, and Simon muttering.

"I have to go," I said.

"Like what?" he repeated. "Talk to me, Chere."

"I can't talk to you. I told you that. This is against the rules."

"And I told you I don't give a fuck about the rules."

"Chere!" That was Simon, out in the hall. "Chere!"

Just as I feared, he'd woken up like a bear. Withdrawal was a bitch. He rattled the knob and pounded.

"Chere, open the door! I told you not to lock me out!"

"Who's that?" W asked. "Your boyfriend?"

"Yes," I said miserably. "I have to go."

"He sounds angry."

"He'll be fine."

"Will you be fine?"

More pounding, more shouting. I wondered how much W heard. I curved my hand around the phone like that might block the huge noise of Simon's meltdown.

I didn't want to hang up anymore. I wanted W to be there so I didn't have to go through this alone. "He takes drugs," I said in a near whisper. "He's so messed up. If he's not high enough, he's unbearable."

"Then why are you there? Why do you live with him?" His blunt questions were just like the damn book. They didn't solve any of my problems.

"I'm in a locked room. I'll stay here until he calms down."

"Fuck that. Chere—"

"It's none of your business."

Simon let loose a string of blistering expletives, and the banging stopped. I heard him stomp away. He couldn't get at my money because I had it in the room with me. He'd leave now, to go bum money or drugs from his friends. From Rich Rachel, who seemed to provide an endless supply.

"He left," I said, because W had sounded worried, and I thought he would want to know. "He'll be gone for a while."

"You should be gone," he said, in the most sincere voice I'd ever heard.

"I'm hanging up." I didn't want to do this with him. I didn't want him in my life. I didn't want him insinuating himself into the other fucked-up areas of my existence, especially since I wasn't seeing him again.

"I need to see you again," he said, before I could hang up. "I know you don't want to see me anymore, but I want to see you."

I rolled my eyes, my sore eyes that were red from crying. "That's too bad."

"What if things could be different? I mean, I'll never really change. I'm a mean bastard. I'm a sadist, but maybe we can sit down before our next session and talk. We'll talk before we fuck. I'll prepare you a little more for what's going to go on."

"You mean..?" I paused and swallowed hard. "Are you saying you *know* what you're going to do to me from the beginning? That all that stuff you do to me is planned?"

"It wouldn't be very safe, otherwise. If I just came at you flailing, and deciding things on the fly."

There was a long moment of silence, then he made a tsk of a sound. "Didn't you know that? Do you think all the stuff we do together is real?"

"It feels real. When you're doing it, it feels really real."

"It's supposed to feel real when I'm doing it. Then afterward we calm down together and decompress. At least, when you don't take off. Next time—" His voice cut off, and he made a frustrated noise.

"What?"

"I was going to say that next time, I'd tie you to the bed so you can't leave. But you don't want there to be a next time, and making threats about what I'm going to do to you next time probably isn't the wisest way to proceed." He sighed. "It's late. I'm tired and worried. I'm worried that you won't see me again."

"I'm not going to see you again," I said, but that time, it sounded like a lie. Because what he was saying sounded kind of like an apology, and a promise to do things better next time, for my sake.

"Are you safe there?" he asked. I wondered what he'd do if I said no. Would he come rescue me? Take me to his mystery abode and reveal more of himself to me? More than his phone number? *No, Chere. No.*

"I'm safe," I said. "He won't be back for hours. I'm going to go to sleep. There's a deadbolt on the door."

"That's fucked up."

"I'm going to hang up now. I've had a long day."

"See me again. Please." He made a rough noise, a laugh or a growl. "No one fights like you, Chere. I need you to fight me. All the other whores are pansies. Excuse me. All the other *escorts* are pansies. You affect me more than anyone else."

I knew what he meant. No one else had ever made me feel the way he made me feel, and I feared no one else in my life ever would.

"You scare me," I said.

"You scare me too."

"You know what I mean."

He sighed. "I'll try not to scare you next time. We'll talk. We'll go slower."

"And then you'll still be mean to me and make me feel like shit."

"I told you why I do that. It has nothing to do with you personally." He paused. "That sounded wrong. It has everything to do with you being perfect at meeting my needs. That's the personal side of it. And unfortunately, my needs are to be a complete bastard to you. But I don't mean to hurt you. Really hurt you." I thought I heard him set a glass on a table. "I was afraid I really hurt you today."

"You did."

"But how much of that was because you already felt hurt by someone else?"

He said it gently, because he knew it was a little mean, but he also knew he was right. "You felt hurt too," I pointed out. "You flew into a rage about the Tony thing."

"Ah. His name is Tony."

I clamped my lips shut. I hadn't meant to give up that information, not that it mattered.

Yes, it mattered. He'd use it to taunt me at some future point.

"And for the record, I wasn't in a rage about Tony," he said, drawing out the name with derision. "I was in a rage because of what you let him do to you. You're sad, Chere."

He didn't say I *looked* sad, or that I'd *seemed* sad earlier, during our session. He said *You're sad*. Which I guess made sense after the way I'd cried, and all the girly, emotional shit I'd poured into his ears. I didn't understand why he'd called, or why he seemed to care enough to be upset on my behalf. I didn't understand what I did for him, or why he wanted another date so bad.

I didn't understand anything about him.

"Listen," he said. "I'm going to call Henry and set up another date. You can come if you like. But if you'd rather not, I'll understand. If that's the case, I won't call, and I won't try to contact you again. But if you come..."

"What?" I asked when he didn't finish.

"If you come, I'll give you more poetry," he said in a soft, compelling cadence. "And I've never given poetry to any of the other ones, Chere. Only you."

8.

THE FOUR SEASONS SESSION

He said he'd try not to scare me. He said we'd go slower. I didn't know what that meant, but I agreed to another date, and even put on a designer dress for the first time since he'd cut off my Lanvin suit almost two months ago. This was trust, if not friendship. For once, I looked forward to our session with more anticipation than dread.

Well, there was a lot of dread too.

I walked across the glitzy hotel lobby and found my way to the elevators. I'd never met a client at the Four Seasons before. The rooms were ridiculously expensive. I felt like I was breathing in expensive air and walking along expensive ground. The Four Seasons seemed too stately, too old-world-wealthy to use for tawdry sex, but here I was. How did W afford these hotels, on top of what he paid for exclusive access to my services? Who was he? What did he do?

Believe me, I'd tried to figure it out. I'd badgered Henry for any scrap of information, but his mouth was firmly shut. I'd searched design magazines and design firms, and researched modern poets. No dice. I'd pored over fetish websites and personal ads, but there were so many profiles to sift through, and so many men in New York who claimed to be rich and dominant and sadistic. A quick scan of each profile, and I'd know it wasn't him because the person was trying too hard, or coming off fake, and W wasn't fake. He was irritating and scary, and unfathomable, but he wasn't fake.

I tried to convince myself that this compulsion to know about him was only natural curiosity, not some deeper feelings. I had a boyfriend, after all, and W was just a client. He was a very small part of my big and complex life, and the fact that he gave me exquisitely mind-blowing orgasms didn't mean I was falling in love. *Oh, Jesus, don't let me be falling in love.*

I walked down a silent hallway to the fiftieth-floor room. W loved his corner rooms. I checked my carefully applied makeup and smoothed my hair, and knocked on the door. My stomach fluttered with familiar anxiety as the lock clicked and the door swung open. He looked stylish as ever, in dark dress pants and a white starched shirt, slightly open, no tie. I stared at the base of his neck, at masculine muscles and defined tendons.

"You came," he said.

I looked up to meet his eyes. He smiled as he drew me inside, but it wasn't a simple, friendly smile. It was a complicated smile, like everything about him.

"Are you being brave?" he asked, and that sounded complicated too, caught between happiness and mockery.

"I'm being stupid," I said.

"No."

That was all he said, *no*, but just like that he was in charge of me and I was scared. He took away my bag and stripped off my dress, barely sparing it a glance. I wore nothing underneath, which he liked.

"Take off your shoes," he said, running his hands over my skin.

I kicked them off, wondering how W made me feel so much more naked than anyone else. He pinched one of my nipples, holding my gaze, and I was already white-hot, already willing to do anything on earth for him.

He backed away abruptly, releasing me.

"There's a beautiful view." His words sounded thick, or maybe my brain wasn't firing on all fronts. I tried to readjust from his presence and control to this view he wanted to show me. We looked out together at Central Park fifty stories below us. So pretty to look at.

The room was pretty to look at, too. There was a polished wood desk beside the window, and a leather upholstered chair, and across the room, a wide king bed with smooth white sheets. But all I really wanted to do was look at *him*.

What's your name? Who are you? His blond hair was dark and light at once, and his blue eyes could seem dark and light too. So many things had become dark and light in my life, good and bad at the same time. Like my boyfriend. Like escorting. Like W. I supposed this whole "view" thing was his attempt to go slower and be easier with me. I didn't like it because it was fake.

I turned away from the window. "Well, I'm here," I said. "What are you going to do to me?"

"Will you let me tie you to the bed?"

"You're *asking*?"

"I'm asking if I can tie you to the bed. After that, you have no more say in what I do to you. And you probably won't like what I do to you."

That sounded more like him. "What if I say no? That you can't tie me to the bed?"

That smile again. "I guess I'd try to convince you to let me."

"With words?"

He shook his head, slowly. Seductively. When had I begun to find the threat of him so seductive? I glanced back at the door.

"You won't make it," he said. "And you're naked. They frown on naked women tearing through the halls of the Four Seasons."

I moved first, toward the door, because I knew he wanted me to. He grabbed me around the waist. Not gently. This wasn't a game. I knew if he got me tied to that bed he was going to do everything in his power to make me regret my life choices, like the choice to fight him when I knew it would only make him excited.

He hauled me over to his briefcase and somehow managed to open it and extract some rope while I flailed and clawed at his face.

"Let me tie you up," he said. "Be a good girl."

I was not a good girl. I was a wild, fighting girl, and I was thrown across the bed so hard it knocked the breath out of me. Before I could regroup, he was on top of me, straddling my ribs. He corralled my arms and looped the rope around my wrists five or six times, leaving a tail. Then he leaned over me, his crotch pressed to my face. I moved my head, searching for air, but all I got was gabardine and balls. His hard shaft pressed against my cheek, over the bruise Simon had put there two days ago.

I didn't want to think about that now.

"I can't breathe," I yelled with what little air I had left.

He moved back, leaned down and grabbed my chin. "Maybe I don't want you to breathe."

"Jesus. No matter how nice you are to me, it always ends like this," I said, meaning the force and roughness.

He frowned. "You have no idea how it's going to end."

While he was suffocating me with his cock and balls, he'd tied me to some tether point in the headboard. I yanked hard. Nope. Nothing. When I kicked my legs he held them down.

"Be still. You'll stay where I want you to stay. You should know that by now."

More rope, more brutal force to capture my legs and bind them together. He wound rope from my knees to my ankles and fixed the end somewhere under the footboard. I was bound tight, barely able to turn or stretch. So much for him trying to be less scary.

He undid his zipper and took my face in one of his hands, and shoved his cock into my mouth, or more accurately, my throat. I choked and tried to sit up, but I wasn't going anywhere. I groaned and sucked him. The bondage took away my choice to comply.

"That's fucking hot, when you groan like that," he said.

He played with me for ten minutes at least, pounding into my throat, rubbing his balls on my face, demanding that I lick or kiss or nibble or suck. He pinched my nipples with excruciating force whenever I did it "wrong." No matter how much I writhed and tried to get away, I was stuck, a prisoner to his will. When he finally shot his load in my throat, I was relieved, not turned on. Well, I was a little bit turned on.

"That was nice," he sighed, sitting on my chest.

"Your vision of nice and my vision of nice are so different," I whispered. "Also, you're crushing me. Please get off me."

"Shut up." He drew a finger across my drool-covered lips. "Jesus, you're a mess. So sloppy and wonderful."

"Your vision of wonderful and my vision of wonderful—"

He clapped a hand over my mouth. "One more word, and you'll be gagged for the rest of this session. And that won't suit my purposes at all."

Oh God, I hoped that didn't mean his purposes included more blowjobs. Or chokejobs, as I'd come to think of them. He got up and went to the bathroom while I waited, still tied to the bed. I wondered if W ever had gentle, caring sex. I wondered if he'd ever tried it, just once.

He came back and cleaned me up in a relatively gentle manner, kissing me and wiping all the drool from my chin, neck, and ears. I stared at him, because I wasn't supposed to talk, but I wished he would talk to me. I wished he would connect to me somehow, with something beyond his cock.

He finished wiping me off and tipped a water bottle into my mouth. I spit some of the water out to keep from drowning, and he went back for the towel, blustering about what a mess I was. As he sopped up the dribble, he took the opportunity to hurt my nipples some more. The truth was, he loved reducing me to the level of a drooling, helpless victim.

And we were only about twenty minutes into this scene.

He stood and went to his briefcase, and dug out his phone. While he scrolled through messages, he unbuttoned his shirt and scratched his chest. My God, so freaking sexy. His cock spilled carelessly from his fly, all his beautiful masculinity flaunted in profile. Sadly, I couldn't do a thing about it. *Just take off the pants*, I thought. *Take it all off. Let me look.*

He stroked his half-hard cock, ignoring me completely. There was something about the careless, confident way he stood there that fired my desire. I was drooling harder now than I'd drooled during the blowjob. I shifted on the bed, pressed my legs together the slightest bit. Of course he noticed.

He threw down his phone with that smile again. Why was he so damn happy today, when he'd been such a bastard the session before? Not that I trusted that smile, or even believed it signaled happiness. It might just as easily signal disaster.

He reached in his briefcase and pulled out a blindfold. Damn it.

"You should be resting," he chided in his evil-Dom voice. "Maybe this will help."

I shook my head, for all the good it did me. He circled my head with the black length of silk and tied it a bit to one side, so I wouldn't be resting my head on the knot.

The darkness and helplessness took me right back to our first session, to the nerves and WTF feelings that had consumed me. I wanted to tell him about those feelings but I couldn't. I just wanted to say one word: *Remember?* But I didn't dare. I hated being gagged, and I couldn't bear it on top of the bondage and blindness. I made a soft, urgent sound instead, and was rewarded with a slap on the cheek.

"Quiet," he said.

That was it. *Quiet,* and then he left me to stew in my horny, dark world, wondering what would come next. More slaps? More face fucking? Nipple clamps? My legs were tied together, which kind of limited what he could do to me fucking-wise.

As I lay there, still and bound, I listened for his movements. I listened for the door (I didn't want him to leave) and the zipper of my purse (I didn't want him to root through it) and the sound of his clothes hitting the floor (because that probably meant something else was going to happen). I listened and waited but I heard nothing for long minutes. Was he playing on his phone? Looking out the window? Staring at me?

I thought he was probably staring at me. He'd trussed me up on the bed, his whore-in-waiting, and now he was studying me, thinking up the best ways to screw with my head. His silence frightened me.

Why was I here, allowing myself to be terrified? Why did I let him take over me this way? But I knew why. For the orgasms. I didn't drool earlier because of his beautiful body, but because my body remembered what his body could do.

At last I heard movement and—*yes!*—the whisper of clothes being pulled off and thrown over the chair. I heard him take steps toward the bed and stop. He tugged at the rope holding my legs and then released the tether point. He unwrapped my lower legs, then ran his fingers along the places the rope had been. I drew in a breath as he caressed my sensitized flesh. How could his barest touch make my whole body shudder?

I pressed my legs together, dreading the next touch but wanting it too. I wanted to protect those vulnerable parts between my legs but I also wanted him to force my thighs open and take me, because no one else made me feel the way he did.

"Why are you shaking?" he asked, running a hand over my tensing muscles. "You're allowed to talk now. I want to hear what you're feeling."

"I'm scared," I said. "I'm worried. I don't know what you're going to do next."

"Ah, but you don't have to know. That's the fun of it. I could tell you right now what I plan to do, but then it wouldn't be as exciting for you when I do it."

He moved. I flinched. I felt him settle against my front, not crushing me this time, but lying above me. He pushed my thighs apart with his knees, pinning me down, not that I'd made the first attempt to escape. My arms were still tied above my head. He kissed the sensitive underside of one of my forearms. I turned my face, seeking his warmth.

"You smell so good," he said. "Like vanilla and woman. Not that you're very vanilla anymore. Do you like this, Chere? Do you like being tied up, subject to my every whim?"

It took me a moment to admit it. "Yes."

"*Yes, Sir,*" he corrected softly.

"Yes, Sir," I said. "I like it."

"Do you want me to kiss you?" He said it so quietly I could barely hear.

"Yes, Sir."

I flinched when his lips contacted mine, not because he was rough, but because I didn't know when to expect the kiss. He licked my lower lip and kissed me again, sweet and sultry. I could feel his hardening cock between my legs. I arched to him, needful, wanting. He chuckled.

"Not yet, my little plaything. My captive. Let's make out for a while."

Just like that I was a captive, and he was my Master, implacable and in charge. I squiggled in frustration and his arm came around my waist with a quelling sound.

"You can't get away," he reminded me. "The most you can do is flip over, although I wouldn't recommend doing that unless you want to be fucked in the ass."

He poked his cock against me again. He was so thick and hard, already ready for round two. He gripped the blindfold so it was tight against my eyes, and then he grabbed my hair and pulled it, and kissed me at the same time. I moaned at the dissonance of pleasure and pain.

"You want that now, don't you? Since I mentioned anal, you want me to flip you over and ream your ass, you little slut. You love when I hurt you."

"No, Sir," I lied. "Please don't."

"You don't get to choose. Shut the fuck up."

He shut me up with his lips, his kisses that grew hotter and more insistent. I whined as he yanked a fistful of my hair. The harder he pulled, the more I ground against him. No one else had ever made out with me like this, rough and painful and soft and tender all at once.

"I'm not going to hurt you," he said against my ear in a hoarse whisper, and at the same time he said he wasn't going to hurt me, his fingers tightened around my neck.

I turned my head. I wished I could see his face. Did he look angry or loving? Was he going to kill me or just scare me?

"You're hurting me," I rasped.

"Calm down and let me choke you."

My body was making involuntary motions to get away. My arms jerked. My legs strained. My neck lengthened under his hands and blood heated my face. "Please don't," I begged. "Please, Sir..."

His grip loosened. I gasped in air at the same time he kissed me. It felt like he stole my breath. "Please," I said, and I didn't even know what I was pleading for.

"I'm not going to hurt you," he said again. "Do you trust me?"

"No," I cried, just before his grip tightened on my neck again. I fought but he held me down. Next I knew, I woke to the sound of frightened keening and realized the sound was coming from my own throat. I panicked because I couldn't see. Oh, God, I couldn't move my arms.

W said my name, stroked my cheeks and kissed me. "Okay, you're back. It's okay."

I calmed, and remembered the hotel room and the blindfold, and the bondage.

"Please don't do that," I pleaded. "Don't make me pass out like that."

"Why not?"

I felt too weak to yell at him. Instead I whispered, "What if I don't wake up?"

"I'll make sure you wake up," he said against my lips.

He started kissing me again, but I couldn't enjoy it any longer. While one hand stroked my hair, the other still rested around my neck.

"You said you would try not to...to scare me," I said when he let me come up for air.

"I told you I wouldn't hurt you."

Because of the blindfold, I couldn't tell if he was willfully fucking with me, or if he honestly thought he wasn't hurting me. I suspected it was a combination of both.

"You might kill me," I said, so aware of his fingertips against my throat.

"I would never kill you," and this time he said it like he meant it. "I just want to kiss you."

As he said it, his fingers tightened a little, but not enough to bring back the tumble into nothingness. It was worse somehow, that restrained threat.

"Please," I begged. "I'm so afraid."

"I know, baby." He nuzzled me, moved his hips against mine and licked a line from my neck to my cheek, and along the edge of the blindfold. "I love how afraid you are. But I swear, I promise, I won't hurt you. I would never kill you."

The more he said it, the more I shivered, because his fingers were pressing on either side of my esophagus, bringing death a little increment at a time. Then he was gone. I heard a condom wrapper ripped open, and the snap of him adjusting the tip once he rolled it on. I was so concerned for my breath, and my life, that I'd forgotten about his cock. Within seconds he was back on top of me, nudging open my legs and sliding deep within me. I clenched around his thick length and remembered. Oh, yes, I remembered.

He moved in me slowly, taking his time. I luxuriated in the feeling of fullness and wished I could hold onto him. My shoulders ached from my arms being bound over my head, but it wasn't enough to overcome the other pleasure I felt. I moaned and groaned and arched to him. Then his hands were back at my neck.

"No," I said.

"Yes," he replied, and gave me just enough oxygen to feel fear and panic and not pass out. At the same time, he kept fucking me, driving me across the sheets with powerful thrusts so the rope tethering my wrists went slack. I struggled like I might free myself, like he might ever let me be free.

"Please, don't," I said, but at the same time, those alternating forces were working on me. Fear, need. Breathlessness, bliss.

"You're mine," he said in response. "I can do what I want to you."

You're mine. I was thinking how weirdly happy and euphoric those words made me feel when his fingers tightened and set off pastel explosions behind my eyes.

The last thing I remembered was his cock filling me up, all of W filling me to bursting. And when I came to, he was still there, deep inside me. "There you are," he said. My cheek felt hot, like he'd just slapped me. "Want to go again?"

"No," I gasped.

"No, *Sir*," he reminded me.

"No, Sir, please. No more."

"Time for your assfucking, then?"

I didn't answer, just let him flip me over and give my ass cheeks a few spanks. I was weak as a kitten. No more fight, no more energy to do anything but cry and lie there as he went for lube.

"Don't choke me out while you're in my ass," I begged. I didn't know why, but the idea terrified me, that he might be in that sensitive, vulnerable place while I was gone to the world.

"*Don't choke me out while you're in my ass,*" he repeated in a mocking falsetto. "Really, Chere, why would I? I want you to feel every minute of this, from the moment I force it in until the moment I come deep inside you."

I cried some more as he pried open my ass cheeks and shoved the head of his cock against my hole. The ritzy white Four Seasons bedspread had to be smeared all to hell with my juices and tears. For $1500 a night, they could deal with it. I braced as he straddled my hips and eased his shaft into my passage. *Ow, ow, owww.*

I was exhausted, but not too exhausted to feel every inch of his length. I tried to be open, especially since he wasn't giving me much choice. I couldn't defend myself or wiggle away, which made it feel worse.

"That hurts," I groaned.

One hand gripped my hair again, and the other clamped over my mouth.

"It ends when you come," he said. "So I suggest you stop whining and figure out a way to get off. This doesn't end until your ass milks the cum out of my cock."

Fuck. There was no way I could come when it hurt so bad. But then, the idea that I *had* to come to make all this stop...that was a very powerful mindfuck.

"I hate you," I said against his hand. I truly hated him, but there was something about his cruelty and perversion that turned me inside out in a wondrous way.

"That's right," he said. "Feel me taking your ass, tearing you up. You can pretend I'm raping you if you want."

I tried to shake my head but he only laughed.

"I'm waiting for you to come," he goaded. "Do you want me to help you?"

I feared what his "help" might entail, but when he let go of my hair and grasped my pussy instead, it felt much better. Way better. He hurt my clit, but it was a good kind of hurt that blended with all the other hurt to make me sub-spacy and hot. I was his, trapped, blind, used, manipulated. I groaned, wanting this to be over, only because the torment and feelings were so overwhelming.

"Please, please," I begged.

"Come on, you horny little bitch. This fucking doesn't stop until you realize this is the only reason you exist. To please me. To amuse me. To surrender to me. To take my cock in any fucking hole I want, however I want." He punctuated each assertion with a pounding thrust, and then he slapped my pussy hard, and my body and my mind decided this depraved treatment was worthy of an orgasm after all. I tipped off the edge of the cliff and fell, fell, fell into a powerful climax.

"Oh God. Oh Jesus," I babbled. He groaned and pounded me harder, and yes, I think I milked his orgasm right out of him. My pulsing release went on and on, too intense to feel very pleasurable.

"I can't. I can't," I repeated weakly. "I can't. Let me go."

I didn't even know what I meant by *I can't*, except that I knew I couldn't bear any more stimulation. I had to be released. I had to recover.

He withdrew from my limp, ragdoll body and went into the bathroom. I heard water running. Not the shower. A bath.

Oh, yes, I needed a bath. When he returned and untied my wrists, and lifted me from the bed, I huddled like a baby against his chest. It wasn't until we were together in the water that he undid my blindfold and let me see. The lights were dim, but they still seemed too bright. There was too much glass and mirror and chrome. I whimpered.

"Close your eyes if it's too much," he said.

I did, just for a minute. He washed me, running hands over my skin and down between my legs.

"I'm finished now," he said. "I'm finished hurting you for today. I'm finished fucking you, I promise. Look at me, Chere."

I blinked my eyes open.

"Are you okay?" He asked it very slowly, and very kindly, and I *was* okay. My body still hummed from arousal. As usual, he'd taken me from too-much to too-fucking-much.

"I need to touch myself," I said.

"Be my guest."

I rubbed one out there in the tub, straddling his legs, pressed against his chest. I could feel him get hard again but he kept his promise and didn't stick it in me. Maybe he rubbed one out too. For a while, I was too oblivious to care.

After that orgasm, it was like my body came back to itself and I was able to settle down. The water had chilled by that point, but it felt good. W watched me steadily, leaning back against the lip of the Four Seasons' fancy soaking tub. This was luxury and depravity, and no one did it like him.

"You weren't better this time," I said when I felt able. "You were worse. Scarier."

"No. You were more scared at the Empire, when you thought I was a serial killer."

I splashed him as he smiled. "You shouldn't be proud of that," I said. "And I came back again today because you said you wouldn't be as scary."

"I don't know if I used those exact words."

I curled up in the water, studying him, trying to understand how someone so sadistic could be so handsomely beautiful at the same time. "You shouldn't choke people out," I said. "It's creepy and sociopathic."

"Breath play is a common enough fetish."

"It shouldn't be."

"That's probably true." He shrugged. "I won't do it to you very often. I did it today because I felt very close to you, and happy to see you."

"You choke people when you're happy to see them?"

"I choke people who move me, who surrender to me and make me feel energized."

I gave him a skeptical glance. "Not energized. Powerful."

He shrugged again. "Yes. It makes me feel powerful to put my hands around your neck and watch you struggle for breath. I'd like to do it again someday, but without the blindfold. Next time, I want to see the fear in your eyes." He touched my leg. "That blindfold was a kindness, by the way. You would have been more scared without it, because you would have seen what was in *my* eyes."

"Murder," I said.

"No. Don't even joke about that. I'm careful with you."

Your vision of careful and my vision of careful are different. I didn't say it out loud. What was the use?

He took my wrists and kissed them, and kissed me. I could always count on the kisses, no matter how much he hurt me beforehand. I used to think the kisses were an apology, a way to make things up to me, but now I wasn't sure. He made no sense. Violence and poetry. Choking and kissing. Degradation and caring.

What's your name? Please tell me.

"Can I stay here tonight?" I asked. "It's really beautiful. You choose the most beautiful hotels."

He smirked at me like I was sassing him. I wasn't. It occurred to me that I'd paid him very few compliments in our escort/client relationship. He at least deserved a few.

"You can always stay the night," he said. "The room's paid for, and I don't mind. You can even order room service and dirty movies." He kissed me one more time. "But I have to go."

The water was cold, and he was suddenly restless. We got out and dried off, and I put on the fluffy Four Seasons robe, while he went out into the other room to dress. When I joined him, he was sitting at the desk, his pen poised over paper. He'd finally turned on the lights.

After the blindfold, and the soft light of the bathroom, it seemed too bright. I walked over to stand beside him. After all I'd gone through, I wanted my poem. I wanted to watch him write it out with his own hands.

"What's our selection tonight, Mr. Cumming?" I asked.

He smiled and looked up at me. "You remember my name."

"Your fake name."

His smile faded. He stood and took my chin, and tilted my head toward the light. "What happened to your face?"

The makeup. My tears. The bath. All my makeup had washed away, exposing the bruise from when Simon backhanded me in the kitchen. It had been an accident, mostly. He hadn't been in his right mind. I said what any self-respecting idiot would say in this situation.

"I walked into a door."

"You're a fucking liar," he said in an icy tone. "A bad liar, too. Your addict boyfriend did this."

I blinked at him. We both knew he was right.

"This happened that night?" he asked, staring between the bruise and my eyes. "That night we were on the phone, and he was banging on the door?"

"No. It happened a few nights later."

"Jesus fucking—" He let loose a string of epithets.

"It was an accident."

His blue eyes snapped. The lights were way too bright now, and his grip on my chin was starting to hurt.

"Are you fucking kidding me, Chere? You're telling me he accidentally hit you in the face?"

"You hit my face all the time."

Now his fingers were around my neck, not my chin. He gave me a sharp little shake. "Do not compare me to him. You have a bruise on your face. I've never bruised your face. I'm not even bruising your neck right now."

I pushed away from him and he let me go. We retreated to opposite sides of the room—I slunk over by the TV, into the shadows, while he stood looking out the window at the dark.

"You're an idiot," he muttered, not looking at me.

"It was an accident," I repeated. "He was raging around and I got in his way."

"Did he apologize?"

"I don't remember. And it's really none of your business."

I could see his eyes close from across the room. He stood like that for a while, with his eyes closed. Then he opened them and turned to me. "You're right. It's none of my business if you want to live with someone who—"

Who hurts you. He couldn't say it. He would have been the world's biggest hypocrite to say it, because he hurt me all the time. He got off on hurting me; he *intentionally* hurt me, which was way worse than Simon, because Simon never meant to hurt me. Simon hurt me for reasons outside his control.

"Do you need money to move out?" he asked. "Is that the issue? Do you need help finding another place to live?"

"I don't need you to rescue me. It's my life. My problem. I'm working on it."

"So what's your plan?"

I could tell from his hard expression that he wasn't going to let this go. I sighed and shrugged.

"He has a show next week. The plan is..." As I started telling W about it, I realized what a hopeless, flimsy plan it was. "Well, the plan is that he'll sell some work, and build up a little momentum so he can take time off to go into rehab. It's all about momentum in the art world. He's trying to get to a place where..." My voice trailed off.

"A place where he can stay high all the time?" W suggested.

"Where he can get better. Speaking of which, I can't see you next weekend. One of the week days would be fine, but we're having a big reception on Saturday at the gallery. I'll have to be there Sunday too. This show is consuming him and he...he needs me. He needs this to be a success. I'm sorry. It's just the one weekend."

W's lips tightened. He looked at me with such anger, such irritation that I added, "If you even *want* to see me again..."

"I want to see you again," he snapped. "Preferably without a bruised face."

"I'll see what I can do," I snapped back.

The nerve of him. He'd choked me until I passed out—more than once!—and he had the gall to judge Simon for accidentally hitting me. I drifted away from the corner to sit on the bed. He leaned over the table and started writing on the Four Seasons stationary. As soon as he started, he stopped and put down the pen.

"You know what, Chere? I'm not in the mood for poetry."

"You promised me poetry."

He gave me a dark look. "I'll give you a poem next time I see you. In the meantime..." He wrote out something quick, ripped it off the pad, folded it over a couple times and brought it to me. He pressed it into my palm and touched my bruised cheek. Then he brushed a kiss across my lips and left without looking back at me.

When the door closed, I unfolded the paper and smoothed it in my lap, and read the two words, dark and bold, in W's handwriting.

Love lies.

IN BETWEEN

Simon might be a fuck-up, but he'd built a lot of relationships in the art world, and everyone came out to support his comeback attempt on opening night. His parents and his sister were there, his family's friends, even former college professors, and art teachers who'd developed him as a rebellious child. There were people who had touted him when he was first appearing on the art scene, and people who had torn him down when his star shone too bright.

There were critics and buyers, gawkers and socialites and glitterati, and the magic of Simon was that he didn't care. He stared through them until he could escape their attention, and then hung out with his current circle of friends, the drug users and losers. When people tried to engage him about the art, he acted disinterested and precious. It worked for him before, and maybe it would work again, but it irritated me.

Why couldn't he be professional? I was trying to be professional. My hair was done up in a neat chignon, and I wore a classy, knee-length Pucci dress with Fendi pumps. Simon was in paint-stained jeans and a baggy black viscose button-up. For weeks he'd been telling me how important this was, and now he wasn't taking it seriously because he was either drunk, or high, or both. Probably both.

Of course Rachel was there, in her raccoon makeup and a sloppy dress carefully designed to look like she didn't care, but oh, she did care.

She followed Simon around, fawning over him and basking in his attention, while I dealt with Boris White, the gallery owner, and Josh Jacobs, Simon's agent. I was also the one who directed the caterers and decided where to set up the bar. I did it because this felt like Simon's last chance, and a little bit like *our* last chance. But under my busy focus, under my frenetic efforts to make this work, two words whispered, over and over.

Love lies.

Whatever. I knew that love lied. If I had a dollar for every time my clients claimed they "loved" their wife while they snuck off to me for twice-weekly sessions, I'd be a gazillionaire.

Sometimes it seemed to me that love was a complete and total lie, but then I'd remember times with Simon that I knew I was in love. Love was definitely out there sometimes, in fleeting moments. Maybe it was more accurate to say that *Love flies.*

Screw W and his platitudes and poetry. He was as precious as Simon in a lot of ways, with his elevated self-worth. At the height of the party, when people were packed into the gallery like lemmings, I stood off to the side and thought about what *I* was worth. I couldn't make art. I didn't have a real career. I didn't have money for a room at the Four Seasons. I barely had money for the basics, thanks to Simon and his money-draining addiction.

Speaking of which, was anybody going to buy his new work?

Some things were selling, some paintings flagged with discreet red dots. There was a lot of talk, a lot of nodding heads and scrutinizing and pointing. Simon's art blared from the walls, irritating me because I didn't understand it. I was tired of not understanding anything about my life. While people chattered and postured with champagne glasses dangling from their fingers, I shrank into a corner and struggled to discern the essence of myself, the purpose of my life and why I was here, and what had brought me here. Chere: vibrant, flexible, caring, pretty.

The one thing I didn't feel was worthwhile.

Someone handed me a flute of champagne. I took it because my emotions were a blur, and because I'd paid for the fucking alcohol, and then the crowd in the background receded. I realized that W stood in front of me, blond and tall in his designer suit.

It astounded me that I'd taken a drink right out of his hands without seeing him. He was so big in my mind, so large. How hadn't I known the second he walked in the gallery door?

I stared at him, helpless to speak. It was so loud all of a sudden, and I didn't understand his expression. I didn't understand why he was here.

"How are you?" he asked when I couldn't muster up a greeting. "How's the show going?"

"Okay, I guess. There are a lot of people here." I gestured around the room, trying to act casual. "I think he's sold a few paintings."

A burst of laughter interrupted our conversation. W turned his head, then moved so he was beside me rather than in front of me. Simon held court across the gallery, surrounded by art groupies and hangers-on. A prominent New York art critic bandied for space in front of him, her wild hair and manicured fingers waggling in unison. She was either chewing him out or enthusing about his work.

"It makes me proud," I said, glancing sideways at W. "I'm proud for Simon, that his work excites people. We didn't expect this kind of turnout."

"Everyone likes a train wreck. It's fun to gawk."

"What does that mean? No one's gawking." I looked around. Were people gawking? "There are a lot of big names here, critics and collectors. They wouldn't be here if Simon's work didn't mean something."

W took a sip of champagne. "Yes," he agreed. "His work means something, and it will mean something years from now. Everyone here knows that, just like they know he's a fuck-up. If I didn't hate the motherfucker, I might buy some of his work myself."

I didn't ask why W hated Simon so much. I knew why. Instead I asked, "How can you look around at all he's done and say he's a fuck-up?"

W gazed at me with the same cool, derisive look he employed in our ritzy hotel room sessions. I turned away.

"You shouldn't be here," I said. "You weren't on the guest list."

"I'm still not on the guest list," he replied with a quirk of his lips. "In case you're thinking about looking through it to find my name."

"I don't care about your name." I hadn't even been thinking about that. "I just don't understand. You make this big deal about privacy, about your boundaries, and then you show up at my boyfriend's art show."

He gave a lazy shrug, his shoulder brushing mine. "I do what I want."

"You shouldn't be here. You're one of my clients."

"Are you ashamed of me?" he asked, joking.

"You shouldn't be here," I repeated. "And you shouldn't be standing here talking to me. It's not respectful to my boyfriend."

He gave a half-laugh, half-bark, and rubbed his forehead. "Jesus fucking Christ, Chere. Number one, your boyfriend is higher than a kite at the moment, and he hasn't looked your way all evening. Number two, I only respect people who deserve it."

He was talking about Simon, but I thought he was also talking about me. I wondered how long he'd been here, if he'd been watching me run around arranging everything, supporting my boyfriend who didn't give a shit about me.

Humiliated tears rose in my eyes. I took a sip of champagne to mask them, and it tickled my nose. "I know it's not...it's not... I know my situation is shitty. I know he's shitty. I told you, it's just for now."

"Peace, Chere." He held up a hand. "You can do what you want, and Simon can do what he wants. It's a shame, though, his addiction. He might have been great, one of those artists who lived on down through the ages."

The chatter rose around us, or maybe it was the pounding of my heart. "He might still be great," I said.

"He'll be dead in a year," he replied. "You know the kind of shit he's using, and you know what he spends on it. I guess the silver lining is that dead artists' work brings higher prices. So keep him painting, if you can."

I knew W was cruel and sadistic, but it amazed me that he could say those words without a glimmer of empathy. I raised my hand, I don't know why. To punch him. To slap him. He grabbed it and pushed it back down at my side.

"Listen," he said in a low voice that was nonetheless perfectly audible above the craziness of the crowd. "I'm not saying anything you don't know. I thought that's why you were staying with him. For the end. The payout. If that's so, you'd better marry him if you can."

"You're an asshole." I angled my body away from him. "Why don't you leave?"

"Why don't *you* leave?" He turned the question back on me with urgent emphasis. "Why the fuck don't you leave him?"

He nodded toward Simon, the barest nod, but I already knew what he was trying to show me. I saw the way Simon fawned over Rachel in utter disregard for my feelings. I blamed myself. I wasn't worthwhile.

"Do you use drugs?" W asked.

I hunched up my shoulders. "No. I never have."

"Why did Simon start?"

"His friends got him into it."

"They're not your friends?"

"No." Bitterness closed my throat, and brought on a second flush of humiliation. "I'm not an artist. I'm kind of shunted to the outside."

"You're the money," he said, parsing the situation perfectly. "But I'm surprised you never caved to drugs yourself. Your life must be miserable."

I glared at him. "Some people make me more miserable than others. Why did you come here?"

He rubbed his lips, took another sip of champagne and thought a moment. "I don't know. I'm not sure why I'm here. To watch the train wreck, I guess, like everyone else. Now I wish I hadn't come. I prefer to see you in other settings." He reached under my flowy skirt and touched the back of my leg, drawing his finger across my flesh as if he traced an invisible welt. "I'll see you Wednesday at the Mandarin Oriental."

"I know." I wanted to throw my champagne in his face and tell him to fuck off forever, but this party wasn't coming cheap, and W was my only paying customer. "I've been to the Mandarin a few times. It's a beautiful hotel."

He stared at me a moment, then looked down at my glass. "You don't like the champagne?"

I gazed past him, at the back of Simon's head. The crowd was growing larger, not smaller. It was so hot. "Not tonight," I said. "I don't like it tonight."

"Come here." He took my hand and led me to the bar, and barged his way through to the front as people made way. He had a commanding presence, even here in this overcrowded room. His gold-blond hair looked even blonder in the gallery lights.

When we got to the bar he took my glass and set it on the counter. I felt a tap and heard a squeal, and turned to find an old friend from Simon's earlier days, when he was the next great thing. Her eyes flicked past me. I couldn't blame her. It was hard not to look at W—he was just that hot.

I couldn't remember her name, so I searched my memory while she chatted at me about Simon's work and the show, and what a huge success it was. She asked what I was "up to these days." I could feel W against my back, leaning over the bar. He was talking to the bartender, asking him for a pen.

I wondered what she would think if I told her I was W's exclusive prostitute, that he beat me and throat fucked me and tormented me at every one of our sessions until I cried. Instead I muttered something about consulting, sounding as vague as possible. I finally remembered that her name was Shelly and that she worked for a museum.

Maybe I could work for a museum. I wondered what kind of degree that required.

"You must be so proud of him," she said, and I thought she must be talking about W, because she kept glancing at him with her round, black-lined, fuck-me eyes like she wanted him. She didn't have a clue. W would leave Shelly-the-assistant-museum-curator in a heap of broken dreams. But then I realized she was talking about Simon.

"I am proud," I said.

W thrust a napkin into my hand behind my back, and closed my fingers around it. A moment later, he moved away. I knew from Shelly's gaze which direction he went, and that he was leaving me here, alone, in this bedlam and noise.

"Jaysus, Chere, you wouldn't believe the guy who was just standing behind you. Oh my God, girl. Sex on a stick. I haven't seen him around before."

I made some nonchalant noise and held the napkin tighter. "I wonder who it was."

"I don't know, but yum. Blond hair and jawline for days, and his suit! Older guys are so sexy. It's like they're old enough to know what they're doing, you know? They have that aura, like, *wow, I'm all rich and successful and I enjoy the finer things.*"

"I know exactly what you mean," I agreed. "Will you excuse me? I'm helping Simon with the catering and I have to...you know...check on something."

"Of course. It was great talking to you. I'll see you around."

She gave a fluttery little wave as I clutched the napkin in my palm. I headed into the crowd, toward the back. I pushed around a clutch of socialites and avoided eye contact until I got to the storage room behind the bathrooms. I leaned against the wall and looked down at the napkin, at the handwriting I recognized by heart.

For I have sworn thee fair, and thought thee bright,
Who art as black as hell, as dark as night.

I thought of Simon's black hair and his dark eyes, which, I'm sure, was exactly what W intended.

Shakespeare. Jesus Christ. He was bringing out the big guns.

* * * * *

It was after three when the party wound down. The caterers left and the gallery locked its doors. Some of Simon's friends lingered, strangely animated. I skulked around the walls, looking at red dots. Those dots should have made me happy because they meant success and more money, but I didn't feel happy.

As black as hell, as dark as night...

"Chere." Simon's voice drew me from my thoughts. "We're going out to a club. Want to come?"

He said it in a surly tone, like he hoped I wouldn't. Tough shit. *We're together until we're not.* They were all off their faces, and way more awake now than they'd been earlier. I didn't want to go with them, but at the same time, I didn't want him to go alone. He was manic and ratcheting up. He'd made a lot of money tonight—and he knew he'd made money. I was afraid he'd do something stupid if I didn't stay with him.

My feet hurt from the Fendi shoes, it was a hot, sticky night, and I had to chaperone wacked out artists and posers around the Meatpacking District. *Love lies.* I was so miserable. *Love lies.* I wanted to go home.

I pushed through his cabal of friends to take Simon's hand. He smiled down at me, high and happy. "Do you want to dance? Let's go dancing."

One of his friends led us to an underground disco, one of those secret-knock, dank-stairwell types of places. It was a cement box with jet-engine level rave music. Simon and his friends surged onto the dance floor while I stared up at the crumbling concrete ceiling and gauged the likelihood of it burying us alive. Wouldn't that be a fitting end to my life, being buried alive? I already felt buried alive. *Your life must be miserable*, W had said.

I wish I'd drunk that champagne now. I wish I'd drunk a whole bottle of champagne so this might be more bearable. I looked around for a bar but there was no bar here, nothing so civilized as that. People brought in whatever they needed to get altered. I saw pills exchange hands, clusters of addicts using needles in the corners. I thought I saw someone against the back wall smoking crack. Simon jerked and jumped in the middle of the crowd. Rachel was near him, smiling up at him. He was surrounded by his adoring posse. I was extraneous here.

What would it take to cross the ever-widening distance between us? I was afraid it would take pills. Needles. A crack pipe. I'd grown up with addicts, and I'd always sworn I wouldn't be one, but standing alone in the middle of hundreds of blissed out people, with my ears hurting, and my heart hurting, I wanted drugs. I wanted to sink down in oblivion and never rise again. *Love lies.*

Love dies.

Someone shrieked in time with the music, an ear-splitting noise that set me on edge. The person next to me reeked of body odor and the beats were endless, *duh duh duh duh duh duh duh duh*, over and over to oblivion. My feet throbbed in time to jackhammering rave music, but I couldn't sit down anywhere or I'd never get the filth off.

I watched Simon on the dance floor, his long hair bobbing, his eyes like deep, black holes in his head. He thrust his hands in the air, waving his arms. His cuffs fell down almost to his elbow. His wrists were so thin. When had he gotten so thin? He was so frail, but I couldn't shelter him anymore. I had to get out of here before I lost my mind.

I turned and headed back the way we'd come in. Let his friends get him home. Or better yet, let them all die here in this concrete rave death box. Let him bury himself here with the people who idolized him while slowly killing him. I didn't care.

I covered my ears and pushed my way to the exit. The doorman laughed at me, but it didn't matter. I knew, finally, that I was doing the right thing. It wasn't his friends killing him. It was me. I was killing him by letting him kill himself.

No, that couldn't be right. My conscience was in knots. It wasn't my fault. It was his. Wasn't it?

After the stultifying stench inside the club, the humid night air felt cool and cleansing. I tottered down the block. No cabs. I was too tired for this. Fuck it. I was going to sit down and rest, and if any of the jacked-up night crawlers around me tried to mess with me, they'd get a Fendi heel in the eye socket. I was done with this shit. I found a spot free of litter and vomit and planted my ass on the sidewalk, and laid my head against the rough stone wall behind me.

Love lies. W had done everything in his power to show me I was a fuck-up, that my thing with Simon was lame and untenable. Not that it was any of his business. I pressed a fist against my heart. What was I feeling? Tears burned behind my eyes, and I wanted W. I needed W. I needed him to hurt me and punish me, and be really *real* with me.

I fumbled in my bag for my phone. I had his number from when he'd called me. I'd never tried to use it, for obvious reasons, and now that I needed to use it, I knew it wouldn't work. He would never have connected us like that, and given me a way to bother him when he didn't want to be bothered. I called anyway, held the phone to my ear and listened to the whole "this number is not in service" spiel before I shut it off.

I thought for a moment, and then I dialed Henry. When it went to voicemail the first time, I dialed again.

"Geez, Chere," he said by way of greeting. "It's four-thirty in the morning. What do you want?"

"I want to know..." My voice wobbled. I was losing it. I couldn't ask Henry for W's phone number. That was so against the rules.

I heard rustling, a soft groan. "Where are you?"

I looked around Meatpacking, watched cobblestones blurring mustard yellow under the streetlights. Where had everyone gone?

"I'm nowhere, Henry." My voice sounded steadier now. "I'm nothing. You of all people should understand."

He sighed. "Are you at home?"

"No."

"Do you want me to come get you? Are you safe?"

"Tell me who he is." I was begging. I had to beg, because I wanted W's number in the worst way. I just wanted to hear his voice. No, that was a lie. I wanted to know where he lived, so I could go see him right now instead of going home to my bleak loft and my bleak life. I was feeling dangerously needy. "It's just...I've been meeting this guy for weeks now, and I don't know his name. Who is E.E. Cumming?"

"He's a poet," Henry replied in a hard voice.

"I'm not talking about the poet. I'm talking about the asshole I see every week."

"I know who you're talking about, and you know I can't share clients' contact information."

"Please tell me his name," I said. "I won't use it. I won't look him up. Just tell me his first name."

"You don't need his name. You know everything you need to know about him. You know where to show up for the dates, and you obviously know what makes him happy." He was silent a moment, then he asked, "Are you falling for him? Is that what this is all about?"

"No, I'm not falling for him," I said, and I sounded like a whiny, needy liar.

"Because if you are, you need to remove yourself from the situation. You know that's not how this works, and you know..." I could practically see him shaking his head. "You know any love for him wouldn't be returned. So if you're falling for him—"

"I'm not!"

"Then why are you calling me at four-thirty in the morning? What do you need?"

His name. His number. Anything about him. "Nothing," I said. "I don't need anything. I'm sorry. Go back to sleep."

I hung up on Henry. He called back a moment later, but I let it go to voicemail. Fuck him and his accusations. I got up, took off the shoes from hell, and started down the street. Eventually a cab would pick me up, and if one didn't, then I'd just walk the fuck home, fueled by my frustrated anger.

Even if I was falling in love with W, it wouldn't matter, because I'd lost faith in love. *Love lies. Love flies.*

Love dies.

Why the hell would I want to start that cycle all over again?

9.

THE MANDARIN ORIENTAL SESSION

Simon and I had a huge fight Tuesday night, when he finally came down from the art opening high. I made the mistake of reminding him of his promises, his plans to go to rehab. His reply was a furious rampage that left his studio—and several of his works—in shambles.

"Is this what you want?" he screamed. "You want me to destroy my career? Give up everything I've worked for?"

It was no use reminding him that we'd planned this all along, that he'd promised to take a break after the show to get better. Addicts had no memory, and no reasoning abilities.

His raging turned to shouting, and we engaged in the usual melee, where I called him an addict and he called me a whore, and told me that I was just jealous. "You won't leave," he said, when I threatened to break up with him. "You're too fucking weak to leave."

I drifted through the Mandarin Oriental's lobby, still numb from the things Simon and I had said to each other, from the vast emptiness that opened between us each time we tried to communicate. It probably wasn't the best time to show up for a date with W, but we'd made arrangements, so I wore my black maxi dress for mourning, a pair of black patent pumps, and nothing else. The last thing I needed was a pair of panties setting off my temperamental client.

He opened the door and my heart gave its usual flip as he fixed me in his leonine gaze. He was already shirtless, and his pants were undone. No underwear. That made two of us.

"Hello," I said.

I couldn't meet his gaze; it was too intense. I fixed my eyes on his chin, staring at a couple days' worth of stubble. He had an amazing, stubborn chin.

"What the fuck are you waiting for?" His growl drew my gaze to his lips as he yanked me through the door.

He shoved me down with one hand and pushed his pants down to his hips with the other. He was hard in an instant, and buried in my throat. His fingers wrapped around the back of my neck when I tried to jerk away. The maxi dress pooled around my knees, and I kicked off the shoes so the patent finish wouldn't be ruined by the carpet. I was so numb, so outside myself that those were the things I thought about: whether my skirt was arranged prettily, whether my shoes would get scuffed.

It didn't take him very long to realize I wasn't present in that face he violently ravaged. I looked up at him when he smacked my cheek, and I wasn't there either. I was back in Simon's studio, watching him rip up a canvas and call me a freak and a whore, and blame me for all his problems.

W pulled out of my mouth and yanked me up by my hair. That finally got through to me, that sharp, screaming pain. He knew the top of my scalp was more sensitive than the sides. He knew all the best ways to hurt me by now. I tried to squirm away and found myself thrown back against the wall.

"Don't fight me today, damn you. Just let me have you."

He pinned my legs open with his knee and yanked my dress straps down. Something ripped, a ragged sound to harmonize with my ragged breath. He grabbed my arms, slapped my breasts and pinched my nipples. He shoved his thigh up against my pussy and I cringed from the pressure, but I didn't pull away.

If he didn't want the fight, that was fine. I didn't have a lot of fight left.

"I'm going to fuck the shit out of you," he said, shoving my dress down over my hips. It fell to the floor, and his fingers were in my pussy, probing me, searching for my spot. I went up on my toes with a moan.

"That's right. I know you've been waiting for this. You've been waiting to be fucked and hurt the way you deserve."

The way you deserve. Yep. I moaned again, because I felt guilty and shitty and sad. I pushed at his waist and he answered by trapping my wrists and popping my cheek again. "Bad girl," he said. "You don't push me away."

He took his belt from his pants. He smacked me twice on the front of my thighs as I danced and cried in alarm, then he turned me around and struck my ass five times while he muffled my screams with his hand. Next, he grabbed my wrists and wrapped the belt around them. More pain to bring me out of my drifting sadness. I loved him for giving me this pain.

"Stop," I said, because I knew he would want me to. "Let me go."

"You don't fucking want to be let go." He held the belt with one hand and smacked my ass with the other. Somehow his hand felt way worse than the leather. I shifted on my toes and begged again for him to stop. He put his cheek beside mine.

"I'm not stopping. You're mine to hurt, to use. Are you my slave?"

How could I be his slave when I didn't even know his name? "I don't know," I cried.

"Yes, you're my slave. Whenever my hands are on you, you're my slave, and I'm your Master." He stopped spanking me and gave the belt a shake. "When we're together, you're mine, Chere."

"I'm not yours," I said, just to anger him. "I'm only your whore."

"You're whatever I say you are, and you damn well better pretend you belong to me."

This might seem weird, but looking back, I think *that* was the moment I broke up with Simon, there with my cheek to the door, with W's cock pressed against my spanked ass, and my hands cinched in a belt behind my back. Not that I envisioned some new future "belonging to" W. I wasn't that stupid.

But that was the moment I realized I felt nothing for Simon anymore, while I felt everything for W. That was the moment I understood that I was falling in love with W, that he was doing all the things Simon wasn't: accepting me, appreciating me, trying to engage with me.

I never would have said any of this to the man gripping my neck, not even under torture. But that was the moment I admitted everything to myself, that I loved W, and that if I stayed with Simon, it would kill my soul. Two facts—and both of them scared me. Jesus, all of this scared me so bad.

W kicked off his pants, lifted me up and carried me to the bed, and I thought, *what the hell am I going to do now?* How was I going to hide these feelings from him when they were so intense, so strong? Everything inside me felt dangerously close to the surface, like a volcano about to blow. W wouldn't be into lava. I knew that.

He rolled on a condom. His cock was so hard it scared me. I turned on my side, away from him. "No," I said, because no had become my word for "*I love you.*"

"You don't tell me no," he snapped, which maybe, a little bit, had become his words for "*I love you too.*"

I let him flip me onto my front and mount me while my hands struggled in the belt's grip. His cock surged into me, driving deep, taking away all my words and willpower. I didn't want to want him. I didn't want to have feelings for him, but when he tugged at my wrists and whispered in my ear that I was his *slave*, his *toy*, I had feelings for him.

The first time he fucked me like this, back at the Gansevoort Hotel, I didn't know how to process it. I interpreted his passion as hatred, anger, fear...but it was none of those things. It was something pure, some drive to break down walls and connect. I didn't understand before, but I did now.

I tried to pull away, but he whacked my ass and kept on going, and I realized that the only reason I ever pulled away from him was to be pulled back. It was so simple, so honest. So pure. When he was in control, I felt peace. How strange, that his violent lovemaking was the one thing that could bring peace to my conflicted existence.

Don't fall in love. Jesus, I couldn't fall in love. But as he fucked me, I felt a yearning that was peace and agony at once. I longed for him, this john who was little more than a stranger to me. I read a saying once: *they call it longing because it doesn't last a short while.* How long would I long for W?

"Are you going to come?" he asked, smacking my ass again. "Don't lie there like a fucking corpse."

But oh, I was a corpse. I was so dead, because the only good thing in my life right now was the man taunting me and destroying my pussy. I'd go home tonight and think of him, and go to sleep and dream of him, because everything else in my life was broken and hopeless.

"I'm not going to come," I said. I was too upset to come. I never should have kept our date today, when all my emotions were pooled up at my nerve endings, waiting to snap.

"What the fuck do you mean, you're not going to come?" he asked. "My cock's not good enough?"

He turned me over and grabbed my face. He wasn't really angry. I think he was going to make some joke, or maybe stick his cock in my mouth, but he took one look at my expression and all the humor went out of his eyes.

"What's the matter?"

"Nothing. Finish!" I ordered. He'd love that, being ordered around.

His eyes narrowed. "I'll finish when *you* finish. You're like a fucking wet mop today, you fucked-up piece-of-shit whore. Who pissed in your mop bucket?"

He reached behind me and undid his belt. As soon as my hands were free I went for his face, his neck, his chest, anything I could scratch or slap, because hurting him was the only thing I could do at that moment besides fall apart.

He grabbed my hands and held them hard. "That's all you got?" he goaded. "Fight harder."

I fought but it did me no good. He had my number. He had my heart and soul crushed between us and he didn't even know. He kissed me roughly, laughing against my lips as I kicked and flailed and tried to break free.

"I'll bite you, you little bitch," he said. "I'll bite the fuck out of your lips if you don't cut it out."

I tried to bite him instead, and he smacked my ass three times, hard enough to bring tears to my eyes, and then he did bite my lower lip until I moaned. Before the moan was fully formed, he left my mouth and crouched between my legs.

There was no finesse with him when it came to cunnilingus, no coy kissing down my neck, between my breasts, down my belly in a trail to the pussy. No, he shoved my legs open and fastened his lips over my clit, titillating my flesh with the deftest talent of any lover I'd ever had.

Fuck. I didn't want to come. I didn't want to try. I pushed him away and got my arms slapped for it.

"Don't make me fuck you up," he warned.

Too late. It's too late for that. You've fucked me up on some cellular, lizard-brain level because ohhhh... What you're doing feels so good...

My pussy was alive from the fucking earlier, and my clit wanted more, and more, and more. My hips bucked. I forced myself against his mouth, but it wasn't enough to burn under this exquisite pleasure. I needed his cock inside me too, jamming into me, joining the two of us together.

"Please fuck me," I cried, reaching down.

He slapped my hands away again. "You don't deserve to be fucked. You're a bad girl."

"Please."

"No."

"Please, I'll be good. Give me another chance."

"No." He teased me with his tongue between words, driving my passion higher even as I begged and pleaded.

"Give me your cock. Please."

He looked up as I grabbed his hair. "My cock wasn't good enough for you before. Remember that? Let go of me, Chere."

He meant it. My fingers opened and I let go. "I'm sorry." *I love you.*

As quickly as he'd hunched between my legs, he was back again, looming over me. I expected a pop on the cheek and I wasn't disappointed. "Who's in charge here?" he asked in a terrifying voice.

"You are. Master," I added, although, as usual, what we were doing felt way more intense than dungeon games.

"I get to do what I want, don't I?"

"Yes, Master."

His cock hovered at my entrance. I shivered with the effort to stay still, to not sink down on him and ride him like the whore I was. "Please," I whispered. "I'll be so good. I'll come so hard for you."

I needed to come with him deep inside me. I needed it to survive. My whole body wanted him, every vein, every vessel, every nerve.

He slapped me again but I didn't care, because he was thrusting inside me too. He drove all the way in and ground against my clit. I reached for him, only to have my arms pushed back on the bed. He spread his palms on my forearms and pinned me like a butterfly, wings spread. That, more than anything, made the orgasm break open.

He sneered down at me and rode me hard. *See? See what I can make you do?* And it was true, I had no shame. I tried to come again as he pounded into me, and when he growled and twisted his hips and reached his own climax, it set off a second set of earthquakes for me. He was shifting my tectonic plates, breaking me up and putting me back together.

I closed my eyes and waited for him to pull away. I felt so sensitive and exposed. He could have killed me, slaughtered me to pieces with the wrong look, the wrong words.

Maybe he knew, because he rose from the bed without saying anything. I thought I heard him mutter *Jesus* under his breath. I heard the bathroom door close. I thought about leaving, running away, but our session wasn't over yet. Plus, I doubted I would have been able to walk.

Instead I turned on my side in a ball, and pulled the sheets over me. The light bled through the fabric, illuminating a dim world. I heard the bathroom door open, and I wanted him to stay as much as I wanted him to go. I lay very still. *Go, just go. I can't take it. I'm falling apart.*

A few minutes later, the bed dipped and I felt him beside me. He pulled down the sheet and showed me a pad of hotel stationary, and a pen.

"*Longing*," he said. "By Matthew Arnold."

And I thought, *They call it longing because it doesn't last a short while.*

He started to read what he'd written. "*Come to me in my dreams and then/ by day I shall be well again.*" He paused and re-traced a letter with his pen. "*For then the night will more than pay/ the hopeless longing of the day.*"

And that went over the edge of too much for me. Ten minutes earlier I'd been thinking about longing, and dreaming, and hopelessness, and here was *this poem.*

I burst into tears and vaulted off the bed, ran into the bathroom and locked the door. *Help me. Oh God, help me. Here comes the volcano.* I couldn't stop crying. I couldn't get his voice out of my head. *Longing, by Matthew Arnold.* My God.

He pounded on the barrier between us. "What the fuck? What's wrong with you?"

"Go away."

"It's supposed to be romantic," he yelled through the wood. "It's a very famous poem."

I turned on the shower to drown out my meltdown. I needed a shower anyway. I needed to wash all of my nonsensical thoughts of love and longing away. I needed to get clean.

"Open the fucking door," he ordered.

"In a minute. I'll be out in a minute. Please..."

I knew he'd leave if I stayed in the shower long enough, so I washed, and cried, and washed some more, and let the water run over my hair and back and shoulders. I could never shower this long at the loft. Our hot water heater sucked. It would have run out of water ages ago. I tried to convince myself that the only reason I felt so much for W was because the rest of my life was such a mess.

After half an hour or so, I turned the water off. My eyes hurt from crying, but I felt squeaky clean, and that was something, at least.

I hoped W wouldn't be mad at me. What had he called it? My girly emotional shit? I dried off and toweled my hair, and stood with my ear against the door. Was he still there? I heard a knock, and "Room service!" and then W's rumbly voice. He'd ordered food?

When I heard the room door close, I pulled on one of the neatly stacked bath robes and unlocked the door. W stood by the table, fully dressed, arranging platters and bowls. I knew a simple fucking sandwich cost forty dollars at this hotel. There was probably five hundred bucks worth of room service on that table, but that wasn't as impressive as the way W looked standing over it.

He glanced up, noticing me. I pulled my robe closer around my waist.

"Are you hungry?" he asked.

He didn't sound angry or accusing. In fact, he sounded like he was trying to keep his voice modulated. I tried to keep mine modulated too.

"Not too hungry," I lied.

"Sit down with me anyway."

I hugged myself. "Maybe I should get dressed first."

He shot me an irritated look. "We're done for tonight. I won't touch you again. Anyway, I ripped your dress. " His frown deepened. "Do you want me to leave?"

"You paid for the room."

"Are you staying tonight?"

I wanted to stay. I didn't want to go home, where depression and grief threatened to overwhelm me. "I'll leave if you want me to," I said.

"I don't want you to leave. I want you to sit the fuck down and eat something."

Somehow, his snapping and frowning was better to me than leaving, so I crossed to the table and pulled out a chair. The food was still hot, and it smelled amazing. He'd ordered Vietnamese pho, and Mandarin chicken on salad, and a burger, and some spaghetti, and some salmon with vegetables. There was wine and dessert. Cheesecake, my favorite.

"I didn't know what you liked to eat," he said as I stared at all of it. "If you want, I can order something else."

I choked back a laugh, because there was *so much food*. He'd done a really kind thing, and the last thing I wanted to do was laugh at him. I wanted to curl up in his lap and bury my head in his neck and tell him how much his kindness meant to me. I didn't. We were off the clock, and Henry wouldn't approve of this.

Not that I cared. I was going to quit.

"Thank you," I said. "I guess I'm kind of hungry after all."

"Did you have a good shower?"

There, that was sarcasm. And a little more irritation.

"I feel better now." I looked up and met his gaze. He'd lowered the lights, or maybe it had just gotten darker outside. "I'm sorry. It was the wrong poem for me at the wrong time. Things have been... It's been a stressful week."

"He didn't go to rehab, did he?" He didn't say it in a mean way. If he had, I would have crumbled into dust, but he said it sympathetically. Of course, he'd known all along that Simon wouldn't go, just as I'd known that he wouldn't go.

"We had a really big fight," I said, and wished I hadn't.

W's face didn't change. He possibly breathed a little deeper, a little faster. "Did you lock yourself in your room again? Your safe room?"

"No," I said, which was a lie. I pulled the sixty dollar burger across the table and picked up my knife. "You want to split it?"

"You can have the whole thing," he said, reaching for the pho.

"I can't eat the whole thing. Plus I want to try some of the salad and spaghetti too."

I sawed the gigantic burger in half and thought to myself that for once I'd be putting something bigger than W's cock in my mouth. Maybe he was thinking it too, from the expression on his face as I bit into it.

It was a great burger. It made me feel better. As for W, he ate the pho with chopsticks—expertly—and it was pure sex to watch. Not just because of his dexterity and beautiful long fingers, but because of his teeth and lips.

Our session was over. There could be no more sex. Neither one of us wanted to cross those lines, but some other line was being crossed. We were eating together, sitting across from one another at a table.

"Anyway, I'm sorry I flipped out," I said. "It was a nice piece of poetry. I always love your poems."

The word "love" felt heavy and guilty on my tongue, because I really meant that I loved him. I just wanted to say the word love. His eyes narrowed, or maybe I just imagined it.

"I think you should leave Simon," W said.

"I know."

"You have your own money, don't you?"

The burger tasted less delicious now. I put it down and poked at the spaghetti. "I have money. But I've been supporting Simon for a while."

"Why?"

"Because I loved him."

Loved. I didn't mean to use the past tense, but the word came out and echoed around the room. Afterward, resounding silence. I ate a few bites of salad. W ate his half of the burger, and the salmon, and the rest of the spaghetti. He poured me a little more wine. It was probably a full five minutes before either of us spoke again.

"This is good wine," I said, to end the silence.

"What do you know about it?" he scoffed.

For real, I knew nothing, but he wasn't being mean. He was being...shy.

There in the dim light, over wine and quickly emptying plates, I saw that he was shy beneath all his violence and posturing. He was insecure, just like I was insecure. He only masked it well. The mask came back within seconds, the hard look, the curve of his lips. He made a motion down the side of his face, a curling finger.

"Your hair looks darker when it's wet. You look different."

"My natural hair color is dark," I confessed. "Dark brown."

"Why do you bleach it blonde?"

"Because men like blondes." I looked up at him from under my lashes. "You asked for a blonde, or Henry wouldn't have paired me with you." I didn't know if I was flirting or lecturing him.

Having pillaged the plates, we moved on to cheesecake drizzled with hazelnut chocolate sauce. I was too full to eat very much of it, but the rich, decadent taste of the hazelnut sauce would stay with me forever. It would bring this moment back to me for the rest of my life.

"Will you leave me the poem?" I asked. "Even though I freaked out, I'd like to have it."

He nodded toward the side table. "It's over there. Along with something else I brought for you. A gift. Are gifts allowed?"

"Yes, gifts are allowed."

"I bet you get a lot of them."

"I used to, when I had other clients."

He downed the last bite of cheesecake with his patented fox-in-the-henhouse grin, and I stood up to see what he'd brought me.

One thing I'd learned about presents...when clients brought them, they wanted you to open it in front of them and enthuse about how cool it was. I'd feigned ecstatic bliss over many a custom negligee or exotic sex toy, although I doubted that was W's style. Maybe a book of poetry? Or a velvet noose, so I could choke myself whenever he wasn't around to do it for me?

But there was no book or velvet noose, just a small ivory box beside the lines of poetry he'd written. I opened the lid to find a silver key on a bed of black satin. I blinked at it as W made his way to my side.

"It belongs to an apartment on Bleecker Street. An apartment for you."

It belongs to an apartment? I tried to figure out what he meant. *It belongs to an apartment on Bleecker Street.* It was a key to an apartment.

An apartment for you.

That part finally registered in my brain. My head shot up. "You're giving me an *apartment?*"

He shrugged. "I have more of them than I need."

He was a real estate mogul. Of course. That explained all his money. I looked down in shock at the key in my hand. "It's still yours though, right? I mean, you're not literally giving me an apartment?"

"Yes, I'm giving it to you. It's nothing fancy."

"It's an *apartment*. It's crazy to just give someone an apartment!"

"It's not yours yet." W tipped up my face and looked into my eyes. "I have this ace lawyer, starshine. He's worked out this deal, although you don't get to see the paperwork. The apartment is yours, legally and officially, one year from now, if you follow two simple rules. First, you don't rent it out. Second, you don't let any drug-addicted assholes through the front door. Ever. I'll take it back if you let Simon so much as step over the threshold." His fingers tightened on my chin. "Remember that. It's not a joke."

I felt a little scolded, but I'd just been given the key to an apartment on Bleecker Street, so my irritation didn't last long. "I d-don't know what to say," I stammered. "I expected, like, a necklace or something."

"A necklace?" He snorted and let go of me. "After all the shit I've done to you, you thought I'd give you a necklace? No."

He moved away from me, back toward the table. "Don't get all bent out of shape about this. The thing is..." He poured a little more wine but didn't drink it. "I kept thinking about you locking yourself in a room, and him banging on the door. You don't have to live that way. You shouldn't live that way."

I blinked hard, swallowing past emotion. "I know."

"So maybe this will help. I hope it does. But don't ever let him in there, or I swear to God I'll make you sorry. Don't tell him where it is. Don't even let him know you have it. Promise me."

"I promise."

The key in my palm was the key to my new life. I knew it and he knew it. I just had to be brave enough to make it happen, brave enough to cut those ties to Simon. I had a place to go, now, tonight if I wanted to. I had no more excuses or reasons to delay.

W was back at the table, holding my dress. I watched him for a while, feeling numb. I had an apartment. He'd given me *an apartment.*

"I can't believe this is happening," I said. "Did I say thank you yet?"

He grimaced down at the tear in the fabric. "No."

"Thank you. I really appreciate this." There was a blank pause after "I really appreciate this" that I would have filled with his name, if I knew it. But I didn't know it. He made a motion with his arm, brought his hand to his mouth and bit something off. I realized it was thread.

"What are you doing?" I asked.

"Fixing your dress. It'll only take a minute. Are you tired? You should lie down."

I needed to lie down. Life was too weird at the moment. First W gave me an apartment—conditionally—and now he was mending my dress. I needed to sleep a while and see if things made more sense when I woke up. I vaguely remembered W touching my hair and kissing my forehead just before I dropped off, but maybe it was a dream.

I awoke hours later to a slew of manic messages from Simon, and the sun in the window, heralding a brand new day.

IN BETWEEN

I didn't head right to my new apartment on Bleecker Street, although I wanted to. Simon had sent seventeen messages between two and four A.M.

Come home, Chere

Where a u

Im to high Ser

Yes, when he was high, he forgot how to spell my name. That wasn't unusual. But the last message read, *Ths is the end,* and that terrified me out of my luxurious hotel room and into a taxi.

The end? What end? The end of us? The end of his life? I imagined Simon alone, too high, haunted by drug demons and surrounded by his destroyed artwork. I'd always feared accidental overdose, but would he purposely kill himself? I shouldn't have left him alone so soon after our argument, and I shouldn't have spent the night at the Mandarin.

I urged the cab driver to hurry. He sneered in the rearview mirror at my frizzed hair, morning face, and low cut maxi dress, and made the obvious, belittling conclusion. Whatever. The last thing on my mind was some stranger's judgment. *What if? What if...*

When I arrived, I found the door to our loft ajar. That wasn't unusual either, unfortunately. We'd been robbed twice, but when Simon was high, he sometimes forgot to close it. Or had the police been here? EMTs? No.

They would have shut the door behind them. It had been four hours since he sent the last text.

"Simon?" I called out to him with a shaky voice. I went into each room, afraid of what I might find, but I found nothing. The last room I checked was his studio. That was where he'd kill himself, if he'd chosen to kill himself. *Please, Simon, no...*

I saw a blanket on the floor behind the couch. I walked over and found Simon and Rachel entwined in each other's arms. They were both naked, still as the grave. I studied them, afraid to move closer. "Simon?" I said softly. Nothing. Dread choked my throat. They looked so gray and stiff, and I couldn't see either of them breathing. Was this what overdose looked like?

Then Simon twitched, and I screamed. I screamed so loud it reverberated off the walls and windows, and the wrecked pile of paintings, but still, neither of them moved.

"Simon." I didn't know why I bothered saying his name when he didn't respond to a scream. I knelt beside him and touched his shoulder. He felt warm and alive, even if he looked dead. Rachel stirred and pulled him closer. There was a bottle of bourbon on the table to their left, and a bent spoon and needles on the floor beside it.

I was glad he wasn't dead, but Jesus. We were so over. He was right, this *was* the end.

I thought about waking him up and confronting him about Rachel, and ruining his blissful high. But then I realized we'd already had enough fights, too many fights, and that our last fight was just that, our last fight. I didn't have the power to save him. Isn't that what all those self-help books said? You can't save an addict.

And then I realized that I was an addict too. I'd been addicted to Simon, to protecting Simon and saving him from the dire consequences of his actions. This was *my* rock bottom, standing over him as he drifted in the arms of his junky girl-on-the-side. Well, she could be his main girl now. It was time to save my life.

I went to our room and packed my clothes and anything we hadn't bought jointly. I had a few DVDs, a few books, my laptop and toiletries and hair accessories. My whole life, without Simon, fit into three suitcases and five boxes in the back of a cab. I left a note beside my key, on the counter where he'd see it when he finally woke up and looked for food.

Dear Simon,
I think it's time for me to leave. I hope you get better one day. I won't forget the good times we had. Please don't call.

It wouldn't matter if he called. I blocked his number on the way to my new home, and started composing another letter in my head.

Dear W,
You can't save an addict, but you can help one save herself. Thanks for the apartment. It was the right gift at the right time.

I mentally crossed that out and started again.

Dear W,
You'll never understand how much your generosity means to me. You've given me the strength to do what I should have done a long time ago. You have literally changed my life.

I mentally crossed that out too. It was too gushy, too many blathering words.

In the end, it came down to this:

Dear W,
I love you.

I sighed, because it was impossible to be in love with someone you didn't know, someone who would never let you know them. The driver looked over at me.

"Such a sigh. You're too young to sigh like that."

"I'm almost thirty," I said. "Not too young."

"But it's a beautiful day."

"It is," I said. The sun was out. There were probably rainbows somewhere. "I'm leaving my boyfriend today. He used drugs. He hit me."

That wasn't the whole story. In fact, it was a ridiculously abridged version of my relationship with Simon, but it made sense to the cabbie. He nodded his approval. "That's good. Very good. You won't go back, will you? You're not the first one of these I've had in my cab. But too often, they change their mind and go back."

"I won't go back. It took me way too long to be able to leave. I'm afraid to go back."

"Don't go back," he persisted. He was older. I wondered what kind of craziness he'd encountered in his life.

"I won't go back," I promised. "I'm only moving forward from now on. I'm going to go to school, get a good job and make something of my life."

He was so proud of my newfound resolutions that he parked the cab and helped me lug my bags and boxes all the way to the elevator, and I was so grateful for his kindness that I gave him a huge tip. The doorman helped me the rest of the way, right to the entrance of my new home.

I held my breath as I turned the key and opened the door. While he dragged in my boxes and suitcases, I looked around at the most elegantly furnished residence I'd ever seen. Two bedrooms, two baths, turn-of-the-century styling. This was exactly the type of building and apartment I imagined W would like. White, glossy, clean, classic. Somehow I knew he'd lived here. At some point, these ecru sofas and gleaming fixtures and white walls had been his home, if only for a few weeks.

It was so beautiful and peaceful, with an open floor plan, lots of windows, and a view of the Empire State Building. I felt protected high above the city, and high above my problems here on the sixth floor. Everything I needed was already here. White porcelain dishes in the kitchen, stainless pots and pans that looked like they'd never been used. There was a king size bed with a huge white comforter, piles of white pillows, and folded sets of linens in the closet. The master bedroom was luxurious enough to be a Four Seasons hotel room, but it wasn't. It was my bedroom, in my new home.

I lay on the bed and thought to myself, *he's slept here.*

And then I thought, *maybe he'll sleep here again someday.*

It was so easy, and so dangerous, to make that leap in thinking. I didn't have a boyfriend anymore. Maybe W and I could develop a closer relationship, a real relationship. He didn't seem like the boyfriend type...but maybe...

No. Pure romantic dreams. I pushed them out of my head. With anyone else, the gift of a three million dollar apartment might look like commitment, but I knew him well enough to know this wasn't a commitment. This was an assertion of dominance. He'd wanted me to get away from Simon, and this was how he accomplished what he wanted. This apartment was an expression of his will.

And it was beautiful, airy, pristine, and freeing.

His will had set me free, and I planned to capitalize on the opportunity he'd given me, starting today.

10.

THE CARLYLE SESSION

I spent the next six days sleeping, eating, bathing, and staring out the picture window of my new place. I needed a little hibernation. I had a lot to work through in my head.

It wasn't that hard to let go of Simon, even after all our years together, and all the memories. I felt as if I'd escaped, so I had no intention of unblocking him on my phone, or telling him where I lived. No, letting go of Simon was the easy part. Picturing him in Rachel's arms helped.

The more complicated part was letting go of the old Chere and finding the new Chere. I spent a lot of time considering what I wanted to do.

Without rent to pay, and Simon's drug habit to eat up my savings, I'd have enough money to start looking into degree programs. I started reading about local colleges and trade schools that offered scholarships to non-traditional students.

Design. I'd always been interested in design.

Not just because W said he was interested in design, although that was part of it. The main reason was that I wanted to do something creative, and design seemed like a way to be creative and practical at the same time. I'd seen Simon scrounge for years as a painter, a *fine artist*, and that lifestyle wasn't for me. I wanted to be a practical artist, and design practical and beautiful things, like the dishware in my new kitchen cabinets or the etched brass drawer pulls in the master bath. I could design wallpaper to cover the white walls, I could design shoes, jewelry, purses. All of these were things I noticed and loved, and things I could create while working for one of the hundreds of design firms in New York City.

And maybe, just maybe, W would respect me more, and start to admire me, and fall in love with me...

No, no, no, no, no.

That was the big complex thing I thought about the most as I stared out the window at the vast city around me. If I stopped escorting, what would happen with me and W? I had to talk to Henry before I started making any plans. My contract forbade me from contacting former clients for one year from termination of service, but Henry was a human being, and maybe W was a special case. He'd paid Henry a lot of money, way more than a typical client, so W might be able to talk Henry into releasing me from my contract so we could still see each other.

But that was assuming W would want to see me outside the agency, that he would want to keep dating me outside our neat, clean, no-strings-attached escort relationship. As I made these plans, and dreamed and schemed, some small voice in my head kept pleading, *but Chere, he's never even told you his name...*

I went to meet him at the Carlyle Hotel exactly one week after we'd shared the burger at the Mandarin Oriental. I put on my favorite black dress, made myself pretty because I owed him, and I wanted to make him happy. He met me at the door and he didn't look happy. He was in one of his moods.

"I want you to wear this," he said, holding out a leather eye mask like the one I'd originally worn.

Nooo... I'd waited all week to see him, to look at his beautiful gold-blond hair and his muscles, and his scrutinizing eyes. I'd waited all week to drool over his body and experience his delicious violence. I was rested and energized and I wanted to *see* him, but he put the mask on me anyway, fastening it extra tight.

The ball gag came next, pressed against my lips. This time I did say no, and I stuck out my tongue and tried to back away from him. That earned me a slap, which rattled me enough for him to overcome my resistance and strap it on.

This wasn't how I'd wanted this session to go, but I knew if I hung in there, I'd be rewarded with orgasms and poetry. *Please let me survive whatever he has planned.*

I felt his hands on my jaw, and then he wrapped something around my neck. At first I thought it was his belt and I started to panic, but then I realized it was a collar. He buckled it in the back and then yanked at the front of it. I stumbled and moaned behind the gag. A slave collar? That was something new. His mood, his voice, his hands, all of it felt new. Unfortunately, I couldn't see his expression, and I couldn't ask how he was feeling.

I heard his pants unzip, detected the rustle of clothing coming off, and then I felt his hands under my dress. He pushed me back on the bed and lifted my skirt. *Please, please, kiss me there.*

But he didn't. He took off my panties with an irritated sound—they were so beautiful, those panties—and tugged apart my thighs. *Now, please, now, go down on me, you magical pervert.*

But no. I felt some sort of leather band or cuff circle each of my upper thighs. He buckled each side with a tiny clink. New, so new. I didn't understand all this equipment.

"Give me your hands," he said.

He put cuffs on my wrists too, and then attached each hand to the cuffs on my legs.

"Stand up," he said, hauling me to my feet.

I tugged at the cuffs, trying to find my balance, but my hands and arms were bound for the moment. I couldn't move them more than one or two inches from my side. If he pulled me off balance, I'd go flying. If he hurt me, I'd have no way to stop him.

I felt him yank at the front of my dress, over each of my breasts. For some reason, I imagined he was going to put clamps on me over the fabric. Then he pulled tighter. I heard the whisper-soft sound of scissors cutting fabric.

Shit. I squirmed and moaned, but he grabbed my face and told me to be still. He yanked on my bra next, and *snip snip snip*. He released the fabric and I felt cool air on my nipple. He did the other side next, cutting a hole through my clothes to expose the tip of my breast. Part of me hated him for ruining my beautiful dress but part of me was fascinated by this objectification. I wondered what I looked like, standing there with my stiff tits peeking from the fabric.

I knew what I felt like. I felt vulnerable and scared, and so excited. When I shivered, he twisted a handful of my hair.

"I know," he said. "I know this makes you horny. You'll get my cock, I promise. I'm not sure you'll like where I put it, though."

I whined, but it wasn't a real whine, because it felt kind of fun to be this scared. I heard the soft metallic sound of nipple clamps clinking together. *Oh, shit, shit, shit, shit.* Even when I was turned on, the clamps were torturous.

"Don't move," he warned me. "Don't you dare struggle or back away from me."

He applied the first clamp, and my whole body tensed at the searing pain. I huffed out breaths and tried not to move. As I stood there, I felt him tinkering with the front of the collar. The chain connecting the nipple clamps was lifted from my skin, and I realized he was threading it through some ring on the collar, probably the same ring he kept yanking to remind me it was there.

"Please, no," I said through the gag. It sounded like *aww aww.* I could picture the sadistic smile on his face as he clamped my other nipple. Ow. *Shit.* My fingers dug into my thighs as I tried to process the pain. I didn't dare try to pull away, in case I fell down. And of course, every time I moved my neck, the chain made the clamps pull tighter.

"Please," I said again. *Aww.* I squirmed and then squealed at the resulting agony in my nipples. I could hear his chuckle through the curse words in my brain.

"You're a helpless little piece of shit, aren't you?" I felt his hands on my waist, and heard the scissors again. "You know why I'm cutting up your pretty dress, Chere? Because I can. Because you can't do anything to stop me." He cut away the bottom half, up to my waist. When he finished pulling the skirt away, he thrust rough fingers into my pussy. "Right now, I can do anything in the world to you, and you don't have a say. It's called slavery. It's called being my pretty set of holes."

I went up on my toes, angling my hips, trying to get him to touch my clit. I was so wet and horny, a fact he was happy to exploit.

"You want it bad, don't you? You want some cock."

"I want *your* cock," I said through the gag. Of course the words were unintelligible, just a garbled series of moans. My nipples were killing me, but I arched to touch him wherever I could.

"No, you're my toy. My sex slave," he said, slapping my ass. "You're here to please me, not the other way around. Let's take that gag off and put you to work."

I was shoved to my knees. When I pitched forward—*ow, my nipples!*— he caught me by the hair and righted me. He removed the gag but not the clamps or blindfold.

"I want to see you," I cried.

"Shut the fuck up. You don't get to see me right now. Nothing I show you is real anyway." He slapped my cheek. "Open your fucking mouth."

He drove into my throat until he choked me, and then he stayed there while I coughed and struggled to get away. I couldn't use my hands to support myself, or seek any leverage. I was powerless, controlled by his palms on either side of my head.

"Just suck me," he said. "Don't be all dramatic."

I tried. I really tried. I drew air through my nose and tried not to throw up as he banged the back of my throat again and again. *He gave you an apartment*, I told myself. *You owe him.* But that just made me feel like a whore.

Not a whore. His slave. I felt his hand tug at the collar, circling it, reminding me of my place. The blowjob got easier after that. *Be a pretty hole, Chere.* Yes, for now I'd be his pretty hole. For the orgasms. For the poetry.

He finished with deep, urgent growls of satisfaction, coming partly in my mouth but partly on my lips, so I had to lick it away.

"Don't say anything," he said, letting go of my face. "Don't say a fucking thing. Sit back on your heels and wait until I'm ready to fuck you again. You're getting it in the ass next."

My whole body clenched, imagining him taking my ass in this heightened mood, with all the gear, the blindfold, the collar, the cuffs. At least he took off the clamps. My nipples throbbed as the blood returned, but I couldn't rub them or soothe them in any way. All I could do was sit there and stroke my thighs with my fingers. If my hands were free, I would have masturbated to orgasm seventeen times in a row without stopping. The fact that I couldn't touch my clit made me agonizingly aware of how turned on I was. I wondered what he'd do if I started humping the bed, or the floor. I was too scared of him to find out.

I listened as he moved about the room. He poured himself a drink, but I didn't know what it was. Maybe he'd kiss me and let me taste it on his tongue. I wanted him to kiss me so badly. Somehow I doubted the assfucking would include kissing, but with W, you never knew.

Ten minutes passed. Maybe fifteen. He didn't need that long to be ready again, although it felt like an eternity to me. I knew he always, *always* lasted longer the second time, which was a very unfortunate situation for my ass.

There was no warning when it was time to go again. I felt his approach, and wobbled to my feet when he pulled me up. He held the front of the collar to pull me closer. His warmth enfolded me. His bristly cheek pressed against mine.

"Are you ready to bend over and give me your ass, slave girl?"

"Yes, Master," I said, although I'd never, ever really be ready.

"Do you love it when I take you in the ass?"

"Yes, I love it, Master." I sounded like I was telling the truth. I think I *was* telling the truth.

I was turned around and bent over the bed. My hands scrabbled against my thighs as my tender nipples scratched across the comforter. I'm sure it was some very expensive, luxury three-thousand thread count, but it felt like sandpaper against my sensitized skin.

I felt his hand on my cheek, and then the gag. Damn it. I opened up for the hard plastic ball because I didn't have a choice to refuse it.

"It's for your own good," he chided when I whimpered. "You'll be able to cry and groan as much as you want with the gag on. But no screaming. Good slaves don't scream."

Shit. Oh shit. He was only trying to scare me, wasn't he?

"Spread your legs," he said, once the ball gag was buckled. He apparently wasn't happy with my good faith effort to spread them since he yanked them wider, so wide apart that they ached from the stretch. He circled one ankle with rope and fixed it to the bed, then tied my other ankle. I was already moaning in fear, and he hadn't touched me yet. I was so trapped, and so open.

"You don't get to close your legs until I'm done with you, so stop squirming. You're not going anywhere." He put a hand on the small of my back and slapped the insides of my thighs with sharp, stinging blows. He paused, and then, oh Jesus, he started using that evil stinging whip instead of his hands.

Whack. *Oh, the burn.*

Whack. *Oh, fuck.*

Whack. *Baby Jesus!*

Whack! *Oh my God, no…*

When the insides of my thighs were alive with stripes of agony, he moved to the backs of my thighs, and it felt ten times worse.

I didn't scream, no. I couldn't catch my breath to scream. I panted and trembled and arched against his hand holding me down. I jerked my arms at my sides, and made frantic sobbing sounds in my throat. He moved to my ass, flicking it with blows, one on top of the other. I clenched my ass cheeks, helpless to escape the fiery pain.

"I want to lock you in a dungeon," he said in a low, dire voice. He paused, and drew the whip up and down my drenched pussy lips. "A real one, not one of those pansy BDSM dungeons. I'd tie you down a thousand different ways and do every hurting thing I could think of to you before I let you go. I'd keep your legs held open with a spreader bar twenty-four hours a day, so I could hurt your pussy and your asshole whenever I felt like it. I'd train you to want it, to beg and plead for sexual pain."

I shook my head, even though I could absolutely see myself begging. I'd be begging right now, if I weren't wearing the gag, begging for him to put down the whip and invade my body. I wanted him to take me, to press deep inside me. I didn't care how much it hurt.

"Please," I said behind the gag. "Please."

I wiggled my ass, offering myself for his use. I felt completely submissive, completely needful of him. The collar impeded my breathing just enough to remind me it was there, and that I was his slave.

When I heard the condom, and the cap from the lube, I didn't brace to resist him. I was scared and I knew it would hurt, but I was ready to be hurt. I *wanted* to be hurt.

When he took my bound hips and jammed the head of his cock against my sphincter, I was drifting in fantasies of his "real" dungeon, and all the things he might do to me there. I wondered if he had a dungeon somewhere, wherever he lived. I wanted to be in it, experiencing all those scary things he'd said.

His cock pressed into my asshole while I pictured dark walls and racks and bars for torture. I fisted my hands against the stretching, cresting pain of his entry. I knew it would subside in a moment, if I could relax. *Relax, relax.*

He wasn't gentle. Thank God for the lube, so when he started fucking my ass in a firm, steady rhythm, I was able to bear it without too much panic. His repetitive thrusting shoved me forward against the bed, and pain mixed with pleasure as my clit rode the sheets. *Yes, yes, yes.* I squeezed around his cock, seeking my own pleasure in his dominance.

My thighs were killing me, not just because of the whip marks, but from being bound open. I thought of a twenty-four hour spreader bar and shuddered. My asshole hurt with a vivid, blissful kind of pain, with roughness and overstimulation. I whimpered behind the gag and arched my back, tugging at the cuffs that held my arms at my sides.

"What the fuck are you whining about?" he said, sounding more amused than concerned. "You love this, you horny slut."

It was true. I loved it. I blinked behind my blindfold and struggled anyway, clenching my cheeks as he drilled into my asshole. He added more lube and kept going, smacking my cheeks from time to time, reminding me that I was his slave and that he could fuck my ass for as long as he wanted.

All the while, my clit throbbed with heightening arousal. I wanted so badly to come, but my legs hurt and my jaw hurt, and my ass hurt. He reached beneath me and tweaked my sore nipples, until I groaned behind the gag like an animal. It was like he was doing everything in his power to keep me hurting and crazed and unable to orgasm, but the more he did that, the more needy I became.

My arousal was like the ocean tide, the eddies on the sand, half advancing, half receding, until finally, the part that was advancing was going farther than the part that was receding, and I thought I might be able to come even through the pain. My whole body shuddered in hornified heat. My hips jerked, my shoulders tensed, and my wild pleas warbled through the gag.

"Come on," he said. "You either come with my cock in your ass, or you don't come at all. You belong to me. I decide how you come, and how much it hurts."

And that was it. Those were the words that sent me over the edge, along with his demand and derision, and his beautiful, thrusting, painful length rending my ass for his pleasure. I ground against the bed and squeezed his cock so hard I'm surprised he didn't smack me for it.

He put a hand around my neck instead, over the collar, and pressed me down, down, down. My orgasm exploded ten-fold after that, so intense it comprised every part of me, my pussy, my clit, my breasts, even my arms and legs and toes. He covered me, driving into me with the last frenetic strokes of his own climax. After one last momentous shudder, he went still.

Both of us were still for long moments. I moved my hand a little, the thigh and wrist cuffs making a chink of a sound.

"Jesus, Chere," he said. "Fucking hell. Don't fucking move. Just stay."

So I stayed in my dark, bound world, waiting for his next command. It seemed like forever before he pulled away from me, but at the same time, it seemed too soon. I didn't want him to go.

I felt his fingers working at the gag. He took it off and wiped my cheeks and kissed me, hard uncomfortable kisses along the edge of the collar and beneath my ear. I was still so blind and breathless, I hardly heard what he said. "God, that you let me do this," he murmured. "That you let me do these things to you."

I turned my head so he could kiss my mouth. "Let me see you," I begged against his lips.

"No."

His fingers twisted in my hair. I wished I knew his name. I wished I knew everything about him. I wished I could see the expression that went along with that ragged murmur.

Please, W, I want more of you. I wanted to cry and scream out everything in my heart, but I didn't dare. My mouth still hurt from the gag. My heart hurt. My ass hurt, though not as much as when he was inside it.

He shifted away with a groan, and released my ankles, and then unbound my wrists and thighs from their connected cuffs. My body felt too free, too exposed now that I wasn't tied down anymore. I'd become comfortable in the security of bondage, and now that security was gone. I reached to unbuckle the eye mask, but he stopped me. "Not yet," he said.

"Why not?"

"Because I said."

He lifted me up and I tried to walk, although it was hard. I felt like collapsing into a ball. He led me into the bathroom, from wool carpet onto cool, smooth tile. He propped me against his body and then he took off the leather mask. I flinched as I stared at the two of us in the mirror.

He looked beautiful, stern and tall and sexy, but I looked like hell. My hair was a wreck and my makeup was smeared by drool and tears. My face was crisscrossed with the marks from the gear straps. My dress was nothing but a scrap of fabric down to my waist, with my nipples sticking out. When I tried to look away, he turned my head back.

"Look at yourself," he said. "Look at what you do for me." He rested his cheek against mine, and reached to trace the collar with his fingertips. "You're so beautiful."

I felt like a failure, because I couldn't see the beauty. I couldn't see beauty in anything but him, with his striking features and his muscular physique. And the collar...the collar was beautiful. I was seeing it for the first time, since I'd been blindfolded when he first put it on.

I'd imagined something black and shiny, but it was weathered brown leather, the same tawny brown color as my eyes. I'd imagined lots of metal but there was only the buckle and one single O-ring. So classic and simple, considering all the complex feelings it gave me.

He finally let me turn away from the mirror. I buried my head against his neck but he made me look up at him. I felt crusty and dirty, and whorish in my adulterated dress. He kissed my forehead and my eyes and my neck, and then he released me so he could turn on the shower. He kept hold of one of my hands, like I might run away. Maybe I would have.

"Let's take the collar off," he said. "Had you ever worn one before?"

I didn't know how to answer. Yes, I'd worn them as part of silly sex games, for clients. No, I'd never worn one the way I had today.

"I've worn collars a few times," I said quietly. "But...not like..." I reached for it as he drew it away.

"Do you want to keep it?" he asked.

I blinked at him. "Aren't we going to use it again?"

He shrugged. "We might. I don't know. I guess I'll keep it."

When we got into the shower, he nudged me under the water first. He watched as I wet my hair, stared as my eyes closed and stared as my eyes opened. His gaze was so intense. He took me in his arms and kissed me, a long, slow kiss unlike any he'd ever given me. I tried not to fall in love. He wasn't making it easy for me. After a marathon make-out session under the cascading water, we got out and dried off, and wrapped up in the hotel robes.

I knew it was time for him to go, but I didn't want him to go. I wished he would order food, like last time. I wanted to sit and eat together, and talk like friends, but instead he got dressed and started re-packing the kinky gear into his briefcase. Cuffs, rope, clamps, gag, mask, the beautiful collar. I stared out the window while he moved around the room, because I didn't want him to leave. When I heard him zip his bag, I turned.

"I'm staying at the apartment now," I told him. "It's so beautiful."

"I'm glad you like it."

"Simon and I are finished." He hadn't asked, and he probably didn't want to know, but it seemed important to tell him. "We've broken up for good. It's a really good thing, and you helped me make that decision. So thanks."

He looked uncomfortable. "It would have happened eventually anyway."

"I guess."

I knew, *I knew* he didn't want me to say any more, but now that I'd started talking, I couldn't seem to stop all my self-congratulatory bullshit from spilling out. "I've been looking into schools. You know, degree programs. I'm going to stop escorting soon, in the next few months, I hope, and go back to school. I'm thinking about a design career, or fashion. Something creative."

"Hmm."

"I know I can do it. There are plenty of scholarships out there, and I have money saved up. But I could keep seeing you as long as you liked. I mean, I guess I could. I don't think Henry would have a problem with it."

His eyes were so blue when he stared at me. So magnificently blue.

"But even if he did...I don't know. I wouldn't charge you. I don't think he can complain if you and I... I mean... If we were just having sex together, not for money."

I pulled my robe tighter around me. W tilted his head.

"But that wouldn't really be a client-customer relationship anymore, would it?" he asked. He touched the tip of one of his fingers, then pinched it, the way he pinched my nipples. "We'd have to figure that out."

"We could definitely figure things out," I said too quickly. "And none of this is happening right away. I just wanted you to know that even though my life is going to start changing, things between us don't have to change. I don't want them to change. I look forward to our sessions. I mean, I do now. I know we had kind of a...a rocky start, but I really enjoy...now..." *Stop babbling. Shut up, shut up.*

"I enjoy our sessions too," he said. "We have fun together."

"But school, and a better career...it's good, right?"

"Yes, it's good," he agreed with a genuine smile. A small smile, but a genuine one. "I'm sure you'll be great at anything you pursue." He finally stopped pinching his finger, and lifted his briefcase. "Are you going to stay here tonight?"

"Maybe. I don't know." I grinned at him. "I have a really nice place of my own to go to now."

"Yes, you do." He walked over and touched my arm, a fleeting caress. "You brought some extra clothes?"

"Yes. I always do, thanks to you and your scissors."

"Good. Because I'm taking the dress. I doubt you'll be wearing it again."

I watched as he crossed the room and picked up the scraps of my bodice and skirt, and shoved them into his briefcase with everything else.

"That was one of my favorites," I said mournfully. "What are you going to do with it?"

He shook his head. That smile again. "You don't want to know. Have a good week, starshine."

He gave me one last kiss, a soft, lingering kiss that ended in a bite. Orgasms, kisses, and...

"Oh." I stopped him on the way to the door. "Aren't you going to give me some poetry?"

He looked at me, then dug in his overstuffed briefcase for a pen. "Come here," he said. He pulled me against his chest, my back to his front, and took my arm. He ran fingers up the pale underside of my forearm, from elbow to wrist.

"I already gave you some poetry," he said against my ear. "You don't listen."

I watched as he wrote. The pen tickled, and sometimes scratched.

Look at what you do for me.

You're so beautiful.

"That's nice poetry," I said when he was done. "I wonder who wrote that."

"Some self-absorbed, perverted jerk," he answered, smacking my ass. Even through the fluffy robe, it hurt. He kissed me and departed, leaving the room quiet. Too quiet.

Although the room was luxuriantly gorgeous, I decided not to stay the night, because I'd just sit around missing W. That was one downside of leaving Simon. I had too much time on my hands to daydream and think about impossible things.

I glanced at the words scrawled on my skin. Maybe not so impossible.

Maybe someday he'd tell me his name, when he trusted me better, and knew me better. In the meantime, orgasms and poetry were enough.

I got out my phone to take a picture of my forearm, standing next to the window to find the perfect amount of light. It seemed important to save everything W gave me, to archive it and analyze it. These words would eventually fade, but I'd have a picture to remember.

Poems, pictures, memories.

I wanted so much more.

IN BETWEEN

Henry met me Thursday afternoon at a cafe on West 3rd. I hadn't told him yet I was quitting, but I think he knew. He hugged me extra hard before he sat down across from me.

"So what's up, love?" he asked, once we'd ordered some coffee and sandwiches. "How's your life?"

"It's good."

"How are things with Mr. Cumming? It's been two months. Is he mellowing at all?"

"Mellowing?"

He poured sugar in his coffee and looked up at me. "Mellowing. I remember you described him in less than glowing terms after your first date."

I thought a moment. "He's mellowed a little, maybe. But he still hasn't told me his real name."

"He just set up a date for next week, at the Gramercy Park Hotel."

I stared down at my coffee. Henry wasn't going to make this easy for me.

"Listen, I asked you to lunch today to let you know that...well... Mr. Cumming is going to be my last client."

In the awkward silence, the waitress sailed by and dumped our plates on the table. "Need anything else right now?" she chirped, eyeing Henry.

"No," he said. "We're good."

I pulled the toothpick out of my sandwich and laid it at the edge of my plate. "Are we good, Henry?" I asked. "Are you angry?"

"Not angry. Disappointed. You're leaving the business?"

"Yes. I'm getting older—"

"Older? You're not even thirty. You're in the prime of your escort life. Young enough to be gorgeous, and seasoned enough to know the sexiest techniques."

"Did you just call me 'seasoned'?"

He waved a pickle spear at me. "Don't try to joke your way out of this. You're not too old. What's the real reason? Is Mr. Cumming getting to you?"

Yes. But not in the way you think.

"If he's too much, I told you, Nina can take him. If it's the exclusive thing—"

"It's not the exclusive thing. I've been ready to leave for a while. I finally broke up with Simon—"

"Good."

"And I feel like I'm on a roll. I just need to keep making changes in my life. I need to keep moving forward while I have this momentum. I planned to start back to school this fall. So I can work a few more months. July and August. After that, I want to be a student. Only a student."

"A student?" he said, wrinkling his nose. "Why?"

"Because I don't want to escort anymore."

"Have you told Mr. Cumming this? That you're leaving the business?"

"No," I lied.

Henry was looking at me too sharply. He took a bite of his sandwich, watching me as he chewed. "Do the two of you have something going on?"

I laughed, and it sounded so fake. "I don't think so. Like I said, he still hasn't told me his name."

"I knew the exclusive thing was a mistake. Is this his idea, for you to leave the business? He wants to set you up in some apartment to play house for a while? You know how these things end."

"He hasn't said anything about playing house." *Although he may have set me up in an apartment...*

196

"These situations last a couple months, and then the girls are back begging for another chance. I've been doing this a while, Chere. Once men can have you for free, they don't want you anymore. The chase is over. The thrill is gone."

"What the fuck are you talking about?" I said, holding up a hand. "I'm not leaving the business to be with W."

"Who's W?"

"That's what I call him," I said. "Because I don't know his name. And I've been doing this a while too, so give me some fucking credit. I'm not leaving the business to move in with my client or anyone else."

I started out trying to convince Henry, but halfway through my tirade I realized it was true. I wasn't leaving for W, although I really hoped to keep seeing him. I was leaving because I wanted a different life.

"Did it ever occur to you that maybe I'm tired of making a living with sex?" I asked. "Before I escorted, I was a stripper. I've only ever done sex jobs. I'm tired of being valued for what's between my legs."

Henry rolled his eyes. "You make a lot of money with what's between your legs. You have a good life."

"How do you know?"

We glared at each other. I loved Henry. I didn't want to end things on an acrimonious note, but he was being more of an asshole than I'd expected.

"You have a good life too," I reminded him. "Because of me and the rest of your escorts. What if you had to make that money with your own body?"

"I did make money with my body," he said, leaning forward. "I understand. I know it gets old, but you're at the height of your career. You make people happy, even if you're feeling some weird, unfounded guilt about making money from your sexuality."

"It's not that. It's not guilt. I'm just over escorting. This isn't what I'm meant to do with my life. I *know* that, Henry. I've felt it for a long time. I always knew there was going to be an ending to it, and that's happening now."

"What else are you going to do?"

"I told you, I'm going to go to school."

"To do what?"

"I'm not sure yet. Design, maybe. Some creative type of career that entails being more than someone's pretty holes."

I was quoting W, yes. Henry wasn't stupid. He suspected W was part of this, but he couldn't stop me if I wanted to get out. He ate a few more bites of his sandwich, and I ate some of mine too.

"I'm not leaving you high and dry, am I?" I said as the silence lengthened. "You have other girls."

"I have plenty of girls, but I hate to lose a good one." He put his sandwich down and brushed his fingers together. "I know I've been losing you for a while, and I understand why, but I don't have to like it." He held out his hand, and I took it. "I'm sorry I freaked on you, love. You have every right to do what you want with your life. So, a couple of months, you think?"

I nodded. "I'd like to work right up until I start school. Build up a little extra money."

"Want me to raise the price on E.E. Moneybucks? I'm pretty sure he'd pay it."

"No." I didn't want him to charge W at all, but I worried he was only interested in sex he paid for. Maybe I could change his mind over the next few weeks, change him the way he'd changed me. Maybe we could find our way to some mutually satisfying place.

You're a dreamer, Chere. An idiotic dreamer. The last thing I needed was another relationship. I'd settle for a friendship. I ran fingers up the underside of my forearm, tracing the memory of his words.

Henry sighed and picked up his coffee. "I think you have a crush on Mr. Cumming. You get jittery whenever his name comes up."

I glanced at him, wondering how much I should reveal. Nothing. Definitely nothing. He'd pitch into more lectures, and I didn't want that. "There's a reason I get jittery," I finally said. "He gives magical orgasms. And by magical I mean what-the-fuck, ruined-forever magical."

He looked pleased. "I'm glad when I hear my girls are enjoying themselves. So you're definitely on for next week?"

"I'm definitely on for next week."

Henry was so trusting, and I'd kept so many secrets, about the oral without condoms, the apartment, and W's involvement in getting me away from Simon. I hadn't mentioned anything about seeing W once I left

Henry's employment. I decided to leave that conversation for another day.

"You've been a great boss," I said. "A great agent. I'm so grateful for everything you've done for me."

"The feeling is mutual. If you ever need anything down the line... If you want to come back..." His voice trailed off. "No, don't come back. Go to school and study for a career that makes you happy. Don't you dare come back."

"I'll try not to." I let out a long, relieved breath. "Thanks, Henry."

"You're sure you want to keep seeing Mr. Cumming? I can tell him you're done, if you feel done."

"No, I'll see him."

He gave me a teasing look. "The magical orgasms. I remember." He signaled the waitress for the check, then turned back to me. "You know, I have men at the agency too, in case you get lonely and horny during one of those late night study sessions. My guys are very good at what they do." He emphasized the word *very*, drawing it out into a suggestive growl.

"I'm going to be on a student budget," I reminded him. "I won't be able to afford your guys, for a while anyway. Whatever job I get out of college won't pay as much as I made with you."

"So why are you leaving again?" He held up a hand before I could answer. "I know, I know. It's clear you've thought this through."

We pushed back our chairs, stood up and hugged. He always smelled amazing, rich and classy like his escort business. He held me tight for long moments and patted my hair.

"You're going to make me cry," I murmured into his chest.

"I'm the one who should be crying," he said. "I'm losing the legendary Miss Kitty. Too bad I'm not one of those evil pimps. I could just rough you up until I convinced you to reconsider your decision."

I gave him an accusing look. "I think deep in your heart you secretly wish you were an evil pimp, instead of a big-hearted pushover."

"I'm not a big-hearted pushover," he said, giving me a little shake. "I'm badass."

I buried my face in his chest again. "You're super badass."

I heard his sigh, and felt it in the rise of his ribcage. "I'll miss you when you go, Kitty darling," he said, "but I wish you the best."

11.

THE GRAMERCY PARK SESSION

The Gramercy Park Hotel was gorgeous, full of art and glittering things. I got there early just to sit in the lobby for a while, with the grand chandelier and rich scarlet carpeting flanked by black and white tile. I'd been there a few times to see clients, but the old Chere hadn't really appreciated how amazing it was. The new Chere noticed artistry and design.

I watched the door. I'd come early enough that I hoped to see W arrive. I sat out of the way, but in view of the entrance, for the secret thrill of watching him walk across the lobby on his way to our date. Of course he'd look amazing, as always, in his dark, stylish business clothes. I wore a form-fitting, deep green dress. It was demure but not too demure. It was classically tailored and fit all my curves to perfection. I hoped he wouldn't cut it off.

I thought back to our first session, to my horror, my naiveté. My blindness. How angsty and stupid I'd been back then. Maybe that was why he'd blindfolded me during our last session, so I could realize how far I'd come. He still scared me a little, but he thrilled me a lot more. He made me feel alive and strong, like I could do anything.

I knew I had to tell him these things one day. Maybe not today, but someday I wanted to explain the ways he'd changed me and improved my life.

His roughness, his violence had cracked me open somehow, made me all new and better, and his kisses had made me realize I was more than a whore. The first day, the very first day, he'd rejected Miss Kitty in favor of the real me. He'd preferred the real me, and was, in fact, the only client who'd ever wanted the real me. Somehow, he'd made me want the real me too.

More than that, he'd helped me find the strength to leave Simon. My ex's gallery show was about to close. I wondered if he'd thought any more about rehab, or if he was going to continue along his self-destructive path. If he was, I wasn't going with him. I was on a new path now.

After twenty minutes, I looked at my watch, and the room number Henry texted me. I would have liked to see W arrive, but he must already be waiting upstairs. Was he getting ready for me, thinking about me? Feeling hot for me?

I tucked my bag under my arm and sashayed across the elegant space, smiling like a minx. The hotness came first. I had to let W run roughshod over my body and exorcise all his demons before I said anything about how much he'd come to mean in my life. That was the type of conversation to save for afterward, when he held me and gazed into my eyes, and made sure, with his gruff and awkward questions, that I was okay.

I'm very okay, thanks to you.

I took the elevator to the tenth floor and took a deep breath as I walked down the hall. He gave me the best butterflies. When I got to the door I raised my hand to knock, then I realized it was cracked open, propped on the bar lock.

I double-checked Henry's text. This was definitely the right room. I pushed it open a little, bracing for W to pounce on me and do something scary.

"Hello?"

The room was moody and lush, done in dark velvet and mahogany wood. I tiptoed inside, looking around. "Hello?"

When I was finally convinced he wasn't going to jump on me, I noticed the dress on the bed, and an envelope with my name on it. I let the door close and walked across the room. I stood beside the bed and drew my fingers along the dress's neckline. It was a replacement for the one he'd cut up last week, new with tags.

I was grateful for the dress, but I didn't want to touch the envelope. I felt afraid.

"Hello?" I called again. "Are you here?"

I strained to hear him speak back to me, to breathe, to growl, to make that low, derisive laugh. I went into the bathroom. Nothing. He wasn't here. No one had been here in a while now. There wasn't the faintest whiff of his cologne.

He's going to knock in a minute, I told myself. He's fucking with me. No, he wouldn't knock, he'd just sneak in and scare the shit out of me. I spun around, the hair prickling at my nape, but he wasn't there.

"W," I said softly, knowing there'd be no reply.

I went back out into the main room and pulled the drapes open. The room looked down on the treetops of Gramercy Park. A park view, of course. Always the best. I looked back at the bed. The dress.

The envelope with *Chere* written on it in W's blocky script.

I went and picked it up, and walked back to the window, unfolding the white paper and angling it toward the light. There was no greeting, no date or name, just one line in the middle of the page.

Good luck, starshine.

I stared at the words a long time, rereading them, trying to understand them past the roaring panic in my brain. He couldn't mean...goodbye? He wouldn't just leave me like this, without saying goodbye. He wouldn't just end us.

I sat in a chair in the still, lush room, and looked at the paper, and the dress, and I knew with a sick, sinking dread that I wasn't going to see him again. He had chosen, for some reason, to terminate our relationship: our working relationship, our emotional relationship, our connection, all the experiences that had helped us bond.

"Why?" I asked, but there was no answer. I covered my face with my hands and leaned over, devastated by emotion. "Why, why, why are you doing this?"

I thought back over our last few sessions. What had I done? Was it because I'd talked about leaving the business? I thought I'd made it clear that I'd be happy to keep seeing him.

I wasn't listening for a knock anymore, or the sound of his footsteps behind me. I knew he was gone, and that this beautiful velvet room was the last room he'd ever reserve for us. I held the paper to my nose and thought I smelled the faintest note of him. In a day, perhaps as little as an hour, it would be gone. Why hadn't I asked what kind of cologne he wore? He might have told me that, if he wouldn't tell me his name.

It killed me that I didn't even have a name to hold onto. I had nothing but a small collection of poems, and fuzzy, adrenalized memories that would also start to fade. Maybe I could find him, with enough money and ingenuity, and persistence, but why even try, when he obviously didn't want to be found?

He'd left me.

He'd deserted me.

He hadn't even given me the chance to say goodbye.

Coward, I thought. *You're a fucking coward. You're chickenshit. I loved you.*

I looked down at the dress, the perfect, new, intact dress lying across the bed as I'd lain across the bed so many times. I didn't understand. I thought he'd come to care about me.

Good luck, starshine? What the fuck?

I left the hotel, and I left the dress, because I knew I'd never wear it again. I went home and arranged all his poetry around me on the bed, trying to figure out what had happened, what had gone wrong between The Carlyle session and Gramercy Park. As I looked at the verses together, themes emerged. Dreams, longing, darkness. Mystery and lust. I read them again, and again, and as much as I didn't want to, I began to comprehend what had happened.

I'd rather have the dream of you
With faint stars glowing
I'd rather have the want of you
The rich, elusive taunt of you

It was a pretty, poetic way of saying he didn't want me, the *real* me, the way I thought he did. It was all right there in the poems. What he wanted was the dream, the fantasy. He wanted Miss Kitty, as much as he insisted on calling me Chere.

And when Chere got too real, too human and complicated, he didn't want me anymore. When I talked to him about continuing to date him as a person, a real, available person and not an escort, he must have been shaking in his thousand dollar shoes. He must have been doing everything in his power not to run away. Well, now he'd run away.

Love lies.

I understood it. I didn't like it, but I understood it. His sexy charisma had blinded me to reality. He'd made me imagine he cared about me, made me believe he might want an actual relationship. God, so embarrassing. He'd wanted sex; that was all. I'd gotten carried away by my fawning, needy fantasies, just as I'd done with Simon a decade ago. Simon seduced me with painting, W seduced me with poetry, but the outcome was the same. Thank God W had been kind enough to save me from my idiocy and fuck off out of my life.

Jesus, this was so hard. My eyes ached from crying, but my heart ached worse. I stood and walked to my window, and made a promise to myself as I looked out at the darkening cityscape. No more relationships. No more co-dependence on others. No more fake emotional shit.

From now on, Chere was going to be in a relationship with Chere, and the rest of the world could go fuck itself. I'd keep his poetry as a reminder, a warning about how awful and wonderful people could be, and how easily they could leave you.

This was it for me. I was finished. I was never, ever letting go of my heart again.

To be continued in *Taunt Me (Rough Love Part Two)...*

TAUNT ME
(ROUGH LOVE PART TWO)
A PREVIEW

It's been two and a half years since the mysterious W disappeared from Chere's life, and things are getting better. Sort of. She's nearing the end of her design program and looking forward to a new career, even if her heart is shuttered for good.

But loneliness is a powerful thing, and she finds herself tempted by a no-strings-attached BDSM partner who happens to be her former professor. She knows it's a terrible idea, and that he could never live up to W's level of passionate mayhem, but she's been waiting so long to be bound and hurt. She's been waiting so long to feel something...

Unbeknownst to her, someone from her past has been waiting too. And when that someone realizes she means to move forward with this new partner, he barges back into her life to express his displeasure in the only way he knows...

W and Chere's story will continue with more ups and downs, more passionate sex and passionate denials, and general fucked-up longing. There'll be more poetry, and more complicated emotions to sort through. Most of all there will be fear about what comes next in their dauntingly unconventional relationship. Her fear...and his...

Taunt Me (Rough Love Part Two) is now available for preorder and will be released in November 2015.

Like it Rough?
You may also enjoy these edgy BDSM romances by Annabel Joseph

Mercy

Lucy Merritt has always defined herself by her body, whether dancing in a small avant-garde company or posing for art. But she has always felt as if something is wrong with her, as if something is missing. She has never been in love.

Suddenly, in the darkness of the theater wings, a strangely affecting man enters her life. Matthew Norris, rich, handsome patron of the dance company, has decided that he wants Lucy for his own. He makes her an offer that both frightens and compels her, and they soon begin an affair characterized by only two requirements, beauty and truth.

But how truthful are Matthew and Lucy? How much of Matthew's strenuous brand of love can Lucy endure? And how long can their rigid Dom/sub relationship stay frozen in time, never growing, never moving forward?

The Club Mephisto series

Club Mephisto... Molly is a 24/7 slave dedicated to serving her Master. When business calls him away on a weeklong trip, he arranges to leave her in the care of Mephisto, the owner of a thriving local BDSM club. Molly is both excited and scared to be given over to Master Mephisto. His power and mysterious intensity have long compelled her from afar.

She finds herself immersed in a world of strict commands, pervasive sex, and creative torments. Over the course of a week, Mephisto strips away privileges Molly took for granted, and forces her to understand and acknowledge the depths to which she can be made to submit. But a surprising conversation the last day threatens Molly's worldview, as does the strange closeness that develops between them. As the time of Master's return draws near, Molly finds herself deeply and inexorably changed.

Note: this BDSM fantasy novella depicts "total power exchange" relationships that some readers may find objectionable. This work contains acts of sadism, objectification, orgasm denial and speech restriction, caging, anal play and double penetration, BDSM punishment and discipline, M/f, M/m/f, M/m, orgy and group sexual encounters, voyeurism, and limited circumstances of dubious consent.

Molly's Lips: Club Mephisto Retold... If you've read _Club Mephisto_, you know the story from Molly's perspective. Now, prepare to relive the experience from Mephisto's point of view in this gripping novella.

When Mephisto's friend Clayton is called out of town on business, he agrees to look after his slave for the week. But Molly isn't your average slave. She and Clayton share a serious, full time dynamic. Mephisto feels a weight of responsibility he isn't used to, and worse, an intense attraction to Molly, the partner of his friend.

Mephisto is determined to sublimate his inappropriate desires and provide a challenging and instructive week for the devoted slave. He subjects Molly to orgasm denial, speech restriction, scenes of erotic torment, even an orgy where she is made to service his friends. Along the way, he experiences unfamiliar jealousy, and deep cravings to possess her himself.

Throughout the week, he is also haunted by persistent questions. Is she happy being a 24/7 slave? Or is there another Molly trapped beneath her submissive, surrendered gaze?

Burn For You... When Molly loses her longtime Master, she feels lost, angry. Confused. She's unsure of her future, even her calling to the BDSM lifestyle. She knows her Master always intended her to go to his friend Mephisto next, but their emotionally—and sexually—fraught history is still a confusion of desire and fear in her mind.

Mephisto wants to help Molly, but he doesn't want to force her into service she's not sure she wants. He owes it to Clayton to help her find happiness, but how? Molly and Mephisto advance and retreat from one another as they try to untangle their complex feelings. More and more it seems their tense standoff will only end one way...

Note: this 63K-word erotic romance novel contains consensual BDSM play, Master/slavery, sado-masochism, anal play, objectification, caging, and other consensual activities which some might find offensive.

The Comfort Series

Have you ever wondered what goes on in the bedrooms of Hollywood's biggest heartthrobs? In the case of Jeremy Gray, the reality is far more depraved than anyone realizes. Brutal desires, shocking secrets, and a D/s relationship (with a hired submissive "girlfriend") that's based on a contract rather than love. It's just the beginning of a four-book saga following Jeremy and his Hollywood friends as they seek comfort in fake, manufactured relationships. Born of necessity—and public relations— these attachments come to feel more and more real. What does it take to live day-to-day with an A-list celebrity? Patience, fortitude, and a whole lot of heart. Oh, and a *very* good pain tolerance for kinky mayhem.

Comfort series is:
#1 *Comfort Object* (Jeremy's story)
#2 *Caressa's Knees* (Kyle's story)
#3 *Odalisque* (Kai's story)
#4 *Command Performance* (Mason's story)

ABOUT THE AUTHOR

Annabel Joseph is a multi-published BDSM romance author. She writes mainly contemporary romance, although she has been known to dabble in the medieval and Regency eras. She is known for writing emotionally intense BDSM storylines, and strives to create characters that seem real—even flawed—so readers are better able to relate to them. Annabel also writes non-BDSM romance under the pen name Molly Joseph.

You can follow Annabel on Twitter (@annabeljoseph) or Facebook (facebook.com/annabeljosephnovels), or sign up to receive her monthly newsletter at annabeljoseph.com. She also loves to hear from her readers at annabeljosephnovels@gmail.com.

Made in the USA
Columbia, SC
08 October 2018